THE LUCK OF FINDING YOU

TAYLOR EPPERSON

Happy Reading!

Tay Epp ♡

The Luck of Finding You

Cover Design Emily Wittig Designs

❁ Created with Vellum

For McKenna,
Without you this book would not exist.
Thank you for helping me say yes to this adventure.

FIVE YEARS, FIVE MONTHS, AND THREE DAYS AGO

If you asked my mom, she would probably say that I am running from my broken heart.

Normally, I try to do everything possible to make sure my mom isn't right about me, but in this instance, she is right. I am running. Running far away from my feelings of heartbreak and betrayal. I'm drowning my sorrows in this cute little café I found in Provo. It's right next to a bookstore, which I plan to check out as soon as I finish eating the chocolate pastries I ordered. It's the first day of spring break, and I have nothing but time.

I grab my book, which is the newest in Simone Sorrows's latest fantasy romance series. Simone has been my mom's favorite author for years, but she wouldn't let me read any of Simone's books until I turned eighteen. But, she gave me a copy of Simone's new book last week for my eighteenth birthday. Dad laughed when she mentioned that she'd purchased a copy for herself too, asking why we would possibly need two copies of the same book in the house. As if he didn't know that we'd both need our own copy.

The café is nearly empty; the only other customer is an older woman who is knitting in the corner. I've barely read the first line of my book when the café door opens and a guy around my age with dirty-blond hair and legs for days walks in.

I try not to notice him. I don't want to notice him. But I can't help it. I look over the top of my book as if it will hide me and watch him as he walks to the counter and starts his order. I frown as the cashier gives him a flirty smile. Moving my eyes away from her, I take a chance to look at the cute guy for a second longer. He's in a fitted white T-shirt and jeans. It's not an outfit that would normally attract my attention, but it's grabbed mine.

"Ugh." I let out a frustrated breath. This is not helping. The whole point of coming here today was not to run to a new guy. Mom says I'm just like her though—I fall hard and fast at the idea of people and what might be between us. She says I'm in love with the idea of romance. My heart has been broken a thousand times, even though I've only really been in love once. He broke my heart too.

Which is exactly why I'm here.

Okay. Well. No.

I'm trying not to let that actually be the reason, even though everyone who knows me knows that I'm here in this new-to-me café with a new book to drown my heartache with chocolate pastries. I start on my second pastry and try not to look at Cute Guy again.

I force myself to look at my book, and I only manage to read the first line again before someone (who I'm trying to convince myself is not Cute Guy) approaches my table.

"Is that book any good?" a deep voice asks. I swear there are butterflies in my belly that come to life when I hear those words. Cute Guy is asking about a book? I think I'm in love. Maybe we can get married and have ten kids.

I squeeze my eyes shut, trying to block out this insane narrative about our future that's happening inside my mind.

I risk a glance up at Cute Guy and immediately regret it. Up close, he's even more attractive. He's got olive-green eyes and his dirty-blond hair hangs down over his forehead. "Um." I swallow. "I just started it." I hold out my book and show him the first chapter, as if to prove that my words are true. Cute Guy nods once, then he does something more insane than the thoughts in my brain.

He sits down across from me. I gawk at him for a moment, and his knee brushing mine under the table sends a jolt through my entire body.

I will not make anything out of this. I will not make anything out of this. I will not make anything out of this.

"I honestly can't wait to read the second book." Cute Guy interrupts my mantra. When I look up to see him watching me carefully, I know I've lost all hope.

We'd have really beautiful babies.

I mentally shake myself. I'm eighteen, for crying out loud. I should not be having thoughts like this, especially about someone I've just barely met.

"You...what?" I'm so distracted by our future flashing before my eyes that I must have heard him incorrectly. "You've...read this?" I hold up the book.

Cute Guy nods.

I drop the book like I've been scalded. From what my mom has vaguely told me about Simone's books, I can't believe this guy has read them. Not that guys shouldn't be reading romance novels; they really are for everyone. But it is shocking to have a guy who reads them sitting in front of me.

"It's my favorite of hers so far." He gives a half-shrug like this information is no big deal. "She's a really fantastic writer."

I gulp. Is this real life? "She is a great writer." Except I've only read one line she's ever written, so I don't actually know that yet.

He nods and takes a sip from his strawberry smoothie. "What brings you here on this fine day?"

I hold back a laugh because no one I know talks like that. From the look on his face, he seems serious though. For a split second I think about lying. There's no reason for me to tell this guy the truth, even though he is adorable. "I'm hiding from my ex-boyfriend." It feels so lame to say the words out loud, even if that is exactly what I'm doing.

Cute Guy watches me for a moment. "He must be a real tool if you feel like you have to hide from him."

Ugh. Why did I bring up Peter? I do not want to be talking about my ex with a guy I just met.

"I'm Noah, by the way." He grins at me and my heart jolts in my chest. Is this just attraction or something more? Do you feel attracted to someone with your entire body? The way he's staring at me makes me feel like I'm on fire. "I'm visiting my grandma for spring break."

I look down at my book, moving it on the table just to give my hands something to do.

"You have a name, Book Girl?" Noah's deep voice makes my belly flip. I try to ignore the physical reaction.

"Book Girl?" I ask him, raising an eyebrow. "That's the best you've got?"

Noah holds up both his hands, and I notice he's got a single dimple on his right cheek. "Working with what I know. I don't know your name yet, but you are reading a book."

"I do more than just read books." I cross my arms over my chest.

"Okay." Noah gives me that grin again. "So tell me about what you like to do, and I'll come up with a better nickname."

If talking about yourself was a test, it would be one that I'd fail. My least favorite thing in the world is telling people what my favorite food is or what flavor of ice cream I prefer. But I can do this. "I'm Tally."

Noah's grin grows wider, the dimple in his cheek more pronounced.

"Nice to meet you, Tally." He holds a hand across the table. It seems so ridiculous that a laugh escapes my lips as I lift my hand to shake his.

His hand is warm and mine fits perfectly inside it. He moves our hands up and down once before giving me a squeeze and slipping his hand away.

My hand stays in the air for a split second before I realize how awkward that must look with my hand just hanging there.

"So, Tally," Noah says, as if he didn't notice my hand in the air. "Tell me about yourself." He puts a hand under his chin and stares at me.

I'm so far gone that I don't know if I remember how to speak. "I've got an older sister. She's five years older than me and teaches art in a high school in California."

"I asked about you, not your sister." Noah says easily, then his eyes widen. "I'm so sorry, I just sat down at your table and didn't even ask if that was okay. Am I making you uncomfortable?"

I shake my head. "No. No. It's not you. Really. I'm just really bad at talking about myself."

"I get that." Noah leans forward on the table. "Would it help if I asked questions?"

I laugh. "Actually, I think that would make it worse."

"Okay, I can start. I'm Noah. I'm from Colorado, and no, I don't like skiing, and I think your eyes are the prettiest thing I've ever seen." Noah looks at me so intently that I go warm all over, but I notice a faint blush on his own cheeks and can't help but wonder if maybe he's not as confident as he seems. I glance down again.

I'm about to blurt something ridiculous, like we should get married and have a bunch of kids and read romance novels together (the two of us, not our children) when the door to the café swings open again and Peter walks in.

My heart drops to my stomach, and I sink low into the seat, wondering if the red polyester can swallow me whole. Peter is with *her*. Sarah.

"You know those people?" Noah asks quietly. I nearly jump out of my skin at his voice.

"Unfortunately," I tell him, still watching Peter and Sarah. That's when the worst possible thing happens. Peter scans the café and his eyes lock with mine. I should look away. I should sit up straighter now that it's obvious I was trying to hide from him.

I watch, horrified, as Peter approaches our table. Sarah, thankfully, is already looking at the overhead menu and hasn't noticed me.

"Hey, Tally." Peter only has eyes for me.

I swallow. "Hey, Peter." I hate the tight feeling that's growing in my chest. He was the first guy I ever loved. And while I've always been a bit of a hopeless romantic, I thought he felt the same. We spent hours planning how we'd go to college together and see what the future held for us.

Then he ruined it all. We haven't talked much since that day three weeks ago when I went over to his house and found him making out with my best friend on the porch. He tried to apologize, but when I wouldn't listen, he started dating her anyway.

I lost my best friend and boyfriend all in one day.

"How are you?" Peter's voice is so gentle that it makes my heart crack in two. But I will not cry, not in front of him. He doesn't deserve any more of my tears.

"Great." I paste on a smile, but I'm clenching my hands under the table to keep myself from shaking or crying.

"That's good." Peter never looks away from me; it's like he's searching for the right words to say. An hour ago, if he'd come crawling back to me, groveling, I probably would have taken him back in a heartbeat.

But five minutes ago I met Noah. And while I have only known him for less than an hour, he seems to be double the guy Peter is.

"Yup." I give him another smile; maybe it'll give him the hint that I'd like him to walk away now.

"Peter?" Sarah calls from the dessert counter. "You coming?"

He stares at me for another beat. "Yup." Then to me. "See you around."

I take a shaky breath as Peter winds through the empty tables back to Sarah. I clench my fists as he puts his hand on her lower back.

"You okay?" Noah's voice snaps my attention back to reality. Back to him.

All the reasons I came to this café today come flooding back and I sink a little in my seat. Noah leans across the table, concerned. "What can I do?"

His thoughtfulness makes my eyes fill with tears.

Noah moves from his seat across from me onto my bench. His arm brushes mine and we sit quietly for a moment. I discreetly wipe at my eyes, trying to get rid of the tears before they fall. Crying is not a great first impression. Noah doesn't seem to notice though, because when I glance at him out of the corner of my eye, I see that he's trying to burn a hole in the back of Peter's head with his stare.

I touch his arm, surprising both of us. "You don't need to worry about him, he's just my ex-boyfriend with his new girl-friend." I say, even though I'm trying to convince myself of the very same thing.

"I'm not worried *about* him." Noah's staring at the spot on his arm where my hand rests. I pull away, suddenly self-conscious.

"Then what are you worried about?" I ask when he doesn't say anything else.

Noah glances over to Peter and Sarah for half a second before facing me, one of his arms moving across the back of the bench and stopping just above my shoulder. "Do you trust me?"

I narrow my eyes at him. "What kind of question is that? I met you like ten minutes ago."

"But do you trust me?" Noah's voice is calm and makes me feel like I'm listening to the ebb and flow of the ocean.

"Yes." My answer surprises me, but I have a good feeling about him.

"Can I kiss you?" Noah's cheeks go a light shade of pink as he asks the question.

"Why?" I ask, but I'm leaning toward him already, trying to ignore the fact that I have indeed been thinking about kissing him ever since he walked in the door.

"You don't need saving." His free hand moves a stray hair behind my ear. I shiver as his finger grazes the side of my face. "But do you want to show him what he's missing?"

My heart thuds in my chest. He only wants to kiss me because Peter is standing right over there.

"I don't need to make him jealous." My voice is almost inaudible, even to me.

Noah nods. "The point isn't to make him jealous."

"Then what's the point?" I ask. I'm so tired of guys not just saying whatever it is they are thinking, whatever it is they want. I want Noah to just tell me how it is.

"I'd like to kiss you." The blush on Noah's face makes me smile. That and his words.

My hormones must have taken over because I answer, "All right."

One of his hands slips behind my neck and Noah shifts, moving closer to me. His other hand is warm on my arm. Involuntarily I shiver. His eyes never leave mine.

"I'm going to kiss you now." Noah whispers just before his lips meet mine.

Then, right there, in the middle of the afternoon in a quiet little café, Noah is kissing me. HE IS KISSING ME.

That's all I can process for the first few seconds until he pulls me closer. The hand on my arm moves to my back, and my hands sit awkwardly in my lap. His lips seem to fit perfectly with mine and he tastes like strawberries. I sigh into his kiss, and my hands move from my lap to his neck, the bottom of his hair tickling my fingers.

"Tally?" Peter's voice sounds far away. "Tally?"

I wonder for a split second if I should pull away, but I feel my insides melting. Kissing Noah is probably a bad idea. I get attached way too quickly, but I don't want to stop. Slowly, so slowly, Noah eases away, his hand leaving my hair and traveling down my arm until it stops at my hand. He's staring at me, and I don't know him well enough to know what he's thinking. I wish I knew what he was thinking.

His chest is heaving and I wonder if mine is too.

I just kissed a stranger in public. Fifteen minutes really isn't that much time to know someone, even though I feel deep in my belly that I'm one hundred percent in love with him.

"Tally?" Peter. This time his voice sounds strangled.

Noah still has his eyes locked on mine, as if he's daring me to look away. Then he squeezes my hand, but I'm not sure why. Reassurance, maybe? He did just kiss a total stranger to help her out, so I'm grateful regardless.

"I, uh, didn't realize you were dating someone." Peter says, and I look up at him to see him eyeing my swollen lips and the boy beside me.

Sarah looks furious. I mean, I would be too if I were her because of how Peter's looking at me right now. Like I'm a tall glass of water and he's just now realized how thirsty he is.

But for the first time, I don't feel a rush of anything toward him. There are no butterflies or hopeful thoughts that maybe he wants me again. If anything, I feel grateful that we're done.

"Can we go?" Sarah asks, tugging on Peter's arm. He doesn't move.

"I didn't know you were dating anyone," Peter repeats.

Noah slips an arm around my shoulders and I lean into him. "It's pretty new." I glance over to Noah, grateful he's playing the part of the doting new boyfriend. I flash a smile in Peter's direction, who has no right to be jealous after what he did. I was in love with him. We hoped for a future together. Then he ripped my heart to shreds.

With my best friend.

"Right," Peter says, as if he doesn't believe me.

"I'm Noah." Noah looks up at Peter. "And I've heard all about you, so I think it's time for you to go."

My heart feels like it might fall out of my chest. Peter looks at me like it's just hit him what he walked away from. I give a little petty wave because I'm feeling pretty good after that kiss.

"Let's go," Sarah hisses, obviously desperate to get out of this situation. Cause, yeah, awkward for her. I doubt they'll last after this.

Peter looks like he might say something, but Noah looks at me, and my eyes are drawn to his as our noses brush. My belly swoops at the realization that he might kiss me again. Peter makes a disgusted noise before heading out the door. Noah doesn't move, even after they're gone.

"Thank you," I whisper, looking down because Noah's gaze is too intense.

His hand brushes across my chin, tugging gently so that I meet his eyes again. "I have a proposal."

"Okay?" I'm breathless.

"I'm only in town for one more night. Spend the afternoon with me?"

That's not what I was expecting. "Yeah."

Noah's still holding my face with one hand and my hand in the other. "I have a few rules."

Intriguing. "Let's hear them."

"No last names. No numbers. Just today."

I hate the rules. I hate them. I want to talk about our future and plan our wedding and ask if he wants to have kids and a dog and if he'll still like me when I'm old and wrinkly.

"Deal." I'm afraid that if I say no, I won't even get an afternoon with Noah.

And I want this afternoon. I push away the guilt that rushes to my chest. I told Mom that I needed a day alone when she asked me to help her in the garden today, something I used to love doing.

Noah grins, and I shove the guilt down even further. I can help her tomorrow. We have a thousand tomorrows, I only have this afternoon with Noah.

"Let's go." Noah tugs my hand, and I follow him out of the booth.

"Where?" I'm laughing as I grab my bag and my book.

Noah smiles. "Maybe somewhere with a little more privacy so I can kiss you again."

My eyes grow wide.

"And there will be plenty of time for talking too. After all, I still only know that you like books, and I'm going to need more than that." I follow Noah out of the door. "So we'll skip that bookstore for now." He points to the one I was hoping to stop by, but I can always come back. "And we'll explore a bit."

"And kiss a bit." I bite my lip as I say it. Noah stops walking and tugs me closer to him, leaving a feather-light kiss against my lips.

"We'll definitely kiss a bit."

I sigh at that. Maybe I can convince him to bend his rules.

1

PRESENT DAY—TALLY

Very few things make me as happy as a cloudy, cool day in fall. Technically, the start of fall isn't for a couple of weeks since it's still early September. The leaves on the trees outside The Book Shop are starting to turn already, and the crisp morning air makes me smile. I've got a small pumpkin under one arm, and I'm wearing a light cable-knit sweater, even though I know I'll regret that choice by noon.

The familiar click of my heels on the pavement also calms me. I take in the trees and breathe in the morning air. I normally hate mornings, but once that autumn air hits, everything changes for me. My older sister, Holly, says autumn is the only time of year that I smile, and she might be right. I used to be the most optimistic person I knew. But after the end of my senior year, when it felt like the universe pulled the rug out from under me, everything changed. And even though that was five years ago, the only time I feel like myself is in fall.

The cowbell above the door clangs as I open it. I don't lock the door behind me, because Olivia, the thirty-year-old who also works here part time, is opening with me today and will be here to cover the register while I'm in my meeting. But I push that thought away, pausing like I do every morning to take in the space.

The Book Shop has been a staple on Center Street in Provo for the past thirty years. We sell only used books, something that Marsha was always adamant about. I let out a short breath, remembering why I'm still standing at the door. I'm waiting to hear her footsteps upstairs, waiting for the door at the far back of the store to open, for Marsha to be standing there, having just come from her small upstairs apartment.

But she won't come down today or ever again. She's been gone for three weeks, and before then, I'd forgotten how much it hurts to lose someone you love. There's another hole in my heart. One for my mom, and one for Marsha. Marsha was the first person who took me in after Mom died, right after I graduated from high school.

"Just open the shop," I mutter to myself, pushing the memories away. It's too much to think about Marsha and Mom today.

I move through my opening routine. The street outside is slowly starting to wake as the bike shop across the street opens and people walk by on their way to work. I flip on the lights and start the hot chocolate machine. Marsha had been serving hot chocolate instead of coffee at the shop since she opened the doors all those years ago. Her favorite thing was to tell customers that they could get coffee at any bookstore, but The Book Shop was different.

Plus, she hated coffee, so I don't think anything would have made her switch to selling it. I was wary at first, but I've come to love having a morning cup of hot chocolate.

I turn on the ancient computer that we use for sales. Olivia has been mentioning for months that we need to replace it. She's right, of course, but there just isn't money to update our systems, so we have to make it work. Even if it will take the next forty-five minutes for it to actually start running. The familiar hum of the monitor calms my nerves.

I grab my favorite mug, purple and blue and covered with Michael Scott's face. Marsha got it for me that first Christmas I worked here because she knew how much I love *The Office*. I stick the mug under the hot chocolate machine, sighing as the aroma of steaming chocolate hits me.

The bell over the door chimes. "Morning!" Olivia calls to me. I wave in greeting but don't turn to look at her. We're co-workers, acquaintances, not really friends, and I need some hot chocolate in me before I have an actual conversation. Some people need coffee in the mornings, I need hot chocolate. Olivia's worked here long enough that she knows this. She heads to the back of the store, where there is a small hallway leading to our tiny office that doubles as our break room. There's a new box of books someone dropped off last night that I left in there. She can start cataloging them while I finish my opening routine.

Once my hot chocolate is ready, I take my steaming mug and a random book to the plush red sofa in the far corner of the store, opposite the office. Customers use it occasionally, but it's become my favorite spot the past few weeks. I tuck my legs under myself and pull out my phone. My heart beats a little faster at the **1** icon hovering over the Twitter app.

I have one new message.

From Mo. Which is perfect, because I need our morning chat today more than ever.

Mo and I started messaging each other about two years ago, when he found my raving review about one of Simone Sorrows's books on my book blog. On the online world, I go by my middle name, Nora, after Nora Ephron. My mom was obsessed with her and all things romance. Dad vetoed it being my first name, but as a romance reviewer online, it works as my alias.

I smile and open the message from Mo. Mo is the name of the main character from Simone's current fantasy romance series, the book that brought us together. I'm about eighty percent sure that it's not his real name, and even though we know a lot about each other, neither of us has ever asked whether or not we use our real names online.

MoReads: Morning! Aren't Mondays just the best? Also, have you seen this?? <<Latest Simone Sorrows Book to be Published in Three Weeks>>

I gasp and click on the link, quickly reading through the article. As a book blogger, I'm sometimes on the in for big announcements like this. I've emailed Simone's publicist several times to offer to help with book launches or reviews but with no response. This is a surprise.

Excitement fills my body as I read the news. "No way!" I shout.

Olivia pops her head out of the hallway. "You say something?"

"Just talking to myself," I tell her, not looking up from my phone. Simone's new book will be out in three weeks, and the last book in the series will be out next year.

TheNoraReview: WHAT!? NO WAY!!!
Also, Mondays are not the best. Especially when you have work meetings. But this news does make it a little better.

It's not completely a lie. I do have a meeting today, and it's likely about the shop. One week ago, a Mr. Thorne, Marsha's lawyer, reached out to me and said that my presence was required at the reading of Marsha's will. That is where I have to go at one today. But I'm trying not to think about it.

I fidget in my seat as I wait for Mo's reply, wanting to jump up and scream and dance. That's when I notice that Simone is doing a book tour along with the release. I click on the event days and times, knowing that there's no way she'll visit anywhere close to me since big authors rarely seem to come to Utah.

"No way!" I say again, quickly tapping to purchase tickets to the event that's a month away in St. George. It's only a four-hour drive, so I can definitely make the trip. It's on a Saturday, but Olivia can probably cover the shop. "Hey, Olivia?"

"Yeah?" Olivia calls from the office.

"Could you come here a second?" I say, distracted because my phone vibrates in my hand.

MoReads: Okay, I am slightly stoked that I am the one who told you about new book! Also, we should read the whole series together to get ready for the final book. And I think you're wrong about Mondays, you just need to find something good about them.

Mo's words make me smile. I love that he's always looking on the bright side of things, even though I can't ever seem to do that myself.

Olivia appears in my peripheral.

"Could you cover the shop on October 1? It's a Saturday and—"

Olivia cuts me off. "I saw the Simone news. I can cover for you."

"And you didn't tell me?" I'm stunned. Besides Mo, Olivia is the one who shares all things from the online book world with me, because even though I'm a book blogger, I try to spend as little time online as possible since it takes away from my actual reading time.

"You don't like to talk in the mornings." Olivia shrugs. "Plus, I figured you'd already seen it."

"You're absolutely right."

"But I can cover—if you're still running the store and I still have a job after this afternoon." Olivia says this with a smile, even though I know she's more anxious than I am. But she loves working here just as much as I do. The shop is important to both of us.

I give her a tight smile. "It's all going to be fine." In exactly three and a half hours, all of this will be over, and we'll know what's happening with the shop. Gran told me to hope for the best, that maybe Marsha left me her shop. My gut is telling me that it won't be that simple. Marsha loved the shop, and she knew I loved it too. But she also has two grandkids who she might have given it to. Two grandkids who have never even visited the shop in the two years I've been manager, I might add. So, yeah, do I think I kind of deserve it? A tiny bit. Okay, more than a tiny bit, but I don't want to get my hopes up. Bad things happen when I get my hopes up.

I've spent the last week trying to convince myself that it's okay if she didn't leave me the shop. Olivia was hopeful at first because she knew how much Marsha liked me, and it makes sense from a logical standpoint. I've been the one running the place for the past two years, but with each passing day, Olivia's nervous energy has mingled with mine, and now there's a tension surrounding both of us that I'm sure customers have been able to feel.

I've put my heart and soul into this shop for the past two years, and even though we're still barely making ends meet, I don't want to lose it.

"We'll know everything in a few hours." I say it more to myself, forgetting that Olivia is still standing beside me.

"I wish we could jump ahead in time so that we could just

THE LUCK OF FINDING YOU   19

know." Olivia tugs on one of the ends of her braids. Her curly red hair is almost always in some sort of braid, and today she's got two. "You're sure Marsha didn't mention anything about you being in her will?"

I let out a frustrated sigh. We've been through this. I've been through this a million times in my brain. "Nope. Not a word."

Olivia nods. "It'll all be okay," she says, repeating my words. "Right."

Olivia heads back to the office, tugging on her braid as she goes. I look back down at my phone, my hands shaking from the anxiety of what might happen today.

TheNoraReview: Yes, I'm glad you told me :) And I'm not much of a buddy reader...but maybe for you.

I push down the uneasiness that's started to bubble in my chest. I don't have time to feel nervous today. It'll all be over soon anyway.

MoReads: Aw ;) That makes me feel so special.

I can't help it, I smile again. This is exactly what I needed this morning. Talking to Mo makes me feel like today is almost a normal Monday.

Dad thinks it's weird that I have an online friend whose face I've never even seen. Holly thinks I'm going to have my own *You've Got Mail* romance happen in real life, and almost every time I see her, she asks when Mo and I are going to meet in real life. Gran hasn't shared her thoughts, but she generally only shares her opinion when asked.

I wonder what Mom would say. I'd like to think she'd be happy that I have a friend who is under the age of sixty—if he really is twenty-six like he said.

But I'm not going to meet him. Mo is my best friend. I tell him pretty much everything (minus the super-personal details like where I live and that my name is actually Tally) and he does the same. I'm definitely attracted to his personality, like how he finds a way to make me laugh, even on my worst days, but you can't really fall in love with someone you've never seen, right?

When we started talking, it was only about Simone's books, but now we talk about more than that. It's perfect that he's the one who told me about the new book. While the idea of reading a book with him sounds fun, I make a terrible reading companion. The only book club I've ever been a part of is completely unconventional, and no one reads the same book each month. I don't really like hearing what other people think as they read whatever I'm also reading. It's part of why I'm not huge on Bookstagram.

Reading is so personal. It's a way to escape, to be in our world but to be somewhere completely different and magical at the same time. Reading is what got me through some of the hardest times in my life, and while I lurk on the online book community, I mainly share reviews on my blog—which does have quite a bit of traction, thanks to Pinterest—but other than that, I'm not super social. I made a Twitter account so I could follow my favorite authors and sometimes share my reviews.

But maybe reading these books with him would be different since we've both read them before.

TheNoraReview: You know I love ya :)

I hit send before I fully realize what I've said. By the time I see the word *love* staring back at me, it's too late. He's already seen it. We've never sent that word before, but I have to trust that he knows me well enough to know that I mean it completely as friends.

MoReads: Of course. Now. Can we talk about what you'll do today to make your Monday great? Even if work meetings are the worst?

I relax. "Thank you, Mo," I whisper to my phone. *Thank you for not making me accidentally saying "love" awkward.* We really are just friends.

2

NOAH

"What are you grinning about?" my sister, Annie, asks as soon as I get back to our hotel room. My dog, Mo, runs up to greet her. When he sees someone he likes, he wags his whole body, not just his tail. He's a west highland white terrier, which is the best kind of dog, in my opinion. Plus, he's adorable.

"Nothing," I say, but I can't stop my smile from growing as I think about Nora, my online best friend. I love that I was the one who told her about Simone's book.

"It's Nora, right?" Annie rolls her eyes. While she doesn't think it's weird that I have an online friend, she thinks that I need to just meet the woman, for how much I mention her and the things she says. But isn't it normal to talk about your friends?

"Yeah. Simone Sorrows has a new book coming out in a few weeks, and I was the one who told her about it." Mo jumps up on one of the beds and curls up in a ball, and I go sit by him.

"Okay, that is cool."

Annie doesn't read a ton of fantasy. I think most of the time she has her head buried in either a classic or a cookbook, but she appreciates all reading.

"And since I was planning to visit Mom in a couple of

weeks, I bought myself a ticket to the event Simone has in St. George."

Annie crinkles her nose, making her look four instead of twenty-four. "Where's that?"

"Here in Utah. South of here. It was the closest event to Colorado." I let out a shaky breath. "I also bought a ticket for Nora; I'm going to ask if she'll meet me in person there. Since Simone's books are the ones that brought us together, it feels like a good place to meet."

"FINALLY!" Annie jumps up and hugs me, a huge grin on her face. "It's about time you meet your mystery lady friend."

"That makes it sound so weird when you call her that." I give her a side hug back, but she's already bouncing away. That's the thing about Annie—she's rarely sitting still, and when she is moving, she seems to be skipping or bouncing through life. A lot of people in my life tell me that I'm one of the most optimistic people they know, but they've never met Annie.

"Well, she *is* a mysterious lady friend." Annie sits on her bed, folding her legs under her. "Is she not?"

"I guess so."

"So, do you think Grandma Marsha left us her bookstore?" Annie changes the subject to the one we've been avoiding for the past two days. We didn't talk about it when we got the call from Grandma Marsha's lawyer last week. Or on the plane here yesterday. Or last night when we went out to eat.

At the funeral two weeks ago, I did wonder about what would happen to the shop, but then we headed back to New York and that was that. Until Mr. Thorne called us.

"What are we going to do with a bookstore?" I bite the inside of my cheek, and Annie gives me a grin that tells me that I'm not going to like what comes out of her mouth next.

"You could always run it. You've been trying to figure out something new to do anyway, and you did say that you were going to start taking more chances after everything happened last summer."

I glance down.

I did say that. I meant it too. After you almost die, it wakes you up to see the life that you're living. It makes you want to do more and be more. But it's been a year, and the feeling has started to fade. I want a change, but moving to Utah to run my grandma's old bookstore? Not exactly the change I was hoping for. "Right. Or we could sell."

"We could sell." Annie humors me. "Or you could work here. You know, the whole 'I'm going to say yes to everything that comes my way!' Did you not tell me that like a month ago?"

I squirm. "I did." I've been trying to live the way I did right after the camping incident, when everything changed for me. But it's one thing to talk about saying yes to everything and another entirely to actually do it.

"Exactly. This can be the first big thing you say yes to." Annie laughs, even though I don't think this is very funny. "Plus, you keep taking all those clients you always complain about, even though you don't actually need to work for them."

I know she's right; this could be the next thing for me, and I do hate most of my clients. I don't technically need to work. Seven years ago, when I was eighteen, I sold a puzzle game app that I'd created from scratch. I could still be living off my earnings—and I still do, but most of it is in savings.

But I like working. For the most part.

"I just need better clients." This is a lie I've been telling myself. The truth is, I'm burned out building websites for hundreds of different clients each year. But I can't imagine myself sitting in an office at a desk every day, which is why I keep taking new clients.

"You've been saying that for years." Annie lies back on her bed, an arm in the air. She can relax in the strangest positions.

"But maybe, because you don't actually do anything, fate is taking over."

"I don't believe in fate." To be honest, I don't know what I believe in right now.

"Well, you should," Annie tells me. "Because it's what brought us here today."

"I don't think that's how fate works."

"How would you know, Mr. 'I Don't Believe in Fate'?" Annie holds up air quotes as she says the name.

I shrug. "Pretty sure we're here because Grandma Marsha left us something in her will. Which is most likely the shop because that's the only thing she really had."

"You can think whatever you'd like. But I'm telling you, fate has something to do with this." Annie proclaims this like she's going to make me a believer. I say nothing; she can think she got me on this one.

"Would you be willing to move out here and run the shop with me if we can't sell it?" Truthfully, I have no idea how any of this works. Our dad left when we were kids, and Mom is still alive and well, though she and Grandma Marsha had a rift between them years ago that was never fixed. I haven't had anyone related to me die before, let alone leave me with something. I don't know what we do with a store once it's ours. Are there rules? Do we have to wait to sell it, or can we just sell it if we don't want to stay here?

"Nope," Annie replies, just like I knew she would.

"I just got the job of a lifetime," Annie starts.

"I know, I know." I am genuinely very proud of her. After years of working as a line chef, she finally got hired on to be a head chef at one of New York's finest restaurants.

I can tell Annie's smiling when she speaks again. "I've wanted this for so long, Noah, and I finally have it. So no, if Grandma Marsha left us her store, and the chances of that are high, I will not be working there with you. No way am I going to give up my dream."

"All right," I say as my stomach growls. "You want to go grab some food?"

"I'm still full from breakfast," Annie says absently. She's looking at her phone. "Plus, I've got three emails from my boss asking me to call her with some info about our new menu."

"You'll be back tomorrow. Does she really need it right now?" I ask. Her boss is just another reminder of why I don't want to go back to working in an office, even if her office involves a kitchen. I work best alone.

Annie's already holding her phone to her ear.

"I'm going to leave Mo," I tell her and she nods, but she's distracted by work. It'll be easier to grab food if I don't have my dog with me. As cute as he is, I've found that most restaurants don't appreciate live animals on the premises.

SINCE WE'RE STAYING at a hotel in downtown Provo, I head down Center Street. As I walk, it feels like I've stepped onto the set of a small-town movie. The buildings all have their original brick, but a lot of the insides have been updated to match the times. The trees lining the sidewalk have started to change colors. It's cozy and quaint, and I know this was part of the charm that Grandma Marsha loved about living here.

I head toward the little café that makes my heart race every time I think about it. The only women in my life are my mom, my sister, and Nora. But always in the back of my mind is Tally. The girl I spent a single afternoon with, then screwed it all up.

Not that I could have found her even if I hadn't messed everything up. I didn't know her last name. All thanks to my stupid rules.

And so I've spent the last five years musing on—though Annie and my best friend, Sam, call it pining over— that single perfect afternoon.

I haven't been back to the café since that day, even though I did come visit Grandma Marsha a handful of times.

Pausing in front of the café next to Grandma Marsha's bookstore, I'm thrown back in time. I can feel Tally's hand that fit so perfectly in mine, the electric shock that went through my body every single time I kissed her that afternoon, and the way her smile seemed to light up the entire world when she laughed.

For the millionth time since that day, I wish I could go back in time and relive those three hours over and over again, from when I offered to kiss her after her slimeball ex was staring at her like he wanted her back to walking down this very street for hours, talking, kissing, and laughing.

If I could go back, I'd end the day differently. I wouldn't have left the way I did. I regretted it immediately, but by the time I turned back, Tally was already gone.

I let out a deep breath before pulling open the door to the café. Unlike that spring day all those years ago when it was empty, today it's crammed full with people. As I make my way to the counter, I see a group of students studying and some ladies chatting. An older couple holding hands across their small table sends a pang through my heart. I've always wanted to settle down with someone, buy a house with a cute little picket fence and a wraparound porch. Despite it being my dream, I haven't been able to settle down with anyone.

My last serious girlfriend gave me an ultimatum to propose or walk away. As much as I dream of that wraparound porch and a life with someone, I walked away. Better to walk away early than leave like my dad did when marriage and kids are involved. It's been years since anyone told me that I reminded them of him, but the idea of being like him still haunts me.

The smell of fresh pastries hits me as I reach the counter. "What can I get for you?" The cashier smiles at me, and I look up at the menu for the first time.

I'm immediately overwhelmed by the expanse of options. "Uh, what's good?"

"I personally love the strawberry-and-chocolate Danish. And if you're wanting lunch food, we have fresh ham sandwiches that just came out of the oven. It'll be the best sandwich you've ever tasted."

"All right." I order a hot chocolate, the ham-and-Swiss sandwich, and a Danish. As I wait for my food, I glance around for a place to sit.

Not much has changed since the last time I was here. There's still a lone booth at the front, the one where I kissed Tally, which is currently full of a family with kids that are jumping up and down and a mom who's trying to get them to sit still, a task that looks impossible. The rest of the café is full of small circular tables with two chairs at most of them. All the seats are occupied except for one.

That's when my heart stops.

Because there is no way that the woman sitting alone with an empty chair across from her is the same Tally who's occupied far too many of my dreams. The woman brushes her bangs out of her eye and turns the page of her book. Her own sandwich sits on the table in front of her untouched. Looking at her, it feels like no time has passed.

I'm still staring when someone touches my arm. "Sir?"

Startled, I turn to the cashier, who's holding my food. I take the tray from her and walk toward Tally. Maybe I should believe in fate.

"Is this seat taken?" My heart is beating so fast, I'm pretty sure it's going to escape my body as I ask her the question. She doesn't even look up from her book as she shakes her head no.

From what I can see of the cover, I'd guess she's reading a historical romance.

I set my food on the small table, hoping that will get her attention, but she still doesn't look up from the page. I force myself to take a slow, deep breath and move the chair so I can sit. Tally looks up in my direction, but I can tell she doesn't look at me, more like through me.

"I didn't think you meant you'd sit at my table." Her voice is exactly the same, soft and low, and even though she's snapping, it's music to my ears and I want to listen to her talk forever.

Her sky-blue eyes finally pierce mine, and I know that the crush I've been trying to bury for five years is still alive and well. Cause that's all this is, a crush. Because you can't be in love with someone you spent a single afternoon with. At least that's what I'm trying to convince myself of.

I shrug. "There are no other seats." There's a flash of recognition in her eyes as I speak, and I watch as her eyes go wide as they skit across my face, taking me in.

"Fancy meeting you here." Her voice has gotten quieter, but it's still sharp around the edges. All the times I fantasized about running into her again, I always imagined the smiling, hopeful girl I met five years ago. Instead, I feel as though I've been greeted by the ice queen.

Which I probably deserve, considering how I left things. I made her promise that it would just be an afternoon, and then I was the one who brought up a future. Something more. Then I ran away without a word.

"Tally, I—" I start.

She holds up a hand and sets her book down with the other. "Don't, Noah. I'm not interested in an apology that's five years too late."

Crap. This is going worse than I ever could have imagined.

"Okay." I nod. She won't quite meet my eyes. "But for the record, I am sorry."

Tally purses her lips. "Too little, too late."

"If I could explain," I start again, because seeing her here is taking me back in time even more than standing outside the café did. Seeing her here makes me feel twenty-one again.

"Of course you want to explain." Tally rolls her eyes. "I've heard all the excuses before. Guys are all the same."

She doesn't really believe that, does she? Something burns inside my chest, a desire to prove her wrong. But I need her to put down her icicles before I can try to melt the frozen wall that's around her heart.

"Look, I am sorry, and I would like a chance to explain. Obviously, that's up to you if you'll let me, but for now, could you just look at me?" I'm desperate to see her eyes on mine, for them to light up or have her laugh at a joke. We've only been together again for a moment, but already I can see that something is different about her. The light that was there last time seems to be dimmer than before. I want to know why.

"Fine." Tally looks at me, her cheeks a little pink. I love that even though something is different, she still blushes easily. "What are you doing here anyway? Visiting your grandma?" She says it as if she never believed that's what I was doing the first day we met.

"Something like that." It's not the answer I want to give, but talking about Grandma Marsha being gone with Annie is one thing; I'm not ready to talk about it with other people. It's too new and fresh. I already heard "I'm so sorry for your loss" so many times at the funeral. I get that people don't always know what to say at funerals, and that is probably better than nothing. But what are you supposed to say after that? Thank you? I'm not really thankful they're sorry because it wasn't their fault. I'm grateful they're supportive, but I still wish there were some other form of small talk we had for after someone died.

Tally blinks once, her face going still as stone.

My answer clearly doesn't win me any points. She reaches below the table and sets her bag in her lap. I'm going to lose her. Again.

"Did you hear about Simone's new book?" I ask, desperate to keep her here and to keep her talking, if only for a few more minutes.

Tally freezes, hand reaching for her book.

"You remember?" The surprise in her voice sends a jolt of energy through my body. How could she think that I wouldn't remember every single moment of that afternoon together?

"Of course." My voice is hushed now, like this conversation is sacred. Maybe it is. Tally blinks at me in surprise. After a moment she sets her book back down on the table.

Her eyes glint when she looks at me again, and all I know is that if I do end up with The Book Shop, I'll take it, no questions asked, just so I can be in the same state as Tally.

"I did hate you for a while," she says, and I gulp. "Probably for all of the reasons you think but also because at some point that day you told me the cliff-hanger would kill me, which it did. But even more so because I'd been anticipating it. This is why I don't like reading the same books as people or for people to tell me things like that. Total spoiler. I was furious."

I bite my lip to hold back a smile.

"But yeah, I saw the news. And I've read all the books so far, so you can't spoil them for me again."

I hold up my hands in mock surrender. "I wouldn't dare. Did you see she'll be down in St. George?"

Tally's eyes narrow again. "Yeah. Why would you know about that?"

"After I'm here, I'll be heading to my mom's in Colorado for a few weeks. It's the closest event, so I bought a ticket." I'm not convinced that telling her any of this will help at all, and I don't know why I'm sharing this information with her anyway. I don't tell many people outside of my circle things this personal, but for some reason I want to tell her.

"Well, maybe I'll run into you there," Tally says, surprising me. Then her phone beeps on the table. "Shoot!" She grabs her uneaten sandwich and purse. "I have to go."

"Big date?" I say it jokingly, but really, I want to know if she's single or not.

Tally smirks. "Something like that." I groan inwardly as she uses my line against me. "And see how easy it was for me to tell you I have to leave instead of just running away?"

The jab stings, and the only thing I can do is hope for her to forgive me someday.

She walks away before I can say anything else. I watch her leave, and once outside, she turns left toward The Book Shop and then disappears from view. I'm left feeling like I just let her walk away. Last time I did the walking away and regretted it for weeks. Months. Years. Still.

I don't jump up to go after her, even though I should. Instead, I choke down my sandwich, not because it's not good but because my stomach is rolling. Seeing Tally threw me for a loop. A loop I don't think I'll be able to get out of. Ever.

Tossing half of my sandwich in the trash, I head outside and walk in the direction of the hotel. I walk past The Book Shop on my way back to the hotel. I should go into the store, maybe warn the manager what's about to happen, that I hope they'll be able to keep their job, but I don't know yet because I don't know them. Instead, I stuff my hands in my pockets and keep walking, reminding myself that I can deal with the manager of The Book Shop once the meeting is over.

3

TALLY

I'm reeling as I drop my uneaten lunch off at The Book Shop. I sink into the uncomfortable office chair, giving myself a minute before I head out to the meeting.

My mind drifts back to the past several years of my life. Starting with the moment Noah sat across from me at the café and leading up to this point. Two months after that day with Noah, Mom died in a tragic car accident and I became a ghost of a person. I worked hard in college and graduated with honors, but it's mostly all a blur. I threw myself into my blog and into reading more than ever. It was both healing and a way of grieving. With every new book I picked up, it was another that I could fall in love with, but one that Mom would never be able to read.

There was no dating. Holly was worried about me, which kind of still makes me laugh because she's almost thirty and has never even kissed a guy. But she was concerned, and rightly so. I went from being obsessed with guys and fantasizing about marriage after every date to dropping out of the dating game altogether shortly after Mom died. I jumped back in a year later, only to completely walk away from love shortly after that.

My experience in love might be limited, but it always seems to end the same—in the fact that it always ends.

Guys cheat or walk away.

Parents die.

I swore off all guys, and because Sarah had been my only close friend, it made it easy not to get close to anyone who wasn't family.

Holly didn't get it because she was already in California and didn't have to see Dad every single day for years after Mom was gone. He was a wreck. Why on earth would I want to do that to myself? I mean, yeah, I love reading romance novels even if I know that happily ever after, the kind that lasts a lifetime, doesn't actually exist. Something bright and shiny that we should chase while reality is much dimmer.

No, I haven't told Holly some of these views because I think it would make her sad. Or she'd try to fix me, tell me that I should be more positive like I used to be. I just don't know how to be that person anymore. The one who looks at the bright side of things, who daydreams about the future or what could be. I still daydream, but it's not like before. I don't think anything will be like it was before.

Nothing has been the same since Mom died. I can't go back to that person; I don't want to.

For a moment though, I focus on this fact. The Book Shop has been my constant for the past five years, and no matter what happens today, I will make sure it stays that way.

"Good luck!" Olivia calls as I hurry through the store and out the front door. I have the sudden urge to turn right back around and tell her that I just saw Noah—*the* Noah—the one who broke my heart and made me swear off dating for, well, forever and who now has my mind whirling. I've heard her give advice to weepy women who come in for some book therapy, but I don't have the time today. Instead, I square my shoulders and walk briskly down the sidewalk, hoping to find some comfort in the sound my heels make as they hit the pavement, but right now it does nothing to calm my nerves.

"Breathe. Just breathe," I tell myself. As soon as the words leave my mouth, I realize why people with anxiety say that telling them to breathe never works. Because I am not calm. I am still very much freaking out, and telling myself to breathe is only making me annoyed.

Sure, I'm super nervous about what Marsha's will is going to say, but I just ran into Noah. HIM.

The guy who has been in way too many of my dreams than I'd like to admit over the past five years. He wasn't supposed to come back. He was supposed to just stay in the little box in my mind that I kept him in. Away from reality, a fantasy, a nice daydream for bad days. But there he was, in flesh and blood. Plus, seeing him threw me back in time and made me miss Mom, and I don't need all of those emotions happening today. I try to think about Noah instead of my mom. It may not be the distraction I want, but it is a distraction.

He's become a man since I last saw him, with his shoulders filled out and his jaw somehow more defined than before. He was also sporting a five-o'clock shadow that I'd be lying if I said it didn't make my stomach flutter just like his laugh did all those years ago.

I pause on the sidewalk, closing my eyes, and let myself picture his smooth, almost wavy brown hair. And his lips. Oh, his lips. What I wouldn't give to feel them against mine again...

My eyes snap open and I grab my phone. I cannot think about his lips. Or kissing those lips. I hit Holly's name and press call, even though I know she's at school. I still hope she'll answer.

"Pick up, pick up, pick up..." I take two steps as I wait for

Holly to answer my call. By some miracle, she answers the phone.

"I've got three minutes until the bell rings and class starts," she says by way of hello. I can picture her sitting at her desk, watching as students filter into her classroom. "This better be important."

"I saw Noah," I blurt.

Holly starts to laugh.

"It's not funny, Holls." Frustration bubbles up inside of me. She clearly doesn't understand what he's doing to my brain, what he's done to my brain already, why I wish he was just someone I'd dreamt up and wasn't real. He is the bad idea that makes me want to be impulsive and carefree. He is not someone I can get mixed up with again.

"It's kind of funny." Her laughter is only growing. This really isn't that funny. Terrible, maybe? The worst timing? Absolutely. But not funny. "You just so happen to run into the guy whose kiss made you swear off all men forever? That's funny. What happened?"

Holly might be my big sister and one of my closest friends, but I never told her the whole story. I told her the part about being in the café, about Noah coming in and Peter showing up. I didn't tell her that Noah and I spent the rest of the afternoon together. Mostly because she would have completely freaked out. She doesn't get why his kiss made me swear off all men, because it was so much more than just a kiss. But I left that part out because his leaving still makes my heart sting at random times. I wasn't about to talk about it.

I quickly tell her about the café. I hear a bell chime from her end of the call.

"Oh, fudge, I've gotta go."

Normally, I'd smile at her creative lack of swearing, but not today. "Holly, what am I supposed to do?" I nearly yell into the phone. She can't leave me like this. I need answers. I need help.

"Go tell him you've been pining for him for years and that you want to marry him and have his babies. Okay, love you, bye."

She hangs up before I can say anything else.

"UGH!" I look at the time on my phone. "Oh, shoot."

I half jog three blocks before I force myself to walk. I don't want to show up out of breath.

The courthouse looms large as I approach. Though I've never been inside, I've driven by a thousand times. Stopping to catch my breath, I stand in the shadow of the tall building and realize that I've already started to sweat. So much for the cool temperatures my phone's Weather app promised me this morning. It was supposed to be cooler until at least three, which is why I wore a sweater, but I'm already dying of heat. I can't take it off though because I didn't wear a shirt underneath, and I can't exactly go to a meeting in only a bra.

Once I enter the building, a massive board across from the elevators tells me that I need to head up to floor three, where Thorne & Ferguson Law Firm is located. The elevator is empty, and I fidget while I wait to get to the third level.

I pull out my phone. There's not a new message from Mo, but I send one to him.

TheNoraReview: I really wish I could read for a living and not have to go to work or other meetings. I'm about to have my meeting, and I feel like I'm about to lose my job.

He responds almost immediately, which is good because I'm freaking out a bit about what I'm going to learn in this meeting. Will this be my last day at The Book Shop?

MoReads: Wait, WHAT!? I didn't realize your meeting was that kind of meeting. I hope that's not the case. Don't you like your job?

TheNoraReview: I love it. Wish me luck.

The elevator doors open and the smell of coffee makes my stomach roll. Or maybe it's my nerves and the fact that I didn't actually eat lunch. Either way, I have no choice but to step out into the well-lit lobby waiting for me. The receptionist smiles at me. "How can I help you?"

"I have a meeting with Jason Thorne. I'm Tally Nelson," I tell her, and she looks at her computer. I glance down out my phone.

MoReads: Best of luck.

His words don't bring the comfort I hoped they would.

"He's meeting you in the conference room." She stands. "I'll take you there." I follow her down a narrow hallway that opens up to a room surrounded by glass on nearly all sides.

My stomach flips when I see someone sitting in the chair closest to the door, facing the windows outside. I've never talked to a lawyer before, so I don't know what to expect.

The receptionist opens the door. "Right in here. Mr. Thorne will be with you shortly." I want to ask who's in the room if it's not Mr. Thorne—but then the person sitting in the room turns toward us.

He and I both freeze.

Noah is sitting at the table, and a gorgeous woman is sitting next to him. A wife? Girlfriend?

Dread fills my stomach. Of course he's taken. Why on earth did I think otherwise after running into him? It's not like I thought I'd actually see him again. But here he is, in the flesh.

It's a good thing I wasn't going to fall in love with him again because now that actually can't happen, not with a woman like that next to his side.

Confusion falls over his face, and I'm still frozen in the doorway. After a beat too long, I'm still standing and now it's awkward. His piercing green eyes never leave mine. There's a magnetic force between us, and I couldn't look away even if I wanted to, which I desperately do want to.

"What..." Noah starts to ask, but then someone moves behind me.

"Oh, good, you're all here. Shall we?" a man asks, gesturing for me to take a seat at the table. "I'm Jason Thorne, Marsha Langford's lawyer."

I nod and make my way to the table, sitting opposite Noah and the beautiful redheaded woman beside him. I regret my choice of seat immediately because Noah's still watching me, confusion in his eyes. It hits me then that he must be Marsha's grandson. I knew she had two grandchildren and that one of them was named Noah. But she'd had a falling out with her daughter a long time ago that never was mended, so she didn't see them all that often.

I've never let myself hope that they might be the same Noah.

I discreetly pull out my phone while Mr. Thorne pulls papers out of a briefcase. I text Holly because this has to be the most insane day ever.

HE IS IN MY MEETING. I REPEAT, HE IS IN MY MEETING WITH THE LAWYER. NOAH IS IN MY MEETING.
Yes. I am absolutely freaking out.
Why do you have to be a teacher?! I NEED MORAL SUPPORT RIGHT NOW, LADY!!

Mr. Thorne clears his throat, and I set my phone down, clasping my hands in my lap to keep them from shaking. Why do I have to have a useless sister who is living her dream while I'm here about to explode with nervous energy? Not that she's usually useless, but I could really use her support in this moment.

Marsha never gave any indication that she would leave me The Book Shop, but now, with Noah sitting across from me, I really hope she did. I won't let him take it away from me.

I will myself to look calm, cool, and collected. Even though I am feeling exactly the opposite of all those things.

4
_____

NOAH

I'm gawking at Tally, dumbfounded as to why she's sitting across the table from me, when Mr. Thorne interrupts my thoughts. "All right. Should we get started, then?"

"Yes," Annie says, her knee bumping into mine. I know she's trying to get me to focus, but I can't stop staring at Tally. She seems even more stunning than an hour ago when I ran into her at the café, and for a split second I'm able to simply look at her before I'm brought back to reality.

"Before I read the will, I'll make quick introductions. This is Tally Nelson. She's been managing The Book Shop for the past two years. Tally, this is Noah and Annie Jones, Marsha's grandchildren." My eyes don't leave Tally, and I watch as she looks at Annie for the first time and then back at me. She glances away quickly when she realizes I'm still watching her. I try to tear my eyes away, but I can't. How is it possible that she has been sitting across from me not once but twice today?

What could it possibly mean? Just because she's managing Grandma's shop doesn't mean she should be at the reading of her will.

I don't get a chance to find out though because Mr. Thorne clears his throat and starts to read.

"The last will and testament of Marsha Bethany Langford. While I don't have much, I do have some. To my granddaughter, Annie Mae Jones, I leave my mother's wedding ring and my cookbook collection."

He pauses, looking at the woman across the table from me. "I have the ring for you to take, and her cookbooks are in her apartment." Annie nods as if she was expecting this.

He continues. *"To my grandson, Noah Jones, my granddaughter, Annie Mae Jones, and my employee Tally Nora Nelson, I leave The Book Shop."*

My heart is thundering in my chest so loudly that I nearly miss Tally's small gasp. "She..." Tally stammers, but whatever she was going to say next dies on the tip of her tongue. My mind is swirling. I instinctively start petting Mo, who's curled up on my lap fast asleep. But the familiar movement does nothing to slow my mind.

Grandma Marsha left us *and* Tally the store? This might just be my lucky day.

Mr. Thorne gives her a smile that I think is meant to be reassuring. But Tally's face has gone a bit pale, so I think it has the opposite effect. Why does she seem so nervous about this?

"Please allow me to continue," Mr. Thorne says, "and then I will answer all of your questions."

Tally nods, embarrassed. "Right. Of course."

I can't help myself; the question that's been burning in my mind slips out. "Why didn't she say anything to us about this before now?"

Mr. Thorne gives me a pointed look. "As soon as I finish the will, I will answer all of your questions, Mr. Jones." He clears his throat again. *"And to all three, thirty thousand dollars each on the condition that they—Tally and Noah or*

*Annie—work at The Book Shop for the next year before
selling."*

Tally's eyes bulge at the mention of the money. It is a lot of
money, more than I ever knew Grandma Marsha had. I wonder
how the shop is doing. In all the years that Grandma owned it, I
never thought to ask. I knew it brought her so much joy, but we
didn't talk often enough for me to know how it was actually
doing profit wise.

"I didn't know she had that kind of money," Annie exclaims
as I shake my head.

"She had some investments that she cashed out before she
died so that she could leave you some money—on the condition
that you don't sell The Book Shop for at least one year from
today," Mr. Thorne clarifies.

"And one of us has to work there?" Annie gestures between
her and me. Tally is pretending like she isn't watching us, but I
can feel her eyes on me. For the moment, I let her look until
Annie asks, "With her?" My eyes fly to Tally, who glances away
just as quickly, her cheeks red.

"That is correct," Mr. Thorne says, a set of keys jingling in
his hands. "The two of you can decide between yourselves who
will stay here and work. Now, Tally already has her own set of
keys to the shop. I'm sure she'll be able to get both of you up to
speed on how things are done." He hands the keys to me. There
are three, one of which I assume will let us into Grandma's
apartment above the shop.

When I look at Tally again, her brow is pinched. She looks
beyond frustrated, which is not a great sign. Does she not want
the shop? Disappointment crashes through me. "So, you've
worked at the shop for two years?"

When her eyes swing to mine, everything else falls away
and it's like we're the only two people in the entire world.
Which is what seems to happen anytime I'm around her.

"I've been managing it for two years." Tally's voice is polite and stiff. "I've worked there for five."

Five years! Five years? She must have started shortly after that afternoon between us. She couldn't have known the connection; I steered clear of the shop that day because I didn't want Grandma Marsha asking questions about my motives or what I was doing on my very last day in Utah. A sudden memory of Grandma asking me if I'd be interested in going on a date with a "lovely young woman" she knew a few months ago comes to my mind. I turned her down because I wasn't interested in dating anyone I didn't live in the same state as. But what if Tally was the woman Grandma Marsha had wanted me to date? She'd never mentioned her by name; I would have remembered if she'd brought up a Tally.

"Oh, Tally!" Annie says beside me, and her recognition does nothing to soothe my pounding heart. How on earth does Annie know who Tally is? Beyond being the person I messed up with all those years ago. Annie looks up at me. "Don't you remember, a few weeks ago on the phone she mentioned how grateful she was for Tally helping in the shop since she'd been so sick?"

I think my heart is going to fall out of my chest. I definitely would have remembered that.

"Wait, I think you were working when I was talking to her, you must not have been there." She turns to face Tally. "I'm Annie, Marsha's granddaughter. Did she ever mention us? I know she was so grateful for all that you did for the shop."

Tally shakes her head slowly. "Well, I mean, I knew she had two grandchildren. I knew your names were Annie and Noah. I just didn't know—" Tally cuts herself off.

She didn't know I was the same Noah.

Tally narrows her eyes at us. "How come the two of you never came to visit?"

I peek at Mr. Thorne to see what he's making of all of this. He seems perfectly content for us to talk, so I look back to Tally.

"It's been a couple of years for me." I hate to admit that fact. I was planning to come again next summer, but I'd been stuck in between the middle of too many jobs to take an actual break—something Mom and Grandma Marsha were both constantly getting after me for whenever I talked to them on the phone. You'd think that working for myself would mean I could do whatever I wanted whenever I wanted, but I have a very specific setup at home, and I don't like to work while traveling.

"I came earlier this year," Annie tells Tally, "but we mostly stayed in the apartment. Grandma wasn't feeling well then. I think that was beginning of it; we just didn't know it."

Tally nods, but I'm not sure she's satisfied with the answer. I can remember her telling me about how her family was—is—everything to her. That she couldn't imagine living in a completely different state as her grandparents. She told me so much that day we spent together, and you might think I'd forgotten it all, but I swear, every single thing she said has been seared into my memory.

She also couldn't believe that I only came to visit my grandma every couple of years. It was easier as an adult because I wasn't living with Mom, but it was hard to change the habits. We talked on the phone often though.

I look at Annie. "Did Grandma Marsha ever mention the will to you?"

Annie shakes her head. "I knew she had one, and I never asked what was in it."

"Same."

"And we can't sell?" Annie's question surprises me, since this morning she was trying to convince me to move here and work in the shop. Mo shifts in my lap, letting out a sleepy dog sigh. I was so worried about how he would behave during the meeting but we didn't want to leave him in the hotel. We'll be heading straight to the airport after this to fly back to New York. But I wasn't sure he'd be happy staying still in a new place, though once Tally walked in, my worries about my dog faded away.

"You can sell it one year from today if all three of you agree on that. Or one of you can simply take over. But at least two of you need to work there for the next year, and one of those must be Tally. Marsha was very clear on that."

"We'll have to go back to New York to get our things." I say "we" even though I already know that I will be the one who will end up coming back here. There's no way Annie is going to leave her job, even for this. She loved the shop and that it was Grandma Marsha's, but I don't think there's anything in the entire world that would get her to move across the country again. "We weren't planning on staying."

"That's fine; I'm sure you can be back by the end of the week. I'll have you all sign here." Mr. Thorne slides a piece of paper and a pen in my direction.

"What if everything isn't fine?" Tally's jaw is clenched, and I wonder why she's getting more and more tense about this. It's not like she has to uproot her life; for her, pretty much everything stays the same. "What if I don't want him working with me?" She jerks her head in my general direction. Annie laughs, then tries to cover it up with a cough. As if she even knew the half of it.

"Maybe Ms. Jones will be the one to come." Mr. Thorne pushes the paper we need to sign closer toward me and Annie.

"I can't." Annie's voice fills the room, but instead of calming me as it usually does, I have a rush of anger. No, not quite anger. Something else I can't quite put my finger on. I clench my fist. I don't want Tally to find out like this. I want to tell her, to talk to her about it, because with the facial expressions she's been making this entire meeting, she's less than thrilled about the news that just got dropped on all of our heads. "I just started a job. The most perfect job, so I can't leave New York. Not yet. But Noah here"—Annie pats me on the arm with her freezing-cold hand—"he was saying just this morning how maybe he could use a change. I think this would be perfect, big brother."

My sister and I have always gotten along fairly well. I'd even call us good friends. But in this moment, I kind of want to strangle her because of the way Tally's looking at me right now.

On her face is a mix of hurt and annoyance. I want so badly to take her in my arms and do everything I can to bring her smile back, to help her feel okay about this. She needs to feel okay about this because this is happening.

I'm starting to wonder if this *is* one of Grandma Marsha's matchmaking schemes. She did love to brag about how she could always see two people who would work well together. Which is probably why she hated my dad so much; beyond the fact that he was just a garbage human being, she knew he wasn't the right fit for Mom.

Tally's clear voice pulls me out of my musings. We'll never actually know what Grandma Marsha was thinking in doing all this. "I know the shop backward and forward. Plus, there's no extra money for us to pay him. Marsha took a huge pay cut so that we could hire Olivia, the other woman who works there. We can't fire her. She loves this job, and we need her. But there's no other money."

A red flag goes off in my head. Is The Book Shop in trouble? "I don't need money."

Tally's eyes narrow at me. "How could you not need money? Everyone needs money. If this is what you'll be doing for work, don't you need to get paid?"

"Money isn't an issue." It would only take her a few seconds to Google me and find out exactly why I don't need the money.

Sure, it'll hurt a bit if I don't get paid at all for a year, but it also won't be an issue.

"Fine." Tally looks back at Mr. Thorne. "I still don't want to work with him."

For a second I think he's going to say that all of this has been a misunderstanding and that we can just go on our way and sell the shop. Instead, he shrugs. "You don't really have a choice if you want the thirty thousand. He or Ms. Jones has to work there for a year with you, and since Ms. Jones has declined, it looks like Mr. Jones will be your co-manager for the year. Then the three of you can discuss what you'd like to do with the shop, as it is yours and you'll have the money also. Mr. Jones has quite the resume, so I'm sure he'll be an excellent associate."

Tally's frown turns into a full-on scowl.

"Will that be a problem, Ms. Nelson?" Mr. Thorne asks her.

"I don't even know the man." Tally's dismay is palpable. "And he hasn't been to The Book Shop at all in the past two years, which I know because I've worked every single day it's been open."

I open my mouth to say that she does know me, at least she did and she could, but instead, I say, "Why didn't Grandma give you time off?"

Fury fills Tally's eyes as she looks at me. "Do you know how long your grandma was sick? Every day I watched her get weaker and weaker. She loved the shop, and it killed her not to be able to be there every day, especially at the end. I worked hard every single day because there was no one else who could do that, who would do that. Marsha and I, and now Olivia, have worked so hard to get the shop to where it is today."

"Barely making money?" I don't know why *these* are the first words out of my mouth. I want to take them back immediately as her cheeks turn pink in anger. They'll haunt me until I die.

"We're doing fine," she snaps.

"Not enough for you to pay three employees?" I can't explain why I'm arguing about this. I just told her that money wasn't going to be an issue. But the shop can't be doing well if money is such an issue.

"You don't know anything about running a bookstore." That, Tally is not wrong about.

"Well, sounds like you're the right person to show Noah the ropes." Mr. Thorne seems oblivious to the fact that Tally resents the idea. "If you'll just sign here," he repeats pushing the pen and paper so that it's now right in front of me. My hand doesn't shake as I sign, even though I should be worried based on the look that Tally is sending me. I pass the paper to Annie. She signs and pushes the paper toward Tally.

Mo whines under the table.

"Is that a dog under there?" Tally asks.

I give her a friendly smile. "He's mine."

"He's not allowed in The Book Shop." Tally stares down at the document in front of her, and I hold my breath until she lowers the pen and signs her name. "I'm only doing this for Marsha, and I'm serious about the dog."

This comment is directed to me, and it lights something inside my chest. She may resent the fact that I have to be here, but she's also still going through with it. Even if it is for Grandma Marsha, even if it is for the money at the end of this.

Hope pulses through my body. Maybe I can show her that even though I left before, I'm not going anywhere now, and this time I can show her exactly what I didn't all those years ago.

That is, if I can get her to stop hating my guts.

5

TALLY

I slide the signed paper back to Mr. Thorne, dread filling my stomach. I'm not sure that what I just agreed to is the best idea. As soon as Mr. Thorne says we're free to go, I'm out of the room.

I hear Noah call my name, but I don't turn around. I take the stairs instead of waiting for the elevator. The sun is glaring harshly outside, and even though it's now a million degrees, I break into a run. I need to get back to the shop as quickly as possible.

There is no way I will be able to work with Noah nearly every single day for a year and not fall in love with him. Which is exactly what I'm planning not to do, and it might be easier if he didn't seem so happy about the prospect of working at the shop. He had no qualms about saying yes. His sister said she couldn't, though she looked like she might have been fun to get to know, and he stepped up to the plate.

Which is why I am going to shove all these feelings that have been bubbling up inside of me back into the hole where they came from. I will not fall in love with him. I cannot fall in love with him.

I'll get on all the dating apps. I'll go on dates every weekend for a year. I'll make Olivia work with Noah as much as possible so I don't have to. She'll be able to resist his charm; she's married.

"Ugh! How could you do this, Marsha? Why didn't you just tell me that I was in your will?" I yell up to the sky and simultaneously trip on the uneven sidewalk. "We talked every single day about the shop, about how it was doing and how much we loved it. Because I do love it."

"You okay, ma'am?" a guy taking out the trash at a restaurant asks me. If I weren't so upset, I might have been embarrassed.

"Yup. Just talking to myself." I give him a forced smile and keep walking. "I really need to stop doing that," I mutter under my breath. I want to call Holly, but I'm not sure what I would even say. That I'm mad at Marsha? I am, a little. But I also feel a bit humbled and grateful that she even left me anything. That she left her most prized possession in the whole world to me.

And to him. And sort of to her granddaughter, but that's not the point.

He's the one who's going to be around.

Marsha still wanted me to have the shop. She knew that I loved it. That I took care of it. I tried new things to keep business afloat since that's what I got my degree in. But Marsha wasn't big on change and didn't want a website or to order in new inventory. She loved that we were a place the community could come to donate books and buy whatever we had on hand. Not buying new books kept the costs down, but it was also hard to guess what would sell and what wouldn't.

Now it feels wrong to change things up so soon, right after she died, even if we are barely making enough to cover my very low salary and Olivia's paychecks. I can't help but wonder why Marsha didn't use some of her investment money to go toward the shop instead of leaving it to me in her will. It would have made more sense to put the money into the shop, right?

We just have to figure out how to keep The Book Shop open for the next year. Our numbers aren't that bad, but I know enough to know that they need to be better for us to stay open.

The Book Shop door is locked when I get back. The *We'll be back soon* sign is flipped, so Olivia must have taken an early break. I quell the rush of annoyance that fills my body; it's too late now to tell her to wait until I was back to take her break.

I unlock the door and relock it as soon as I'm inside, leaving the *We'll be back soon* sign up.

"Seriously, what were you thinking, Marsha?" I look up to the ceiling. As if she can hear me from wherever she is now, as if she weren't gone. "What were you thinking?"

I head to the back of the shop, where I won't be seen by any potential customers, and sink into the red couch, my body melting into the cushions. I pull out my phone. I may not be able to talk to Holly, but talking to Mo really is the next best thing. Even if it's a one-sided conversation until we can actually talk later.

TheNoraReview: We're going to have a lot to chat about tonight.
TheNoraReview: Do you ever have those days that just make you want to scream? Those moments when you feel like you have no control over your life and where it's taking you?
TheNoraReview: Also, I didn't lose my job, but this almost feels worse. GAH. I'll explain everything later.

I log off and flip my phone over because I'm not ready for a reply, even if he's available to give it. I am so tired of feeling like I have no control over the things that are happening in my life.

I text Holly, telling her that Marsha left me The Book Shop. I don't tell her that she also left it to her grandchildren, which means Noah. I leave out the fact that I will probably see him every day for the next year because thinking about that makes me more annoyed than I already am. I know I need to talk to someone about it, preferably Mo or Holly, but for the moment I simply sit and wait for the annoyance to fade from my body.

My solution? I'll pretend he's not here. Pretend he doesn't exist. I'll teach him the basics; I'll do the schedule so that he can work more with Olivia and I can see as little of him as absolutely possible. And I will not fall in love with him.

It might be impossible to completely ignore him, but I'll do my best. Because the more I avoid him, the easier it will be not to fall in love with him, even if it's just in my brain. There might be a small part of me that wants to be interested in him, that remembers the way my hand fit perfectly in his and how easy it was for him to get me to laugh.

"I'm not interested." Maybe if I say it out loud enough times, I'll start to believe it.

I really can't fall for him because when the year is up, he's going to be gone, just like before. Just like my failed engagement that happened a year later.

The memories flood my mind before I can stop them. My whirlwind romance with Grant. We'd met the year after my mom died and got engaged only a month later. I was barely nineteen, but I'd thought I'd found the one. I decided that maybe giving love a shot was actually worth it.

Until he showed up the week before the wedding to tell me that he had to call it off. His high school sweetheart was back in town, and he'd be an idiot if he didn't marry her.

So I got left again.

Which is why I will not fall for Noah. I don't want my heart to be broken, so I'm not going to even give it the chance. I'm not going to give him the chance to leave me.

There's a tapping on the front door that makes me jump out of my thoughts. I sigh and make my way to the front of the store, frowning when I see Noah standing on the other side of the glass about to unlock the door.

I unlock the door but head toward the register by way of greeting.

Thankfully, he's dogless as he enters. His sister must have the dog. "Tally, we should talk," Noah starts, but I hold up a hand.

"Nothing to talk about."

"But about…"

I can't bear to hear the words. "Nope. Nothing to talk about unless it's about the shop—which, welcome to the shop, I guess."

"Tally." Noah's voice is a plea. One I won't give in to.

"Noah—" Saying his name seems to startle both of us as he looks at me with wide eyes. I recover first. "I don't want to talk about what happened that day. We can have this new start; we'll work together and I'll show you the ins and outs of the shop and that's it. We don't need to be friends."

"But what if I want to be friends?" His voice is light, but his words come crashing down like the weight of an ocean wave. His eyes are so sincere, but I remember the promise I made myself. I will not, I cannot, fall in love with him again.

"I don't." Being friends could lead to something more.

Noah takes a step toward me, his blue eyes never leaving mine. I swallow hard. "I'd like to be your friend. But if that's not what you want, I'll respect that."

I blink in surprise. You'd think that a man doing the bare minimum, respecting what I say, wouldn't be completely shocking to me. I read a lot of romance novels, so I've seen a lot of men written by women. But it's been a long time since I met a guy like that in real life. I'm so shocked that I can't seem to find the words to say next.

Noah takes a step back and looks around the part of the shop we're standing in. I suddenly wonder how he'll take it all in. Will he notice how most of the shelves are slightly crooked and always overflowing? How the counter we use as a checkout stand was part of the building next door that we took when they remodeled a few years ago? He opens his mouth to say something, but I'm saved from hearing his words as an older woman walks in the door.

"Hi, welcome to The Book Shop." I smile at her brightly. "Can I help you find anything?"

The woman holds up a list. "I've got a few books I'd like to see if you have for my grandson. He's eight and has been loving reading so much that I needed some more books."

I smile and lead her toward the children's section. Thankfully, Noah stays standing near the register. Because most of the books in our store are donated and secondhand, there's no way of knowing if we'll actually have what she's looking for. I do know we have a good selection though, so I give her a few recommendations as well as finding two of the books on her list.

Noah is leaning against the counter with a steaming mug of hot chocolate when we make our way to the register. The cowbell above the door rings as she heads out, and I face Noah because I have no other choice now.

"Guess you found the hot chocolate machine." This sounds like something you'd say to a new co-worker. Or maybe it's something you'd say to a friend. It's been so long since I had a new one of either, I don't know how to navigate this.

Noah's mouth twitches, but he doesn't smile. "Grandma Marsha was always trying to convince the world that hot chocolate was superior to coffee."

His comment makes me smile. "She really was. Thankfully, she didn't have to work too hard to convince me."

Noah lifts a single eyebrow. How do people do that in real life? I could have sworn it was just a thing that happened in books because no one I know can only lift one eyebrow at a time.

"Yes, I've always been on team hot chocolate," I say in answer to his unspoken question. I have to look away from his curious stare because this feels too much like friends after I just said I don't want to be friends with him.

He doesn't say a word for a moment.

"Do you carry any new inventory? Or just used books?" Noah asks.

"Only used," I say, wondering why I'm so bothered that he's already asking about the shop.

"Have you ever considered selling new books?"

"It's just all business for you, huh?" I grab a stack of books that someone dropped off this morning and carry them to the nearest shelf, where I start shelving them. I already wrote them in our records this morning. And even though part of me agrees with him, my heart tugs at the words, because changing anything makes me think of Marsha and thinking of Marsha makes me think of Mom and thinking about how both are gone makes me want to cry.

Noah grunts. "Did you not just say you didn't want to be friends? I figured I can ask a few questions while I'm here."

Can he just go away? "Didn't you say you had a plane to catch?"

"Annie's walking my dog. Once she gets back, we'll head up to the airport." Noah gives me a smile that doesn't show his dimple. Not that I noticed. That much.

"We only have used inventory," I repeat.

Noah takes a sip of hot chocolate. "We really need to start carrying some new inventory."

"You've been here all of what, five seconds, and you're already telling me what to do?" I turn away with my stack of books.

Noah follows me as I start shelving books. "If you want to sell the shop in a year, we have to have something to show for it. Right now? No one's going to want it. If someone does buy it, it'll be to tear the building down or at least all the shelves and make it something different."

This makes my gut twist. "Who said I would want to sell?"

Noah cocks an eyebrow at me. "You seemed less than thrilled in the meeting about this new arrangement, so I just thought..."

"You assumed. Which, frankly, I shouldn't be surprised by, but no. I don't want to sell. And the reason I was less than thrilled is because I don't want to work here with you." I turn and head swiftly to the travel section, where I shelve a book that we already have three copies of. Why don't people just use library books when they're planning a trip? Seems like a waste to buy only to use it once.

"I could front some of the cost of the new books, at least for the first month or so," Noah says, and I hold back an eye roll. Right. Mr. "Money Isn't an Issue" can cover the cost of the books. How much money does he have, exactly?

"No," I say, purely out of spite.

"We could start a book club." Noah takes a step closer to me, and I don't let myself react. We have one loyal and true book club that meets once a month. All the members besides me and Olivia are over the age of seventy.

"We have one," I tell him.

"Just one?" Noah asks. "We could start more, have a few different themes. Or host a writers' club or something. Get more foot traffic."

I hate that we're even talking about this. We do need more foot traffic, it's true. We make enough to get by, but barely. Plus, the next few months are always the slowest. Things pick up in the summer, but now that school has started again, business will slow down. It's happened every year I've worked here.

I turn away from the romance section to find Noah half a foot away from me. I step back, bumping into the shelves. "Freak. Why are you standing so close?"

Noah smiles. He *smiles*. Again.

Can someone please take away this man's sunshine?

I frown. Nothing about this situation makes me want to smile. "You've been here all of five minutes and already you're talking about how we need more foot traffic? How do you know we don't already get a ton of foot traffic?"

"Maybe because you said you couldn't afford to pay me much. That's a bit of a clue that you aren't rolling in money or customers," Noah says, and I brush past him, back to the front counter. The bell above the door chimes.

"Hey, Tally!" Olivia says from the door, and Noah looks at her.

"Hey, Olivia." I try and fail to keep the dismay I'm feeling out of my voice.

"What's going on?" She glances between me and Noah.

No time like the present to make this very awkward introduction. Awkward because several weeks ago, I may have blurted out the entire story about Noah after she asked me if I was dating anyone. "This is Noah Jones." My eyes don't leave hers. I'm not sure she'll make the connection, and I'm not sure why I care so much. "Marsha's grandson. She left both of us the shop."

Olivia assesses Noah for the first time. "Nice to meet you." She holds out a hand to him, glancing at me as if to ask, *Is this okay?* My eyes are as wide as saucers. When Noah is looking at her, I point to Noah and mouth, *That's NOAH!*

Olivia's eyes go wide for a split second, then a sly smile slips onto her face. I'm not sure what that look means, but it makes me nervous. "Noah, you said? Nice to meet you. We'll probably be seeing lots of each other. I'm the only other employee here. I'm Olivia."

"Nice to meet you, Olivia." Noah is polite, friendly, and I shove down the twinge of jealousy that floods my body. He's not mine to want. "I look forward to getting to know you."

"Nice to meet you too," Olivia tells him. Noah turns back to me, and Olivia mouths over his shoulder *He's hot!*

I know my cheeks are a dark shade of pink.

"We were just discussing how we should sell some new inventory to increase sales," Noah tells her.

"We sell enough books." I know the only reason I'm trying to defend the shop is because Marsha didn't want to sell new books. She said it would make us lose our small, used bookstore feel. Olivia and I talked about it in private every couple of months though, trying to figure out a way to bring it up with Marsha, a way we could keep the same small-town-store atmosphere and also make more money.

"The draw of new books would bring more people in." Noah's eyes search mine. I want to ask him why this is such a big deal. If he's going to be gone in a year anyway, why does it really matter?

"We'd never sell enough to compete with the big chain stores." I fold my arms across my chest.

"You don't know that." Noah takes a step closer to me. I fidget but don't move away. Olivia is standing next to us still, but it's as if we're in our own little bubble. Will it always feel that way around Noah? "Plus, we don't have to compete with the chain stores. That's not really the point of this shop, right? But it could draw in a few more customers, which would increase profit."

"Marsha hated the idea of bringing in new inventory." Yup, I'm using the dead woman as a way of shooting down his idea.

Maybe it's a low blow. I hate it, but because it's Noah standing in front of me, it makes me want to fight harder for what Marsha wanted.

Something flashes in Noah's eyes and when he talks, his voice is sad. "Well, she's not here, so I'm going to guess that means we can do whatever the heck we want."

"I kind of agree with that," Olivia pipes in.

I scowl at her. She's supposed to be on my side.

"She loved this store." My voice softer is now. "She loved what it meant to the community, and bringing in all that new inventory would change that."

"What if it didn't change that?" Noah asks, his tone matching mine. "What if we could keep the small-town-bookstore feel and still offer new books? Indie bookstores do it all over the country."

I keep forgetting that he also likes to read, that even if he's never worked in a bookstore, he is part of this world. There goes my heart again.

"We can think about it," I say in resignation. "I'll think about it, I mean."

"Okay," Noah takes a step back.

"Okay." I lean against the counter, exhausted from the news of today and the fact that my heart is hammering like a woodpecker inside my chest. It's going to be a long year.

6

NOAH

My phone vibrates and I pull it out to see Annie calling me. I hit decline and put the phone back in my pocket. I'll call her back in a second.

"It's time for me to go." It hits me then that now I have to go and pack up my life back in New York. Even though I've been living there for the past several years, it will only take a few hours to pack up the one large suitcase I brought with me. I never settled there because it never felt like home. "I guess I'll need your number?"

Tally stares at me with wide eyes. She looks so adorable and cute with her flushed cheeks. "Is that how you ask for every woman's number?"

"So that I can let you know when I'll be back?" I clarify, tentative now as her face turns hard.

Olivia, the other woman who I forgot was still standing there, barks out a laugh. "Just give him your number, Tally." Olivia gets the ice glare this time.

Tally lets out an exasperated sigh. "Fine. But you can only text me when you're coming back. I am nearly always here though, so it shouldn't be too hard to find me."

She grabs a bookmark by the register and writes down her number. A number I should have asked for five years ago.

"Thank you," I tell her, gently folding the bookmark and tucking it in my pocket. Tally gives me a grunt in return. Olivia laughs again. At least she seems like she'll be fun to work with. "I'll see you both in a couple of days."

"It was really nice to meet you," Olivia says with a wave.

"Thanks, you too." I turn to Tally. I wish I knew what she was thinking. When her eyes meet mine, a spark shoots through my entire body. Does she feel it too? "I'll see you later this week."

"Take your time." With the grimace on her face, I'm reminded that she's not the girl I used to know. She's not the same woman I've dreamed of for years. I want to know why—what happened that made her put up all her walls—even if it isn't a good idea. Even if she does have a boyfriend and that's why she's acting like this. I haven't intentionally flirted with her, but I want to, even with the cold shoulder she's giving me.

I wait for a moment to see if she'll say anything else. When she doesn't, I nod once and make my way to the door.

"See you." I open the door a fraction, my phone vibrating again in my pocket, and look back to the two women. There's one thing that's been on my mind since I walked into the shop, and maybe I should wait until I get back, but I can't seem to hold the words in. "We really should have more of the romance books up at the front—romance sells."

"That's incredibly sexist." I think Tally has a permanent glare etched on her face now.

Oops. Not at all what I meant. I hold up both hands in surrender. "I wasn't meaning to be sexist. Romance books sell. In case you've forgotten, I also read a lot of romance. They seem to sell the best, moving them to the front is just a suggestion."

A suggestion that I definitely should have kept to myself

until everything about this situation settled down. I happened to notice when Tally was shelving some of the books that the romance section was in the back and that the main display table was biographies. I may not have ever worked in a bookstore before, but in a world where people love to read things to escape, it makes sense to move a more popular genre to the front.

"You are not the boss of me." Tally folds her arms across her chest, and I bite back a smile.

"Never said I was," I say, and I catch Olivia whispering to Tally, "Stop acting like a four-year-old."

"We'll move them!" Olivia offers loudly. Tally's frown gets deeper by the second. I would give anything to make her laugh or smile right now.

"At least think about it." I'll have to ask Olivia what I can do to knock Tally's wall down since they seem to be friends. "I'll see you later."

"Bye!" Olivia waves again as I leave the store, but Tally is all statue.

"Noah!" Annie calls, and I turn to see her and Mo walking down the street. "I tried to call you, but you didn't answer."

"I was talking with Tally." Annie knew immediately that the Tally sitting across from us in our meeting was the same Tally I'd brought up again and again over the years. She keeps telling me that I acted like a complete idiot (in the past and today) and that I should have said something.

"How'd that go?" Annie asks, passing Mo's leash to me.

"About as well as I could have hoped after she ran out of the meeting without a word."

"She didn't want to see you?"

I give her a look that I hope says, *Would you have wanted to see me?*

"Right. Well. Now you get to work with her. Seems like that

will be a super fun time." Annie's sarcastic tone does not go unmissed.

"I've got a lot of making up to do. The last time she saw me, I literally ran away from her without a goodbye. Not my proudest moment." We've reached the rental car. "I'm hoping I can show her that I'm not that guy, not the one who walks away without a word. I just can't believe it."

"The part about you running away or that you ran into Tally?" Annie asks as she gets in the driver's side of our rental car. The words *running away* make my stomach turn to lead. "Hey, I didn't mean to imply you're like Dad."

"Am I really that easy to read?" Even the idea of being remotely like our dad makes me sick to my stomach. The fact that I ran away just like him makes me want to vomit.

"You're nothing like him." Annie's words are gentle, but now I'm reminded of where I came from and how easily I could end up being just like him.

"I'm going to ask Nora to meet in person."

Annie frowns at me as we pull onto the freeway. "But you just ran into the love of your life again. Why would you want to meet Nora?"

"Nora and I are friends." I try to say it casually. The reality is, up until a few seconds ago, I was all for doing everything in my power to get Tally to like me again, even if it's just as friends. Because I can't believe that after all these years, she's been right here—where I left her.

But thinking about how much I'm like Dad is making me realize that if I don't want to fall harder for Tally than I already have, I need to have some sort of distraction. I'm not proud of this solution. But I did already buy Nora a ticket to the Simone Sorrows event, so why not meet?

"Plus, I'm pretty sure Tally isn't the love of my life. She hates my guts."

"I don't think that's what she was thinking about when she first saw you in the meeting." Annie waggles her eyebrows. I hate when she does that.

"She was surprised to see me, that's all." That's what I'm trying to convince myself of anyway. All we can be is friends. We've got to work together for a year, then I'll leave and head out on my next adventure, whatever that may be. Tally loves the shop, and while I love reading and all things bookish, I don't know if working in a bookstore was what I had planned for the rest of my life.

It'll be easier not to get involved.

Even though I want to.

I shake the thought from my head and pull out my phone.

MoReads: I have an idea, let me know what you think. How about we meet in person at the Simone Sorrows event in St. George? I already bought you a ticket, so we can meet in person and see what happens.

I log off after that because if she says no, I don't really want to read it right now. I'll wait till we're back in New York or maybe even until tomorrow to see what she says.

7

TALLY

"I cannot deal with this today!" I set my phone on the desk. I've spent the past hour trying to focus on going over numbers and figuring out an easy way to organize all the random files we have so that I—er, Olivia—can show them to Noah when he gets back.

"What's going on?" Olivia is nice. Fun, even. Maybe if we hadn't met as co-workers, we would have been really good friends. And it's not that I'm not comfortable talking to her, she just wouldn't be my first choice. I want to talk to Holly, but she has a faculty meeting, so I can't talk to her for another hour or so, and the only other person I'd talk to about something like this is the one who is making me feel like every single thing in my life had to shift today.

So I decide to tell Olivia. "Mo just asked if we could meet at the Simone Sorrows event. He knows that I live somewhere in Utah, and he bought me a ticket for the St. George book signing. It's not like I just ran into the guy who I've been trying to forget for five years! Why not add more to the table?" I lay my head down on the desk. Saying the words out loud didn't help me feel any better; in fact, I think I feel more overwhelmed.

"Mo, like your online best friend?" Olivia asks.

"Yeah," I mumble. Can the world swallow me up now? That'd be great. Then I wouldn't have to deal with any of this.

"And I know the Noah story." Olivia sinks onto the hardwood chair in the corner, the only available seating option in the small office. "That is a lot for one day. What are you going to do?"

"Schedule you to work with Noah as much as possible so that I don't have to see him ever."

Olivia laughs, a sound that usually fills me with some sort of joy, but today it has the opposite effect. "Would it really be so bad to get to know him again?"

I frown. "Yeah. Because he's the type of guy who walks away without a word. Is it still considered ghosting if you only were together for a single afternoon?" The sting I felt that day washes over me again. I hate that seeing him reminded me of everything, the good and the bad.

I try to forget about the part when he left me, not bothering to say where he was going or even to say goodbye. I blocked it from my memory because other than that part, the afternoon was perfect. But now I can't forget that part, the fact that he just left. He got a phone call and took off running.

After Mom died, I tried to make up an excuse for him. My best theory was that the person on the phone was calling with news of a terminally ill parent. I tried to ignore the thought that the person on his phone could have been a loving girlfriend and he just happened to cheat on her with me. I really hate that option.

But I can't let go of the fact that he just up and left. And I've never been able to let go of the guilt of not hanging out with Mom that day when she wanted me to.

Olivia's been letting me sit with my thoughts, but I'm still surprised to see her watching me when I finally look up at her.

"I say meet Mo." Olivia smiles at me. "He's one of your best friends, even if you haven't met in real life, and who knows what could come from that?"

"I'm not sure I want our relationship to be anything more than friends. I've always only thought of him as a friend, even though we do flirt sometimes."

Olivia nods. "That's fine. But still, keep an open mind about him. And about Noah."

I scowl.

"I know, probably not what you wanted to hear from me, but I think it could be good for you."

"I don't need a man in my life, Olivia." The words sound forced, even to my ears, even if they are the truth. Mom may have loved all things romance, but she also made it clear that both Holly and I were great people all on our own, and we didn't need anyone to complete us.

"I didn't say you did." Olivia is still watching me carefully. And she may not have said those words, but that's definitely what she implied. "You are a rockstar of a human, even if I do think you could be a little less grumpy at times. But when was the last time you were really happy? That you did something for yourself? You give so much of your time and yourself to the shop, which is great, but when have you done something for you?"

Her words make me think back to earlier when I mentioned I hadn't taken a day off in three years. For so long that's felt like something I could brag about. Now I'm not so sure.

"I'm not saying a man will make you happy. But going out and meeting people, doing something a little crazy..." I give her wide eyes and she laughs. "For you that would be going out to eat instead of ordering in. Doing something different would be good for you. So I say tell Mo you'll meet him in real life, and try not to completely shut Noah out. He seems like a good guy."

"You were around him for all of ten minutes."

"I'm a good judge of character." Olivia stretches and stands up. "And if you ever need a girlfriend to hang out with, I'm pretty open, my husband works a lot."

I nod. Maybe I'll take her up on that.

───

WHEN I GET HOME, I FaceTime Holly.

"Hey, Sis." She's on her bed with a tub of ice cream, and I can hear *Criminal Minds* on in the background. How she can watch that show and still sleep at night is beyond me.

"How was school?" I move a pillow to get comfortable on my bed. It's barely eight and I'm already in my pajamas. My face has been washed and moisturized, and I'm ready for a nice evening talking to my sister and then reading a book.

"Today was another day that reminded me how grateful I am to teach art," Holly tells me, pausing her show. "Mr. Rossi, the teacher across the hall from me, teaches some regular history classes along with some art history classes, and he seems to have it rough. Art is at least fun."

I know better than to comment on her calling Drew "Mr. Rossi." They are in the same friend circle, but whenever she brings him up, she only calls him Mr. Rossi, never Drew. I secretly think she's got a crush on him because she always turns bright red whenever I tease her about it. "Didn't you minor in art history?"

"Fun for the kids, I mean," Holly clarifies. "Most freshmen hate art history. It's not exactly fun for everyone. Art though, art is fun for everyone. Because the act of creating art can be fun, even if it turns out badly. Art history isn't really everyone's thing."

"Right." I don't always get it when she talks about the art

stuff. I am not a super creative person, though Holly tells me occasionally how creative my blog is. It's not really though. I feel like it's just me spouting out my random thoughts after I read books and sending it off into the online abyss, wondering if people actually read it and whether I care if they don't.

Holly and I are wildly different. The only things we share are our matching blue eyes that we got from Dad and the fact that we both love rom-coms because Mom did, though I don't watch them as much as Holly does. But unlike me, Holly is still holding out hope for her perfect love story.

"So, what's up?" Holly asks me. "Other than Marsha leaving you her store."

"I might have left out a pretty big detail." I groan. "Or two."

Holly stares at me, waiting for me to continue.

"Noah *is* Marsha's grandson. That's why he was in the meeting."

"Just like you always hoped!" Holly says this like it's the best news in the world. I might have mentioned that Marsha told me about a grandson named Noah and said something like, "Wouldn't it be crazy if they were the same person?" But I wouldn't really call that me hoping for them to be the same.

"No. Not like I've always hoped," I mutter.

She frowns. "This is bad?"

"Super bad. She left both of us, and Noah's sister, the store and some money. Okay, a lot more money than I've ever seen at once in my bank account, but we only get the money if I work with either him or his sister at the shop for a year. His sister can't because she's got her dream job in New York, so I'm stuck with Noah."

"What's his last name? I want to see what he looks like. Does he have an Instagram?" Holly's phone glows in her hand, then her laptop must slide off her lap because I get a nice view of her bright yellow pillow.

"Holls."

"Right. Sorry." Holly adjusts her laptop and puts her phone down. "You have to work with Noah and you're freaking out about it."

"Pretty much." I don't want to tell her about Mo, but I have to. "And Mo asked if we could meet in person."

"That's HUGE!!!" Holly seems to share the same excitement level as Olivia exuded earlier when I told her about Mo. It's not that I'm not excited about meeting him. I've been wondering if we should for a while now. But today it's all too much. "Did you say yes?"

"I haven't responded."

"But you want to meet him, right?"

"Yes. No. I don't know." I sigh. "If he'd asked me yesterday, I think I would have been much more excited. But after running into Noah, everything in my brain is all jumbled. Why did Marsha do this to me?"

Holly pushes her glasses up the bridge of her nose, which is something that's so familiar and so much like Mom that I'm hit with a wave of grief. I miss Mom. And right now, I miss Holly and wish she weren't ten hours away from me. "Is there any possible way she knows about the kiss?"

I sigh. "I never told her."

"Could he have?"

"I don't know. I'm not going to ask him. We decided before any of this even happened that we were going to pretend the kiss never happened." Though we should be talking about *kisses*.

"Sounds like you've got yourself a love interest," Holly says, but instead of laughing with her, I frown. We both inherited Mom's ability to fall in love or at least fantasize about a future. I grew out of it, mostly. Holly did not. "Or two."

"Holls, this isn't funny. This is my life. Suddenly, this guy who walked out of my life just after he got in it is back, and he's all smug and cheerful and thrilled about being here. He acts like he knows everything about running a bookstore, but I don't think he's ever worked in one and now I'm stuck with him for a year. I don't know what to do." Even as I'm saying the words, I know they aren't a fair assessment of Noah. He did mention moving the romance section near the front, which made me mad at the time but was actually not a bad idea.

Holly is quiet, eating her ice cream and thinking. "I'm sorry," she finally says. "What can I do?"

"Help me not fall in love with him." That, I am sort of joking about, but she knows my history of fantasizing about marrying random strangers, so she also knows there's a part of me that's serious. She can't be here to help me get through the next year because that would be impossible. I can't just ask her to uproot her whole life, even though I really hope that someday we'll at least live in the same state.

But she can help me with this. She can be my moral support.

"I can do that," she promises.

"How?" I ask, because he really does have dreamy eyes.

"Okay, kick things up with Mo. Flirt a lot. Talk about what you'll do when you meet in real life. Ask if he wants to date."

"I don't want to do that!" I tell her. She doesn't need to hear my explanation again; she already knows. I don't want to ruin our friendship.

She gives me a little shrug. "Well, you're screwed."

"Ugh."

There's a knock on my door before it opens and then Gran is standing there. "Join me for some ice cream?"

"Hi, Gran!" Holly yells through the phone.

"Hi, sweetheart," Gran says back. "I'll call you on Friday!" They have a weekly phone date every Friday afternoon.

"You should go get some ice cream, clear your head." Holly smiles at me and it hurts my heart how much she looks like Mom. "You've also got to stop running from love."

"I'm not running from anything," I say. "I'm stuck to the ground. Not literally, but no running is happening."

"Uh huh."

"You can't tell me to stop running from love when you're doing the exact same thing!" If I weren't so emotionally drained from today, I probably would have kept this to myself.

"I'm not running from anything. I'm just waiting for the right guy. There's nothing wrong with that."

I want to tell her that yes, it actually is the same thing and that it's just a different excuse, but instead, I smile at her and tell her I'll keep her updated.

Then I head upstairs to eat some ice cream with Gran. I moved into her basement after Mom died, when I wasn't ready to face the world alone yet. It's been five years now, and I'm still here. Some days I day dream about what it would be like to get my own place, but for now I'm grateful for the company in the evenings. And tonight I'm grateful when she fills up my bowl for seconds and relieved that when she asks about my day, she doesn't probe when I don't give more than "It was fine" as an answer.

Instead, we spend our evening talking about the latest season of *Survivor* that we've been watching together.

8

TALLY

I don't hear from Noah until Friday morning, when he tells me that he's landed and he'll be at the shop later that afternoon once he gets unpacked.

Unfortunately for me, Noah's text wakes me up and I have ten minutes until The Book Shop opens. I have never been a morning person, and since I was reading the historical romance I needed to read for book club, I stayed up most of the night because I couldn't stop reading. Instead of showering, I decide that I'll just use my key to Marsha's apartment and shower up there during my lunch break.

I open the shop ten minutes late, but there are no customers waiting, so I'm able to do a simplified version of my morning routine as I help the three customers who come in before lunch.

Slowly, noon rolls around and I lock the door, turning the sign to say that I'll be back in a half hour. I go through the back door, head up the staircase on the outside of the building, and let myself into Marsha's old apartment.

The apartment is the same as the last time I saw it: Marsha's mugs on her open shelving, her faded afghan draped across her couch, a neat pile of books next to the TV. The flowers on the windowsill are dead, but other than that, it's exactly the same. I grab the towel she always saved for me from the hall closet and lock myself in the bathroom. I sigh as the hot water hits my shoulders. I don't have the time for a long, luxurious shower that my mind is aching for, so I quickly scrub my body and am rinsing the shampoo out of my hair when I hear a door.

Not just any door, but the door to the apartment.

I freeze.

The door that I know I locked behind me when I came up here.

I have no idea what to do in this situation, so I turn the water off because that seems like the best idea. As far as I know, no one else has a key to this apartment, so it's got to be a burglar. Or a murderer. Was someone watching as I came up here and just waiting for a moment to follow? The shower head drips its final drops, and I listen closely for the murderer approaching the bathroom now. Because, yes, now I am one hundred percent convinced that I am about to die.

I grab my towel and wrap it around my body. I don't really want to die naked, but I don't think I have enough time to put on my clothes before whoever is out there comes bursting in here.

I twist the doorknob, adrenaline pumping through my body. Maybe I can talk the murderer out of killing me.

I step into the hall and look both ways; no one is there. My heart is thundering in my chest. I tiptoe to the right, toward the main room, and the floor creaks under me, making me cringe. Why do old buildings have to have the loudest floors?

No one is there.

"Hello?" I call out, wishing my voice wasn't shaking. A dog starts barking and I scream, turning to go back into the bathroom, where I should have just stayed, but I run into something hard and muscular instead.

I scream louder.

Warm hands grip both of my shoulders. "Tally?"

I jump back, startled. "Noah?"

My hair is dripping water everywhere and I'm in nothing but a towel. We stare at each other for a heartbeat.

"What are you doing here?" Noah asks, confusion in his voice but his eyes never leaving my mine.

"What are you doing here!?" I ask, my voice coming out louder than I expected. The dog starts to bark again, then comes and starts licking my toes. "Stop that," I say to the dog.

"I'm living here."

"This is where you're living?" I ask, again remembering that I'm wearing only a towel, clutching it tighter around myself. "When did you get here? You weren't here when I got up here!"

Noah blinks at me. "I flew in early this morning. I just got back from taking my dog on a walk and then I was going to head down to the shop. Why were you showering here?"

His explanation makes sense, but how did he get in the apartment? "When did you get a key?"

Noah stares at me like this is a dumb question. "Mr. Thorne gave keys to me during our meeting. It's how I got into the shop on Monday."

Now it's my turn to stare at him, trying to remember everything that happened on Monday. I knew he had keys to the shop. I didn't realize that meant he got keys to the apartment. Then I remember I never answered his question.

"I shower here sometimes. I'm not a morning person, and some days that makes me almost late—but I always open on time—so Marsha let me shower here on my lunch break when that happened. So I have a key." The words come out in a rush.

I really need to get back inside that bathroom because I. Am. Naked. And do not want to be anymore.

THE LUCK OF FINDING YOU   77

"What exactly were you going to do to me?" Noah bites back a smile. "You know, if I hadn't been me?"

"I have no idea," I tell him honestly, and without another word, I skirt around him and into the bathroom and lock the door behind me. Noah's low chuckle from the other side of the door floods my body with heat.

"Am I really feeling something toward him right now? Really, body?" I whisper-hiss at myself. My face is the color of a tomato as I pull on my clothes and stare at my reflection, shaking my head. Part of me wants to laugh because this situation is exactly the type of thing that would happen to Holly. But me? Things like this never happen to me. Except for today, apparently.

My skin is flushed as I blow-dry my hair. It's not quite long enough to put into a bun on the top of my head, so wearing it down will have to do.

I'm angry that Noah showed up. I'm embarrassed by my loud scream and by the fact that he saw me wrapped up in a towel.

"Ugh," I groan as I put the blow-dryer back under the sink.

"Everything okay in there?" Noah asks. I jump but thankfully don't make a sound.

"Why are you standing by the door?" I ask.

"I'm not." His voice is farther away now. "I was just walking by."

I wait in the bathroom for a few more minutes because I'm still not quite ready to face him. I grab my hair tie from the counter, changing my mind about leaving it down, and I pull it into a ponytail. I square my shoulders and take a deep breath. I can do this. I have to do this. As much as I'd rather spend the rest of the day in this bathroom hiding from Noah, I have to leave.

Noah is sitting on the couch watching TV when I make my

way down the hall. He glances at me once, then looks back to the TV. I think he's trying to ignore me.

"I'm sorry I was in the shower." I break the awkward silence. Noah's dog stares up at me from where it's sitting on the couch. "I didn't realize you'd be here. I mean, I knew you'd be in the shop later, I just didn't know you'd be *here* in the apartment, and Marsha was always fine with it. It won't happen again."

Noah's face is soft and kind when he looks at me. "It's really okay, Tally."

"Right." I get hot all over as he stares at me. I really hope he's not thinking about me being in a towel. Gosh, am I ever going to be able to live this down? I give him a tight smile. "It still won't happen again. I'll get back down to the shop. Do you want to start training tomorrow?"

Noah stares at me for a moment. "Sure. I've been looking over some of the numbers that you sent over, and I've got some ideas on how we can get them up."

"We can talk about it tomorrow." I need to get out of this apartment before I die of heat or embarrassment. I move to grab my jacket, then I realize the dog is lying across it. I take a step toward the couch, which startles Noah. He jumps up as if he's going to hug me goodbye. "I, uh, just need my jacket." I point to the gray jacket half-hidden under his dog.

"Oh. Right. Mo, get down." Noah snaps his fingers and the dog is up and moving, tail wagging.

My mind snags on the name. "Mo? Like in Simone's books?"

"Yup, the very same." Noah smiles down at the small white dog. It's bigger than any pet I'd ever want, but it's kind of cute.

"You really do like those books." Great, we're back to talking about books.

"I do." These words snag on my heart. I blink away a scene of me in a white dress as it appears in my head. I'm supposed to be over daydreaming about the future and what could be. I will not start again just because Noah is standing in front of me and saying regular words. They don't have to make me think of a wedding, ours or the one I thought I'd have with Grant. I won't let them.

I grab my jacket. "See you later, then." I'm moving like the speed of light to the door when a hand catches my elbow, sending sparks through my body. I pull away as if I've been shocked because I might as well have been.

"Tally, I..."

I risk a glance at Noah. He seems flustered, which makes me feel a tiny bit better. I've been flustered since he sat down at my table on Monday. Olivia has asked me four times this week if I'm all right because I've been so spacy. Noah's eyes meet mine and I see something flash in them. He swallows. "I'll see you tomorrow."

I'm going to bet that's not actually what he was going to say. What changed when he looked at me? "Okay."

Then I turn and I'm out the door, flying down the stairs and unlocking the back door of the shop.

Okay? I didn't even say goodbye. I bury my face in my hands. That man is going to be the death of me, or at least he's going to crush my heart.

I hear my phone chime from where I left it in the office. I hurry to it, grateful for the distraction. It's a message from Mo. On Wednesday I asked him if I could think about his request to meet in person. I'm not sure how he took it, but he hasn't messaged me since he told me to take all the time I needed.

MoReads: Hey. You around to chat right now? I could use a friend.

His words remind me that we are still friends. Just because we've introduced the idea of meeting in person doesn't mean anything has changed, even though it feels like everything has changed.

> **TheNoraReview:** What's going on?

MoReads: I'm in between jobs right now, and I feel like I've lost my footing.

TheNoraReview: I totally feel that. Not exactly between jobs, but I've had a big change at work too.

And that, my friend, is the understatement of the century.

MoReads: If you could do anything, what would you want to do?

I blink at the sudden conversation change. It makes sense, I guess, because we don't really go into details about what we do for work or more personal stuff. But I decide to be really honest.

TheNoraReview: Travel to Scotland. I've never been, and my mom always wanted to take me because her family is from there. But we never got the chance.

The three bubbles appear and I wait for his reply, but a customer knocks on the front door and I let them in before getting a response.

9

NOAH

"Saturdays are usually our busiest days," Tally is telling me as we wander around the shop. We open in ten minutes. Her hair is pulled back in a loose ponytail, and I'm wondering how it stays because her hair doesn't seem that long. "We have one book club that meets once a month on Tuesday evenings. The next meeting is this Tuesday, if you want to watch. But you don't really need to be there because I'm in the book club and Olivia sometimes comes, so someone from the shop is always there. If we do more book clubs, you can help host a couple to even out the load."

I nod my head. "That sounds fine."

Tally bites her lip like there's something she doesn't want to tell me, but all it does is draw my attention to her perfect pink lips that I haven't stopped thinking about kissing for over five years.

"We read romance novels," she tells me. Why is that embarrassing? I've all but declared my love for the genre. "But the book club is very unconventional. After each meeting we all go over to the romance section and pick a book, a different book for every person. Sometimes we swap after, but we always pick a new one for the next meeting."

"Sounds like fun." There's a grin on my face, and I wonder how exactly I can get myself invited to this book club.

"You have no idea." Tally looks up at me. She's not wearing the heels she was in yesterday or on Monday. Her face is glowing with childlike joy. It's obvious that this book club is something that makes her happy. I feel the urge to find out all the things that make her happy, just so I can get her to smile.

Friends. We're just friends, I try to remind myself. *But friends can make friends smile, right?*

"What did you read this time?" I grab a picture book that does not belong in the history section to distract myself. I expect a glare, but what I get when I look back at Tally is a face that is redder than a strawberry. "What? You're not going to tell me?"

The blush on her face spreads to her neck. What I wouldn't give to know what's going on in her head. I have to know what she's been reading and why it's got her acting this way.

"It's, um—" Tally clears her throat and won't meet my eyes. "It's a very steamy historical romance."

"Intriguing," I murmur, and only then does she look up at me, her eyes wide. I smile at her. "I happen to be a huge fan of historical romances." This last bit isn't exactly true, seeing as I've never read one. But why haven't I? Even though I read a large variety of genres in general, when it comes to romance, I tend to pick up books that have fantasy elements as well.

Tally swallows hard. I take a step closer to her—for what, I'm not actually sure. I should probably stay away, but I don't want to.

Tally doesn't step back, and there's about a half a foot between us when there's a loud banging on the door. Tally jumps, dazed, and hurries to the front of the store. I watch her until she disappears behind one of the shelves. Only then do I turn and try to shake the tension from my body.

ON MY LUNCH BREAK, I slip out the back door and up the stairs to take Mo out and have a moment alone. Tally has been cordial all morning. Giving me the ins and outs of how they very informally track what books come in. Tonight I'm planning to start designing an online website so that we can not only sell potential inventory online but also have a better system for tracking the books we do have. I'll also figure out a code to create the system we have within the new website.

I put a cookie sheet full of pizza rolls in the oven and open Twitter. I haven't talked to Nora much this week since I am trying to give her space. But I had to talk to her after I ran into Tally in my new apartment yesterday. I mentally shake myself; I will not think of how she was wearing nothing but a towel, how smooth her shoulders were when I reached out to steady her, her skin warm and pink from the water.

"Nope," I tell myself, and Mo tilts his head as he looks at me. "Sorry, buddy, but I've got to get Tally out of my head. She's definitely not interested. Maybe she's got a boyfriend."

I haven't asked her outright, and from what I can tell, she spends most of her time at the shop, but the thought still makes my gut clench every time I think about her being with another man. It also makes me want to laugh because what type of normal person gets jealous when a woman they've got a crush on and barely even know might have a boyfriend?

But I'm also not just some random guy. I know Tally, the real one. At least I did. I know the one from five years ago, and at first I thought I had remembered wrong all these years because I didn't want to admit to the fact that Tally has changed, that she is different than how she used to be. Harder around the edges, she doesn't smile like she used to. Back then, she gave away her laughs so willingly, so easily. Now trying to get her to laugh is like pulling a tooth that isn't even loose. I don't want to stop trying though, because her laugh lights me up and I might also be a bit concerned about the permanent frown on her face.

Olivia can get Tally to crack a smile, but the smile never reaches her eyes. What happened in the last five years that made the light go out of her?

Without thinking about it, I type out a message and I've already sent it to Nora before I remember I'm trying to give her space.

> **MoReads:** Hey, I know we haven't been talking much (that's okay, seriously, take all the time you need to figure out if you'd like to meet or not. I know I kind of sprung that one on you), but I've got a friend who's pretty down in the dumps and I'm not sure how to help them.

There. We can talk about it, but she doesn't have to know my friend is a woman who I'm also kind of trying not to fall for.

I asked Nora to meet me at the Simone Sorrows event because it felt like the perfect place for us to meet since her books are the ones that brought us together in the first place. But she's also been my best friend for the past two years. I've always got Annie and Sam, but Sam hasn't even been in the country for the past year and Annie just started dating this guy I hate, so they're not always around. Nora is the one person I've been able to count on. Which is why it's so easy to reach out to her and ask her what she would do in this situation; she's always given the best advice.

While I wait for her to reply and for my pizza rolls to cook, I decide to call Sam. My expectations are incredibly low when it comes to my best friend since high school. I love the guy and the crazy adventures he's always taking us on, but he's not exactly the most reliable person in the world.

At least he's consistently unreliable.

The phone rings and rings and finally goes to his message. "This is Sam, you know what to do." *Beep.*

"Hey, man." I run a hand through my hair. "I could really use some guy advice right now. Remember Tally? Well, turns out she worked for my Grandma Marsha, and now we're running my grandma's old bookstore together. She pretty much hates my guts. Oh, and I asked Nora to meet me in person, but she hasn't responded yet, and mostly, I'm really freaking out. And I don't know how to talk to Annie about this, so give me a call back when you can."

I hang up and look at Mo. His eyes light up. "Ready for a quick walk?" He runs to the door. Mo is not a fan of sidewalks—at least that's what I thought while we lived in New York. I practically had to force him out the door to go on walks. Now he sits by the door multiple times a day to go out.

I'm starting to think that maybe it was New York and all the people outside that he wasn't a fan of.

I force myself to leave my phone on the couch when we go out for our walk. If I bring it, I'll be checking every five seconds to see if Nora responded or if Sam is going to call me back today. I should have texted him. Even if he doesn't respond that day, he's usually pretty good at texting back in a reasonable time frame.

Mo stops to smell a tree and I reach for my phone, groaning when I remember I left it upstairs. "This is torture!"

"Maybe you shouldn't have a dog, then." I whirl around to see a girl about seven staring up at me. "If taking a dog outside is torture, maybe you shouldn't have one."

I'm about to defend myself, to tell this child that I love my dog and nothing about him is torture, when a man appears.

"There you are," he says to the girl. "It's time to go."

The girl gives me an angry stare that could put Tally's to shame. Then she waves to Mo. "Bye, little doggy. I would love you."

Once she's out of earshot, I say, "Well, that was weird, buddy. Come on." We head back to the apartment, much to Mo's dismay. "I'll take you on a longer walk when I'm done with work." I feel bad. He's used to being able to go out whenever he wanted to. Working for yourself has its perks, this new schedule will take some getting used to,

Maybe I can convince Tally to let Mo hang out in the shop. He's the best dog. I could put his bed in the little office and he'd mostly just sleep all day. Plus, he doesn't bark at strangers, so being around people in the shop would be totally fine.

If only I could convince Tally of that, then I wouldn't feel so bad because I wouldn't be leaving him alone all day.

The oven timer is beeping when we get back up to the apartment. Mo pouts as he settles into his small bed right by the kitchen table.

"It's not my fault I have to eat," I tell him. I should have waited to take him out after I was done eating. I burn my tongue on my first bite, which annoys me. But I will not get up and get my phone until I've finished eating.

I scarf down my food because what's the point in waiting for them to be cooler if I've already burned my tongue?

There are three notifications on my phone.

Sam: Sorry I couldn't answer, bro, about to head to bed because tomorrow I start a weeklong backpacking trip.
I listened to your message. I'll call when I'm done with this trip. But quick advice, maybe figure out which woman you want to date before you tell either one you've got feelings for her.

Of course Sam is about to go on a backpacking trip. He's been a travel vlogger since we graduated high school, and his most-watched videos are when he goes backpacking on these hard trails, just him and his camera. I send him a quick text saying thanks and telling him not to get struck by any lightning on this trip, then I open Twitter to see the last message I got while I was out.

TheNoraReview: Thanks for giving me time. I'm still thinking about it. Mostly, I'm nervous about ruining what we have by meeting in person. And that stinks for your friend. Maybe get them their favorite treat or dinner or something. Good food always helps me when I'm feeling bad. I'm not really sure how to help someone else out of a hard time though. I've been a bit stuck in one myself and I can't seem to get out of it.

As I'm reading her message and wondering what she's going through right now, a new one comes through.

TheNoraReview: And maybe I shouldn't say this, but you always make me a little happier. Seeing your name in my notifications makes me smile, even on the worst days. It probably helps that you're great at telling me stupid jokes.
TheNoraReview: What I'm trying to get at is that if your friend is down, maybe you should go tell him a stupid joke, it would probably make him smile.

If Nora's still online, she'll be able to see that I've seen her messages, so I know I need to respond, but she just gave me a lot I need to unpack. It never even crossed my mind that meeting in person might ruin what we have. And I doubt Tally would appreciate my dad jokes, but it could be worth a shot to see if she'll laugh.

MoReads: I don't think seeing each other will ruin anything, but still, it's up to you if you want to meet or not. And thanks for the advice. I'll definitely try that.

I don't feel the need to correct her about her calling my friend a guy. What would be the point of telling her it's a woman anyway?

When I finally make my way back down to the shop, Tally is humming along to the overhead music. Maybe she's not entirely unfeeling.

"I'm ready to learn how to use that ancient cash register." I grin at her. I'd like to crack a joke, but for some reason it feels too soon to try and be funny with her. I want her to know that I'm serious about this job and being here, with her.

She looks at me quizzically. "Are you always so happy?"

"Yes. And you seem to be doing better than earlier," I say, because humming isn't a sign of a grumpy person, no matter how much she wants me to think she's a grump all the time.

She gives me a shrug and moves over to the register. I remind myself that we're co-workers and that I shouldn't get attached. *But maybe that was Grandma Marsha's whole idea about this anyway.* The thought comes out of nowhere, and I push it away. I can and will focus on being friends with her and nothing more. If my heart can catch the memo, that is.

A few minutes later my phone vibrates with a message from Nora.

TheNoraReview: Glad I could help. And I've decided that I do want to meet you in person.

And just like that, I'm the happiest person in the world today. Nora said yes. She said yes!

10

TALLY

TheNoraReview: What do you do to calm down when you're about to do something totally nerve-racking, not like speaking in front of hundreds of people, but my heart kind of feels like that's what is about to happen?

MoReads: Take a deep breath. (I know. Worst advice ever, but I swear it'll help.)
MoReads: I also like to think of a favorite memory. Visiting the lake we went to when I was younger, making one of my friends smile, the time I was totally spontaneous and had the best day of my life. Remembering those times usually help me feel calm. Hope that helps. And good luck with your not-speaking or whatever!

It's Tuesday night and I'm buzzing with a nervous energy. The Book Shop is closed to customers, and Noah and I are waiting for the book club ladies to arrive. Olivia opted out tonight because one of her friends from college is in town. She left me alone with Noah about ten minutes ago. I've been pacing at the front of the shop ever since.

I'm trying to think of a happy memory, per Mo's suggestion,

but the only one that keeps coming to mind is that afternoon with Noah, probably because Mo mentioned something about being spontaneous and I immediately thought of that afternoon. In the past it has been a memory that makes me calm (as long as I pretend it didn't end the way it did). But tonight, thinking about Noah's lips on mine and how he lit up every time he smiled at me or tugged me closer isn't helping.

Instead, the memory, combined with the fact that all of my favorite people are about to meet Noah, makes me want to throw up. I'm fluttering around the store, tucking in scattered books as a distraction. For some reason it felt different tonight when I shut and locked the door. Maybe because Olivia is normally here. Or maybe because ever since Noah came back into my life, my feelings have been all over the place.

Noah was always my "what might have been" guy, and now he's sitting on the red couch in the back of the shop, in my usual spot, and I'm not sure if I want to go yell at him or kiss him. Either way, both thoughts scare me.

"I know that look." I whirl around to find Shirley standing in the doorway. I was so wrapped up in my thoughts that I missed the chime of the bell.

"What look?" I can totally play this off.

"You've got man trouble." Shirley grins at me. All of the ladies in book club, Marsha included, have always tried to set me up with their grandsons or their friends' grandsons. But I don't date and they know that.

"Who has man trouble?" Gracie hollers as she, Pam, and Collene all push their way into the shop.

All four women stare at me. I try to divert their attention away from me and my unfortunately obvious men problems. "Not me. Where's Donna?"

"Parking the car." Pam closes in on me, not skipping a beat. "Now what's this about man trouble?"

"Don't know." Even though I do know. Even though these ladies would definitely be able to help me out of this sticky mess I seem to have found myself in. But Noah is in the shop, and I'm not one to talk about my men troubles.

"She's lying." Collene pats my shoulder as she passes by me and heads toward the back couch that is now surrounded by a few folding chairs set up for those of us who don't make it back there quick enough.

I'm saved from responding because Donna chooses that moment to enter the store. "I have chips and salsa!" Food is always provided by The Book Shop, one of Marsha's hard-and-fast rules about the book club, but Donna usually ends up bringing something. Usually whatever she's been craving.

"Tally's got men problems," Shirley tells her. They are not going to let this go, are they?

"Men really are the worst. I raised three boys on my own, now they're decent men, but still men," Gracie chimes in, helpful as always.

"I. Do. Not. Have. Men. Problems," I say through gritted teeth. But Collene has made it to the couch.

Where Noah is sitting.

"Who are you?" I hear her ask. "Gals, there's a gentleman here. Maybe he can tell us about Tally's man trouble. Are you the one causing her problems?"

Noah laughs, a deep chuckle that I feel all the way to my toes.

Noah is definitely causing me problems.

I haven't seen him since Saturday, thanks to Olivia telling me I could go early yesterday and not to come in until this afternoon today. But still, he's a big, bad distraction.

"There's a man here?" Donna and Pam nearly run to see him, as if they've never seen a man before. As if they don't both have husbands at home. Shirley is still watching me closely.

"Who's this fine gentleman?" Gracie wraps an arm around me.

"Marsha's grandson." Thankfully, that's the truth. I don't have to talk about our past at all. If I can get through the next hour without any of the ladies reading my face and all the secret feelings I've been trying to bury that I have for Noah, everything will be just fine.

"Oh, that's sweet of him to come help out." Gracie gives me another squeeze. Marsha's death was hard on all of us, but Gracie had known her the longest. They'd been friends since they were in high school.

"Marsha left him the shop."

"She did?" Gracie pulls away from me a bit so that she can gauge my feelings about this.

"She also left it to me. And, technically, her granddaughter, but only one of them has to work here in order for us to inherit some money Marsha left." We've reached the couch and circle of chairs. I will not look at Noah, but I can feel his eyes on me as I sit in one of the folding chairs.

"He's handsome!" Pam sits on the other side of me. "Wouldn't tell me who he is, but he looks a little like that Captain America guy. What's his name?"

I bite my cheek to keep from smiling. Pam has always been a talker; she probably didn't give Noah a chance to introduce himself. And she's not wrong about him looking a little like Chris Evans. They've both got the same jawline and hair color.

I sneak a glance at Noah. His cheeks are red as he's taking in all the women who are now staring at him and shouting out questions, mostly about who he is, if he's dating me, and if he knows why I'm having man trouble.

"Ladies." Time to rein them in. "This is Noah Jones, Marsha's grandson. She left him the shop, so he'll be around for a year. Give him some space though. Noah, these are the book club ladies."

I don't introduce them individually; I know they can do that all on their own.

Noah gives them all a grin that shows off his dimple. I swear Shirley swoons. "Nice to meet you all. But I don't know about Tally's men problems. She's been pretty tight-lipped about her dating life."

All five heads swivel in my direction.

I lick my lips nervously. "Like I said. No men problems."

"You were fine last month. Something is definitely going on," Shirley declares. "So it's either his fault or your online—"

"Okay, fine, I finally listened to your advice and set up a dating profile." I do not need Noah to find out that the only "relationship" I've had in the past two years is with a guy I've never met and am not actually in a relationship with. Now I'll have to make an online profile just so I don't feel guilty about the lie. "A few guys have reached out, but I'm not super interested in any of them."

I can tell right away that Shirley doesn't buy my story. From the other ladies, I get the words, "Good for you, honey."

I glance at Noah, who's got a single eyebrow raised at me like he's daring me to call my own bluff. I glance away, hot all over from the lie.

"What book did you ladies read this month?" Noah asks, saving me from my own embarrassment. I don't need saving, but I'm thankful. He hasn't seemed to notice the variety of books that are in our laps.

Pam grins as she holds up her book. One by one the ladies show their covers, all of which are different.

"Isn't the point of a book club to read the same book to discuss?" Noah looks confused, even though I swear I remember telling him about how this book club worked.

"No, dear." Collene, who's sitting next to him on the couch, pats his leg. "We all pick a new book every month before we leave here, read it, and then we talk about what we read."

"So you all read different books?"

"Right," Shirley says. She picked out a pirate romance last month, and I'm kind of dying to hear about it. Sometimes the ladies end up swapping books if the ones they read sound interesting. "This one, for example, completely flopped. The story had no plot, other than the fact they were on a pirate ship and they fell in love. Very steamy."

Shirley hates steam. She only comes to the book club because Collene is her neighbor and invited her. She always tries to pick books that won't be steamy, but she also loves every single cover that has a half naked man on it, so I'm not really sure what she's expecting.

"I'll take that, then." Gracie reaches over to take the pirate book from Shirley. Gracie will read anything and everything.

I risk another glance at Noah and see he's taking it all in.

We move around the circle slowly. Pam didn't like her book, but Gracie says hers is a new favorite. Collene laughs when she starts telling us about how her cat sat on her book and then knocked over a glass of her husband's coffee onto the book, so she only read about fifty pages.

"Tally, what book did you read this month?" Pam asks. All eyes turn to me, and for once I'm at a loss for words. Usually, I can talk about a book for hours and hours. Usually, I do. But the room is sweltering. Maybe we should go back to talking about my man problem.

"I picked a historical romance," I start. "With a guy who's got a bad reputation."

"Not your go-to," Gracie pipes in. She's right. I mainly read contemporary romance, rom-coms, or fantasy.

"No, but it was really good." I pause for a beat. That's all I can say? I write book reviews online as a hobby, and all I can say is that it was good? It was swoon-worthy good. Gran caught me squealing. Twice. All the women and Noah are staring at me expectantly. "It was steamier than I thought it would be."

"Those historical fiction ones always get you, but aren't they so great?" Gracie is gushing. Historical romance is her favorite. "It makes me wish I were young again. Not that my new wife has any problem—"

"Okay..." I interrupt her before she can share any more details about her intimate life, which she tends to do more than anyone else I've ever met. Mom would have liked her. Gran would probably be friends with her if I ever introduced them, but Gran has no interest in the book club. I finally stopped asking her if she wanted to come last year because I realized she wasn't going to change her mind. "But it was good," I finish my thoughts lamely.

Worst. Book review. Ever.

"I'll read it." I blink, and Noah is standing in front of me, tugging the book out of my hand. His fingers brush mine in the process, lingering a half second longer than they should. His eyes are daring me to challenge him, to not let him have the book, but it slips through my hand and into his.

He returns to my—his—spot on the couch and flips the book over to read the synopsis.

"You're blushing," Pam whispers.

I'm not blushing. My body has turned into molten lava. I could melt an iceberg.

It takes me ten minutes to breathe normally again. Once my breathing returns to a normal pace, I know a blush covers my face every time I think about Noah reading the book he's holding in his hands. Because then when I start to think about him reading the book, I think about him kissing me, of his hands caressing my face and kissing me like the love interest does in the book.

I miss most of the conversation.

It's only when Donna nudges me that I realize everyone is standing up, moving toward the front counter where I set out the pastries. "He really is darling."

I pretend not to have heard her because I am not going to have this conversation when *he can hear me*. I head toward the romance section and grab a book at random. "I think I'll read this one."

Donna smirks at me. "I think he'd be good for you. Have fun reading that one."

I peek at the book I just grabbed and nearly groan. Another historical romance, coincidentally by the same author as the book I read last time. I know it won't be bad. I know for a fact it will be excellent. I also know I'll end up thinking about *him* while I'm reading it, which won't make for a good time.

"Anyway, think about it." Donna is walking toward the treats. "You could use a guy like him."

What does that even mean? A guy like him? Does she mean someone who always seems to be smiling? I don't need a man to make me happy. I can't even make myself happy, so how on earth could a man do that?

11

NOAH

The ladies are laughing as they pick out their books for the next month. The worn paperback I took from Tally is still in my hands, which I don't plan to let it out of my sight until it's safe in my apartment. Tally keeps glancing at it like she's going to steal it away from me the second she gets the chance, which makes me want to read it even more.

"It was so good to meet you, dear," Shirley—or maybe it's Pam—says to me. "Take care of our girl for us."

Tally is chatting with one of the ladies. There are only five of them, but I can't remember who's who.

"I will."

"That's a good boy." She pats my cheek, and now I know how my dog must feel all the time. "We'll see you in a few weeks."

One by one, the ladies hug Tally and head out the door. She waves to them through the window before locking the door and turning to face me.

"That was..." I trail off because I have no words to describe the past hour.

"They're something else." Tally glances over at me. Instinctively, I lick my dry lips. I regret it the second her eyes drop to my lips and stay there longer than they should.

I know exactly what it feels like to have her in my arms, and regardless of what I keep telling myself, I don't want to stay away from her. I want to hold her and kiss her and prove that I'm not the kind of guy who walks away. That not all guys are bad.

"I like them. I can see why you enjoy this book club so much." I flip through the pages of the novel I took from Tally.

"Really fun. They're great." Tally smiles. Her cheeks are flushed, like they have been all night. She seemed so comfortable around all the women that were here tonight, except when they asked her about the book. I am dying to read it to know why she was so flustered. "Now you can see why that's one of my favorite nights of the month."

"It was definitely a good time. We should do more. Host more of these. We could even do a similar thing, just with mystery novels or YA. It's kind of fun to have everyone read something different. I didn't think I'd like it, but it was cool. We'd also want to start a book club where we actually read the same book because I'm not sure everyone would go for the unconventional kind, but I think it's a great way to get some more business."

"Yeah," Tally says, but she's stiff. I'm pushing too much, too fast. Now that I've started to spend a little more time with her, I've noticed that she does not like anything that changes too quickly.

"We don't have to do all that right away." I try to backtrack. "We can start slow."

Tally lets out a breath. "Slow would be good. There are only three of us here, so we don't want to rush into anything."

"Right." I squeeze the book in my hand, just to give me something to do. "I was also going to ask, do we have social media?" Once I can get the site up and running, we'll want to connect everything together.

"Yeah, we've got Instagram and Twitter. We don't have huge followings. I feel like Marsha always wanted the shop to be a word-of-mouth thing or a cute shop people saw as they walked or drove by. But we do have them."

"I'm thinking we should do a website." I'm bringing up way too much tonight, but Tally acts as if she's going to run anytime I talk about anything that isn't shop related, and I'm not ready for her to leave.

"I don't know if we have the resources or bandwidth to take on a project like that." Tally bites her lip as she says this, drawing my attention to the one place I've avoided looking all evening. Now I don't think I'll be able to look away. "And there isn't money to pay someone to make one for us."

"I'm a coder. I build websites for a living. When I said we should do a website, I meant me." *Do not think about kissing her. Do not think about kissing her.*

"Oh. Right," Tally mumbles. Crap. I've been staring at her lips for too long. When I meet her eyes, I know she knows exactly what I've been thinking. She takes a step back, right into a shelf. A few books tumble onto the floor. "Sorry."

I can't tell if she's apologizing to me or the bookshelf. "It's fine, are you okay?"

She nods, her eyes wide. She blinks and her face clears. "You wouldn't be overwhelmed by taking on the project?"

Right. All business.

"Nah." I shake my head. I can do this. "It would be something to do in the evenings. I'm not taking on personal clients right now, and my fingers are always itching to do something. Code something, I mean."

Why did that sound dirtier in my mind than the way I meant? I've been reading one too many steamy romance novels.

Tally swallows way too hard and loudly because my eyes snap to her lips again.

"Okay," she says.

"Okay," I say. I think she wants me to kiss her. She's staring at my lips, and I can't take my eyes off of her. Her gaze snaps to mine. The shop shrinks. Neither of us move.

"I should go," Tally says, breaking the connection.

It is a thousand degrees in here. "I hope you like the book," she says, and I know she immediately regrets it because her face goes bright red.

"Does your boyfriend know that you read smutty books?" I tease, still trying to figure out if she's single or not.

Tally lets out a shaky breath. "Is that what we're calling them these days? A good story is a good story regardless if there's sex on the page or not."

I grin at her, and she takes a step toward the counter where her bag is. I take a step. It's like a game of cat and mouse. "I agree. But you didn't answer the question."

"No boyfriend," Tally says casually. "Lots of dates though."

Lie. At least I think that's a lie.

"I have one this Friday!"

She doesn't, does she? I narrow my eyes at her, trying to call her bluff. "With whom?"

Tally scoffs. "An old friend. Why does it matter to you?"

I take a step back, remembering my place. Maybe she did just look at me like she wanted me to kiss her, but I promised her I'd be her co-worker, not even a friend. I won't push this if she really doesn't want it. "It doesn't. Anyway. Cool. Have a great time on your date. I'll see you later."

And with that, I turn and head to the back door. I lock it behind me, watching as the lights in the shop go off as Tally heads out the front door. I head upstairs to my apartment. Mo greets me, happily wagging his tail.

I try to forget about the conversation. I try not to think about Tally going out to dinner with another man, laughing, flirting. Is it too soon to admit that just thinking about it makes me physically sick?

My phone chimes, pulling me from my thoughts. Nora.

Talking to her always gets me out of my head. Hopefully, tonight will be the same.

TheNoraReview: Ever feel like you just keep messing up things in real life so badly?

I run my hand through my hair before responding. I know exactly what she means. I wish she'd tell me what she thinks she's messing up so that I could help her. Or at least be here to listen.

MoReads: All the time. But I don't think any of us have any clue what we're doing, so we're all just doing our best.

TheNoraReview: I really keep saying the wrong thing to people in my life. I know what I want to be saying, but I'm holding back.

MoReads: Why do you think that is?

TheNoraReview: IDK. Maybe I'm scared.

MoReads: You're not scared of me, right? Want to practice saying what you'd say to the people in your life?

TheNoraReview: Definitely not scared of you. But maybe I will practice with someone. (It's not that I'm scared to tell you or anything, it just feels weird. To talk about stuff that isn't book related.)

MoReads: We talk about more than books.

TheNoraReview: I know. SEE? This is what I mean. I can't even say the right thing over a DM.

MoReads: You haven't said anything wrong.

TheNoraReview: I know. I'm tired. I can't think straight. Maybe I really just need sleep and all of this will blow over.

MoReads: Sleep makes everything better. I never let myself make any big decisions at night. Sleep will help. I promise.

TheNoraReview: Night, then. Because I need all the help I can get.

MoReads: Goodnight, Nora.

12

TALLY

I smooth my gray sweater one more time before heading upstairs. Gran is at the kitchen counter, eating a bowl of cereal.

"You have your big date tonight?" She eyes me closely, knowing me well enough to know the real reason I set up this date.

"Yup." After telling Noah on Tuesday that I had a date tonight, I downloaded three dating apps, which I deleted the next day. I ended up scouring Facebook and reached out to a high school friend after he posted that he'd moved back to Utah. Luke was Peter's best friend in high school, so we were in the same friend group, but I was never interested in him back then. He was always the player of the group. I haven't seen him since graduation.

I have a tiny sliver of hope that he's changed somewhat since then. It has been over five years, after all. I'm not the same person I was in high school.

I'm going on this date because I feel like I need to follow through on the lie I told Noah. But it also feels like I'm somehow betraying Mo, even though I'm not committed to him in any way. We've only agreed to meet.

My stomach rolls with nerves as Gran stares at me. It's been a long time since I went out on a date.

"It's with that boy from high school?" Gran asks, her eyes narrowed.

"Yes," I tell her.

"And you're wearing those?" She means my heels.

"Yup. Always." I need all the confidence I can get tonight, and these cheetah-print heels are my favorite.

"What about that man from the bookshop?" Gran changes the subject from my shoe choice and I groan. I shouldn't have told her that the Noah I kissed all those years ago is the same Noah that I now see almost every single day.

Everything about this plan to go on a date tonight is see-through. A guy from my past shows up, and for the first time in over three years I'm going on a date? Yeah, no one would believe me if I said it was a coincidence.

Gran and Holly have zeroed in on the fact that Noah is back in my life and keep saying that since he gave me such an earth-shattering kiss the first time, maybe I should kiss him again.

I was trying so hard not to kiss him the other night that I blurted out I was going on a date tonight. Noah didn't even flinch when I told him, and that was slightly disappointing. That he didn't even seem to care. Which is exactly why dating will be good for me. At least until I can meet Mo and maybe we'll see if there's a spark of something more than friendship.

The doorbell rings. "I'm going on my date now," I tell Gran and grab my bag.

"You should go out with Noah. Or at least invite him to dinner on Sunday. A grown man needs to be fed, and with family."

"He has his own family, Gran."

"Not here! He needs a family here. Invite him, will you?" I know she won't let this go until I agree.

"All right." I'll mention it last minute tomorrow. That way maybe he'll have plans and won't be able to come, but I can tell Gran that I did invite him.

I open the door and smile at Luke.

He looks exactly like I remembered. His dark hair is longer than it was in high school and it curls around his ears. His smile reaches his deep brown eyes as he takes me in. "Tally Nelson," he says and then whistles. He actually whistles. I didn't know that people did that in real life. "Tally Nelson," he repeats, as if he can't believe it.

"Hey," I say, because I don't know how to respond. I close the door behind me and follow him down the front walk, stopping short when I see a small cherry-red scooter parked in front of the house. "That's your ride?" I frown at him and he grins.

"I'm saving up for an actual bike, but I mostly drive around town, so the scooter works! Her name is Apple."

I swallow. I have no words. He named his scooter Apple? Who names a scooter at all? What kind of grown man owns a scooter anyway?

"Plus, she gets great gas mileage."

"We can take my car." I point toward my sturdy Honda Accord. It may be fifteen years old, but it runs. Our restaurant reservation is thirty minutes away if you take the freeway. In a car.

Luke shakes his head. "I'm gonna ride this, but you can drive your car if that makes you more comfortable. I do have a helmet for you." He lifts the seat and grabs two identical bright-orange helmets that clash with the color of the scooter.

I hate the idea of riding on the back of his scooter with him, but I also don't really want to drive myself. We're supposed to be on a date. How can we talk in the car if we're not taking a car?

"It's fine," I grumble, grabbing the helmet. My hair is going to be completely flat by the time we get to the restaurant. *It's too late now*, I think as I pull on my helmet.

My fingers are frozen by the time we get to the restaurant forty-five minutes later, and I'm starving.

The waitress sets a basket of rolls on our table, saying she'll give us a minute. I slide onto the bench, surprised when Luke bumps my shoulder as he slides in next to me.

"Oh," I say, because I can no longer form actual words.

"It's more fun this way!" he says in an annoyingly high pitch that makes me a little nauseous. I'm not sure who he's trying to impress right now. I watched him act this way with so many girls in high school. I can't believe I thought tonight would be any different.

As his arm brushes mine, I'm thrown back in time to a different booth and a different boy, but I pull open the menu because Noah is the last person I want to be thinking about right now.

I'm deciding between a burger or a steak when suddenly my menu disappears. Luke is smiling at me, now holding both of our menus tucked under his elbow so I can't grab it from him.

"Tell me about what you do these days," he says, and I can't hate him for it. He is completely here and present in this date, and I'm so in my head that conversation will help me get out of it.

"I manage a bookstore," I tell him, and confusion crosses his face.

"Oh, you're still doing that? I thought you'd started something else," he says, and I wonder who exactly he's been talking to about me. Or how he even knew I worked at a bookstore to begin with since I'm fairly private about my real life online.

"Nope." I force a smile. "I'm managing a bookstore. It's not what I expected, but I really like it."

"Huh," Luke says, and our waitress appears, saving me from having to come up with something else to say.

"What can I get for you?" she asks us.

"I'll get the twelve-ounce sirloin with double fries," Luke tells her, and before I can put in my own order, he says, "and she'll have the Cobb salad."

I don't mind a Cobb salad, truly; it makes a great lunch when I'm craving it. But right now? Right now I want a burger. A big juicy burger covered with toppings. I know for a fact that this place has the exact burger I want. Piled high with tomatoes and lettuce and their signature sauce. Thinking about it makes my mouth water. Our waitress is gone before I can correct the order.

I feel a small burst of rage start to burn inside of me. "Why did you order for me?"

Luke shrugs, oblivious to my anger. "I saw you were looking at the burgers, but a woman like you needs to keep her figure."

I open and shut my mouth twice, staring at him. I cannot believe he just said that to me. The rage burns brighter. Does he really want a woman who looks like a trophy wife and then he leaves her once she has kids or gets a wrinkle?

Luke doesn't stop me when I reach for the bread basket, probably because he's launched into a monologue about how he just left his cushy job to come back here to start a nonprofit that helps underprivileged kids learn the skills they need to get jobs. "These kids just need a chance, you know?"

I catch the tail end of his spiel. He can't be all bad if he works with kids, right? I feel my anger start to fade as he tells me about some of the kids he's been working with. We'll have to have a conversation about how it's rude to order someone else's food and to comment on their bodies.

"They really are great, and it's not their fault they don't have the resources as someone who, say, has two devoted parents at home. We're really going to help these kids. Which is why I knew I had to be a part of it as soon as Peter told me his idea."

My heart stops. It's not that I've been obsessing over what Peter did to me, because I haven't. I forgave him a long time ago. I just hoped I'd never have to think about him again.

Which I probably should have thought about before I asked his best friend out on a date.

"He's actually going to come meet us tonight, if that's okay. I thought a double date with him and his wife would be fun, like old times, you know? Oh, there they are!"

I don't have time to process his words before I see Peter and a very pregnant woman walking toward us. They slide into the bench across from me and Luke.

"Hey, man!" Luke and Peter do some weird handshake-high-five thing, and I use the moment to send a text to Olivia.

> SOS. BAD DATE.
> *I need you to come get me.*

I send her my location and slip my phone back in my bag just as Peter looks at me.

This night could not get any worse.

I forgave him a long time ago for everything—not that he ever apologized; it was just something I had to let go of. But seeing him now brings back feelings I'd forgotten. Mostly, though, all I feel is rage.

"Tally, good to see you." Peter smiles at me and I hold back a grimace. Why on earth would Luke think this was a good idea? Why on earth did I pick now of all times to start dating again, and with Luke? I think tonight I might need to re-evaluate all of my life choices.

I give Peter a small nod and stare at my glass of water on the table.

The woman beside him, his wife—wow, that's a weird thought—claps. She *claps*. "Oh, this is so much fun! I've known Luke for a long time, but it's always so fun to meet Peter's high school friends."

I look at her for the first time. She can't be more than twenty, if that.

"So, you were friends in high school? Did you always like Luke? He was so excited when he told us about his date with you."

"Um."

"Tally actually dated Peter in high school," Luke announces to the table. He seems so proud to be the one to share this fact. "We all thought they were going to get married."

Peter shifts uncomfortably. His wife grins at him. "What? No way. That's so cool."

My eyes widen and I grab the glass of water in front of me so I have an excuse not to reply.

"My high school boyfriend dumped me right after graduation. Then I met Peter the next week, and I knew it was all meant to be."

"How long have you been married?" I ask.

"It'll be a year in October." She grins at him, and he, realizing she doesn't hate him for being on a double date with his ex-girlfriend, smiles back. He leans forward and kisses her on the cheek.

Peter and his wife, who he introduces as Ava, order when the waitress comes back with our drinks. My phone vibrates on the bench next to me, distracting me from my one opportunity to change my order. The waitress is gone before I realize it. I pull my phone out of my purse. It's a message from Olivia

Help is on the way!! Not me, my husband ordered pizza just before you texted so I'm busy. But help is coming. ;)

That can only mean one thing.

Noah. Noah is coming to save me from this horrible date. A date that Olivia no doubt told him I needed saving from.

And I thought this night couldn't get any worse.

13

TALLY

"You okay there?" Luke asks, eyeing my knee that can't seem to stay still. It's been bouncing since I realized that Noah is on his way here to help me. I hoped for a moment that Olivia would have called one of the book club ladies to come and pretend there was a family emergency, but that winky face told me everything I need to know.

They brought our food about ten minutes ago, but I can't bring myself to eat. Not when the smell of fresh fries keeps assaulting my senses every time I move. I take a breath and twist my hands in my lap to keep from grabbing one. I am incredibly jealous of the large basket of fries that sit in front of Ava.

I see Noah before he sees me—he's walking through the restaurant looking for me. If I weren't so mad about Olivia sending him, I might offer him a wave. Before I have the chance to actually do this, he calls my name and the chatter in the room dies.

I raise my hand, making me feel like a timid student who doesn't actually want to share the answer with the class.

"You know that guy?" Luke asks, suddenly sitting up straighter. He flexes his arm as Noah approaches the table.

Is this guy for real?

"Tally, Olivia said I could find you here." Noah only has eyes for me, which I appreciate because I really, really hope he doesn't look at Peter and recognize him. "There was a bit of an accident at the shop, and she thought you should know about it, and you weren't answering your phone, so I came instead. This your date?" Noah finally looks at Luke.

"Oh, what happened? And yes, this is Luke. He's an old friend from high school." I want to say, *Look! I didn't lie! I'm actually on a date! See! Me and a man, on a date!!*

Then Noah does something I didn't anticipate; he grabs a chair from a neighboring table and sits at the end of ours.

"Do I know you?" Peter asks him right as Luke says, "We're on a date, man."

Noah ignores both of them and continues to stare at me.

"A date, huh?" Noah's still staring at me. "I thought you meant a date with a book."

I swallow and take my time answering because that is truly the kind of date I wish I were on right now. "I do spend a lot of weekends doing just that, but then I saw that Luke was in town and thought I'd see if he wanted to get together."

Now everyone at the table is staring at me.

"That's not completely true," Luke starts, but I ignore him. I have no idea what he was going to say because that's exactly what happened.

"Is that so?" Noah says, looking between the two of us. "What do you like about him?" Noah clasps his hands in front of him on the table as if we're in some sort of job interview that I know I'm about to fail. This isn't a job I even want, let alone one I would get.

"He's good-looking," I say, because now my anger is back and I'm a little peeved that Noah is here, asking these questions. Like he knows exactly what I'm doing.

"You don't seem like the type of woman who goes out with people just because you find them attractive." Noah cocks an eyebrow. His eyes are like a forest I could get lost in.

I've been caught. I shrug, trying to brush it off.

Peter snaps his fingers. "I know, you're that guy from that diner or café or whatever. You dated Tally."

Oh, fudge, as Holly would say.

Noah turns slowly to Peter, scans his face, and then looks back at me. "Anyway, the shop, the hot chocolate machine broke."

"What?" I'm so confused by this information and the fact that Noah said nothing to Peter's remark that I don't know what else to say.

"A lady brought in several large boxes full of books, and as I was moving them off the counter, I kind of bumped the hot chocolate machine and it fell."

I don't know if Noah is being serious or not right now, but if he is, I can feel my heart cracking in two. Marsha told me how she had to custom order the machine because most companies make coffee machines, nothing specific for hot chocolate, even though it's a similar concept.

"It fell?" I know I sound crushed because I am. I love that machine, and now it feels like another part of Marsha that's just gone.

"Wait, you two work together and you dated?" Luke asks.

"Yes" is all Noah says. I'll have to thank him later for sticking to the story we made up five years ago. "I said we should wait until tomorrow, but Olivia said I should tell you right away."

"You should have waited until tomorrow," Luke cuts in. "We're on a date, and we were having a great time until you showed up."

"Olivia didn't think we should wait to tell Tally." This is all Noah offers by way of explanation.

In this moment I should say something, thank him, maybe. But my stomach decides it's had enough and growls so loud that I'm pretty sure people in Antarctica hear it.

I watch as Noah glances at me, then at the salad on the plate on the table, then back up to me with a raised eyebrow.

Luke touches my arm. I'm hoping he'll offer me some of his fries, redeeming himself once and for all. "Are you really gonna listen to this guy? He's just trying to break up our date."

"I think our date ended the second you ordered for me." I jerk my arm out of his grip and motion for him to get out of the booth so that I can also get out.

Luke looks at me like I've just taken away his puppy. "That wasn't that big of a deal."

"It was to me." I give him a little shove, but he's a solid mass on the vinyl seating. "I wanted a burger."

Luke raises his voice, and now more than the people at are table are looking in our direction. "It wasn't a big deal! You really didn't want that burger. A woman like you shouldn't eat burgers regularly."

"A woman like me?!" I repeat, my voice matching his volume. "How dare you! You didn't even ask. You can't read my mind, so why on earth would you tell me what I actually wanted? You don't know me at all."

"Dang, Peter, you were right, she is a handful." Luke looks across the table at his best friend, who's watching all of this happen with wide eyes.

I let out a sound that comes out half cackle, half scream. Then I manage to stand on the bench. If Luke won't move, I'll find another way out of here. I step onto the middle of the table and immediately regret it as it wobbles and my salad hits the bench. Ava lets out a squeal as her food slides across the table.

"Hey!" Luke shouts as a glob of salad dressing hits his pants. I ignore him and take a step in Noah's direction.

Noah's hand catches mine and he helps me, very ungracefully, off the table. For the second time tonight I'm grateful that I chose to wear pants and not a dress.

"Hey, where are you going?" Luke asks, and I turn to see him still sitting at the table. Not that I want him to chase after me, but he's not even going to get up?

"The date is over," I tell him simply.

"Oh, it was so fun to meet you!" Ava says, and I can't make myself fully look at her. This whole thing has been too awkward.

"Why is the date over?" Is Luke really that dense?

I don't even bother to give him an answer. "Just lose my number, 'kay?" Before he can reply, I'm hurrying through the restaurant. I pull my phone out of my pocket. I'll call Gran or Dad; I don't need saving from Noah.

Luke yells the whole time as I'm walking away about how ungrateful I am, how my hair looks terrible, and how I'm just the same as I was in high school. How he understands now why Peter cheated on me.

I ignore him, but with every step, my confidence is fading as more people turn to look at me because of all the commotion.

"Hey, wait up." I startle at the sound of Noah's voice; in the midst of all the insults Luke is throwing at me, I forgot that he was here, witnessing the whole thing.

"I don't need you to save me." I don't mean to snap at him, but Luke's words are echoing in my head. How I'm a handful but not enough of anything else to be worth dating. That because of who I am, Peter had every reason to cheat. I wish the words didn't hurt, but they do.

The night air is cool when we step out into it. I hope that Luke is freezing by the time he gets home.

I wait for Noah to snap back at me, but his voice is soft as he tugs on my wrist and I meet his eyes. "I know you don't need saving, Tally. You can do that all on your own. You did do that all on your own. Olivia texted and said you needed to be picked up after a bad date. When I didn't see you waiting at the front, I went in to find you. I am sorry if I said anything in there that embarrassed you or made you feel bad in any way."

My heart warms a tiny bit around the edges. "Did you really break the hot chocolate machine?"

Noah shakes his head and sticks his hands in the front pockets of his jeans. "I almost knocked it off, but I caught both the box and the hot chocolate machine before there was any damage."

I let out a breath, relieved that I can still have hot chocolate in the morning. I'm relieved that I don't have to sit through any more of that bad date.

"Want to grab something to eat? Like an actual burger?"

I should say no. I really, really should say no. "I'm starving."

"Let's go." Noah holds out a hand, but I shake my head. No more physical contact. I do follow him to his car though, which has heat and does not make me feel like I'm going to die every time he accelerates.

———

WE END up sitting outside an In-N-Out after going through the drive-through. I sigh when I take my first bite.

"That good, huh?" Noah asks, smiling into his own burger.

"You have no idea." I take another bite and watch a group of teenagers come out of the restaurant, all talking and laughing. One of the girls looks a little lovestruck as she looks up at one of her friends. I remember feeling like that once. That's how I used to look at Peter. And probably how I looked at

Noah during our afternoon together. Everything changed after that day. I should probably be over it by now. I was only eighteen at the time. Mom would be sad that I gave up on love so soon. And sure, I often entertained daydreams in my mind where things worked out with the cute guy at the grocery store or the Noah from my dreams, but I didn't actually believe in true, lasting love. Maybe for some people, but not for me.

"Tally?" Noah asks, and I think I've missed something he said.

"Yeah?"

"Why are you staring at those teenagers?"

"What?" I ask, trying to play it off. "I think I kind of was just staring into space."

Thankfully, Noah accepts this explanation.

"So, why did you really go out with that guy?" Noah asks, and part of me hates how straightforward he is. This would be a lot easier if he didn't seem so open about what he wanted because there's a tiny part of me that's thinking it's *me* that he wants, but I don't let that thought take root in my mind.

"Like I said, I knew him when we were younger. He posted something online and I saw that he was in town, and I thought it might be fun to go out," I say, shuddering at the words. "But that was the opposite of fun."

"Which part? Him ordering your food for you or your ex-boyfriend also being there?" Noah takes a sip of his shake.

I start to laugh. The whole thing was so ridiculous. "He showed up to my house on a scooter, you know, those little moped things. He said her name is Apple. Who names a scooter?"

"Me. I named a scooter," Noah says, straight-faced.

"What?" I never liked motorcycles or scooters; Holly thinks they're cool, but I am not a fan. I look down at my half-eaten burger. Would it worth it to jump out of the car and leave right now?

Noah's laugh fills the car. "I'm kidding. I've never owned a scooter."

I roll my eyes. Of course he would joke about that, but I'm grateful he's lightened the mood.

"I'm not sure what the worst part of that date was—the scooter, the ordering my food, or the fact that he said a girl like me shouldn't eat burgers."

"Yeah, that guy's a dirt bag," Noah says as he frowns. Feels kind of nice to have him be angry about something since he's always so calm.

"Or something like that. I was pretty mad, and I don't remember exactly what he said because I blocked it from my memory already. But that was the gist." We're quiet for a second.

"This is why I don't date," I say, right as Noah starts talking.

"I hate men like that," he says vehemently. "You need a guy who accepts you for you and doesn't try to do things like that for you. You can eat whatever you want. You are your own person; you don't need someone making choices like that or about anything."

I blink, watching him carefully. I reach for my fries instead of replying, instead of looking at Noah, because why did he have to say the perfect thing right then? I guess it makes sense, on some level, that he would say something like that. He seems like a decent enough guy and he reads romance novels.

"If your dates treat you like he did, I can see why you'd hate dating." Noah is watching me carefully now. "You deserve so much better."

"Better than you?" The words are out of my mouth before I can catch them.

"I definitely deserve that." Noah sets his burger in his lap.

"Would it help if I told you that I've never been sorrier for anything in my life than for running away from you without any sort of explanation?"

It does help a little, but I don't tell him that.

"Because I am sorry. I want to show you that I'm not that guy."

"I'm not interested in dating anyone, not after tonight."

Noah frowns. I'm surprised that this is what upsets him.

"I'm not like that guy in there," Noah murmurs. "I know you have very little evidence to the fact that I'm not that kind of guy, but I'd like to show you. If you'll give me a chance."

What do I even say to that? That I'd love for him to show me, to prove it to me that he's actually a decent man? But I don't want him to do that. I'm not ready for any type of romance in my life. It will only make things more complicated.

I'm saved from responding by my phone ringing. It's Holly. I texted her after the disaster with Luke while Noah and I were waiting for our food.

"Hey, Holls," I say, glancing at Noah. He's looking at me with so much care that it makes me wish I hadn't put up so many walls around my heart. I have to look away from his gaze.

"YOU'RE ON A DATE WITH NOAH!?" Holly shouts into the phone.

"Not exactly," I say, praying she'll lower her voice and at least not mention my ongoing daydreams about the man I cannot fall for. I give her a rundown of the events.

"But you're with him? In his car?" she asks.

"Yeah."

"Then get off the phone, Tally Nora Nelson! Call me later." Then she hangs up.

"That was my sister," I tell Noah. I can't seem to look at him. I don't know why, but I think it's because I know he heard

Holly call this a date and I'm not sure I want to classify it as that.

"I heard."

Great. Perfect. Absolutely wonderful.

"I'd like to be your friend, Tally."

I've lost count of how many times Noah has surprised me tonight. It also feels a little like a rejection, but that's not what I see when I look at his face. He's got a determined look, and I'm almost positive that being friends is not what he wants. But I can do friends.

"I'd like that." The air in the car rises a few degrees as we stare at each other. I'm the first to look away. "Oh, also. Gran insisted I invite you to her Sunday-night dinner."

I guess I'm also full of surprises tonight.

"I'd love to come." I can hear the smile in Noah's voice. "And I'm looking forward to being your friend."

14

NOAH

MoReads: Have I mentioned that my dog loves waffles?

TheNoraReview: That is the most random thing ever. But no, you haven't mentioned it. Are dogs allowed to eat waffles?

MoReads: I rarely make breakfast for myself, but I did today and he was going crazy! Anyway, I hope you're having a good Sunday and that something makes you as happy as waffles make my dog.
MoReads: Yes, they can eat waffles, but should he? Probably not. ALSO, did you start book one yet? Have we ever talked about the cliff-hanger ending?

TheNoraReview: I'm on book two right now. I KNOW. I started it before telling you. I told you I'm bad at buddy reads. The end of book one is the worst.

Nineties country music blasts from my car speakers while I make the short drive from my apartment in Provo to where

Tally lives with her grandma in Orem. The songs are comforting and remind me of home. There's a longing in my chest for that feeling. It has been so long since anywhere felt like home, even when I was living in the same town I grew up in. For the past couple of years it has felt like something was missing. Annie and Mom think it's a woman, I don't think that would make a difference. All the women I've dated haven't fixed that missing piece. And I know that it's not a woman who makes a place feel like home, but rather the life that you have together.

The neighborhood where Tally lives is older and reminds me a little of the neighborhood where I grew up. The house is white and bigger than I expected. There are two tall trees in front and some empty flower beds that I'm sure are full of bright flowers in the summertime.

My palms are sweating as I get out of the car. The cool breeze tonight feels good, and leaves crunch under my feet as I make my way up the front walk.

I take a deep breath before ringing the doorbell. A few seconds later a man in his fifties answers the door. Tally has his face, which means this must be her dad. Crap. How did I not realize that tonight I'm not just having dinner with her and her grandma but that I'm probably about to meet her parents?

"Noah?" the man asks, and then he grins at me. I nod. He reaches out and pulls me into a hug. If I weren't so surprised or shaking with nerves, I might have cried. It's been a long time since any type of dad gave me a hug.

"Nice to meet you, sir," I say as we step onto the small landing. I note the pile of shoes and slip off my own. There's music playing somewhere up the stairs and I hear women laughing.

"Call me Joe." He holds out a hand, which makes me smile, considering the man just gave me a bear hug.

"All right, Joe."

"Everybody's upstairs." Joe leads the way up the stairs to a family room with a dining room toward the back. Laughter comes from what I assume is the kitchen.

We walk in together and the laughter stops. There's soup simmering on the stove, and a woman who I assume is Tally's mother is pulling bread out of the oven.

"You know Tally," her dad says, pointing to where she's sitting at a barstool. She gives me a shy smile that makes my heart flip. "That's my mom."

"You can call me Gran, sweetheart." The older woman who was talking to Tally steps closer to me. "Why didn't you tell me he was so darling?" She looks back to Tally, whose face is now a deep red. I hold back a smile. Gran turns back to me. "Has anyone ever told you that you look like Chris Evans?"

I shake my head, laughing. "I haven't heard that one much."

"Well, you do." She pats my cheek and goes back to cutting up tomatoes for a salad.

"And this is Beth." Joe's voice has gone soft. "My fiancée." I shake her hand, my mind spinning. I'm going through all the conversations I've ever had with Tally and she's never mentioned that her mom was out of the picture. She's told me how her mom was the one who introduced her to romance novels and how she and her sister love watching romance movies because of their mom. It never occurred to me that she wasn't going to be here tonight. I would like to meet her sometime. I notice Tally's smile has gone from relaxed to stiff, and I wonder if I'm the reason.

"Hey," I say, bumping her shoulder with mine. The small touch sends a jolt of energy through me. I need to figure out a way I can casually touch her more often. You know, in a friendly way, now that she's agreed we can be friends.

"Hey yourself." Tally smiles and seems to relax a little as I stand next to her, so maybe I'm not the reason for her being so on edge?

"Thanks for coming." Gran smiles at me again. "You're a growing boy, you need food. You have to come every Sunday."

Gran doesn't seem like a lady to be messed with, so I say, "All right."

Tally's cheeks are pink after that, and I don't know what to think. I'm still wrestling with my own feelings. Sam texted me yesterday, telling me that I should tell Tally that I'm interested in her. It was only a few hours after I'd told Annie that Tally and I had decided to be friends. I love Sam and Annie, but I don't like how much she talks to him.

Either way, I'm not telling her how I feel, not yet.

Soon we move to the dining table. Gran has me sitting right next to Tally, which I can't say I mind at all.

"So, what were you doing before you started at the bookstore?" Gran asks and all eyes but Tally's turn to me.

"I'm a coder," I start, suddenly missing the work I used to do. I've been sort of working on the shop's website, but it feels weird to be working on something that is sort of for me rather than for a client. Besides the app I made, I've always been doing projects for other people. "I sold an app when I was eighteen, and I've been doing a lot of freelance stuff since then."

"And how old are you now?" Joe asks me.

"Twenty-six," I say, and Tally looks at me in surprise.

"I thought you were my age." I can see the wheels calculating that I was, in fact, twenty-one when I kissed her that day.

I shrug. "A lot of people think I'm younger than I am."

"That's how old Tally's sister, Holly, is," Joe tells me.

"Cool," I say, because I'm not really sure what else to say. I knew that I was older than Tally, does it matter that I'm her sister's age?

"Could you pass the butter?" Beth asks, and Gran is briefly distracted.

"You were twenty-one?" Tally whispers to me. My heart

flutters slightly knowing that she's thinking about kissing me, even if for half a second.

I nod.

"I could have been a minor," she says, still whispering. No one is paying attention to us.

"But you weren't." It had been a risk, one I hadn't thought about at all until I was on a plane and headed back to Colorado. We'd only spent the afternoon together and mostly in public.

Tally is still glaring at me out of the corner of her eye when the conversation comes back to us.

"Are you liking Utah?" Beth asks me.

"Yeah. I like being so close to the mountains," I say. "I came a few times when I was younger to visit my grandma. My mom lives in Colorado. My dad left when I was a kid, so we were always with mom. My grandma was her mom, but they had a bit of a falling out when my mom and dad got married, and my mom didn't love it when we came to see Grandma, even after Dad left. I came out more than my younger sister, Annie."

And now I am rambling like an idiot about my chaotic family life.

Gran doesn't miss a beat though. "Well, I'm glad you like it. I know Colorado has mountains, did you live by them too?"

I laugh. "Kind of. Where my mom lives, it's a little over an hour away, so we can't really see the mountains from her house."

"Where did you say that was?" Joe asks.

"Kersey," I tell them. "It's a really tiny farming community just outside of Greeley."

"Never heard of either." Gran grabs the potatoes.

"Most people haven't." I laugh a bit. "It's about an hour north of Denver." That's the easiest way to explain it.

The conversation moves away from mountains and into books, then our favorite foods, and holiday traditions. Tally is quiet through most of it.

I poke her shoulder as her dad is clearing the table. "Everything okay?"

"Fine," she says quietly. Beth and Gran are talking about Halloween plans. It's already only a few weeks away.

The faint pink I've gotten so used to seeing on Tally's cheeks flushes her face, but this time the reason for the color isn't because I smiled at her. "I don't believe you."

"Well, I'm fine." There's an edge to her voice. I try to force the concern off my face. Something is obviously wrong; she's more closed off than usual.

"Am I making you uncomfortable?" This feels like the only possible explanation. This is her family, and I know that personally, I'm most comfortable being myself around the people I care about most. From how Tally has talked about Gran and her dad, I assumed that she'd be the same way. But it's like she's a completely different person. I am the only different factor. I've intruded on her family life, and I knew she didn't like me. I just didn't realize how much.

Tally snorts. "Don't flatter yourself. It's not you."

I frown at her. "Then, what?" I ask as her dad comes back into the room.

"You're sure quiet tonight, Tally." Looks like I'm not the only one who noticed how she's acting.

"Just tired," she says, and then she forces a yawn. I know it's fake because her eyebrows scrunch when she actually yawns and they don't do that this time, but no one else seems to notice. "I think my period is coming."

Another lie.

I'm pretty sure, anyway, because she was complaining about cramps the other day to Olivia at the shop, and I happened to be getting back from my lunch right as she said it.

Gran frowns.

"I'm sorry, kiddo," Joe says as he sits back down beside Beth.

"Well, I would have loved to do this when Holly was also here, but since she won't be here until Christmas, I'll tell you all now."

Tally tenses beside me. I briefly wonder if I've missed a vital clue about what is about to happen.

"We're engaged!" Joe and Beth grin at each other. I would think their interaction was sweet except for the fact that Tally's fists are clenched around the folds of her dress. By the time Beth and Joe look at Tally and Gran, Tally's features are completely blank again.

Beth is smiling from ear to ear.

"Well, it's about time!" Gran says, clearly happy for them.

"Congratulations," I say. It would feel inappropriate not to say anything, even though I don't think I'll earn any points from Tally by saying it.

"Why so soon?" Tally asks quietly.

Beth's smile becomes more tentative now and she looks at Joe.

Tally's hand starts to shake under the table, and when I reach over and wrap it in mine, she doesn't pull away.

Joe is staring at his daughter as if he doesn't know the right words to say. It's obvious the man loves Beth and that he's happy but also aware of Tally's feelings.

"It's time, sweetheart," he says finally, his words so gentle that it breaks my heart.

Tally is silent for a moment. "I am happy for you. But I don't understand why you are rushing this. You guys have only been dating for a few months." Tally pulls her hand from mine and stands. "I'm going to go to bed. Thanks for dinner, Gran."

"Tally..." Joe obviously wants to say more and I'm surprised he doesn't. Her outburst isn't something that should just be ignored, right?

Tally just shakes her head. Joe stands and gives her a hug. "I love you, baby girl," he tells her quietly, and she nods, then turns. Her eyes fill with tears.

"Night, Dad. Gran. Beth." She looks at me briefly. "Noah." Then she heads down the stairs.

We're all quiet for a minute.

Beth looks sad now; this clearly didn't go the way she'd hoped. Joe rubs her shoulders. "It's going to be okay. That actually went better than we thought."

That went better than they thought? What were they expecting to happen? I know I'm missing a lot of info here, but if Tally thinks they're rushing it, maybe they are.

Beth sighs. "I guess so. I know she likes me. I like her. I know it's hard...I'm not trying to replace—"

Joe cuts her off. "No one thinks you are. It'll take the girls some time though. We'll pick a date and everyone will have a chance to warm up to the idea."

"Do you think I should go talk to her??" Beth looks up at him. I pull at my sleeves; this feels like a conversation that I shouldn't be a part of.

"No," Gran declares loudly before Joe can answer. "When Emily died, it was like the life went out of you. Your light is back, Son. Your daughters know that; they see that. It might be hard for them, yes. But they'll survive. They both love Beth, you know that. You both know that."

Then Beth is crying and hugging Gran, thanking her.

"I'm going to go say bye to Tally, then head out," I say, but the women are still hugging and don't hear me.

"Her room is the first door on the left, downstairs," Joe tells me. I give him a grateful nod.

"Thanks for dinner," I say, but the women aren't listening. They're already talking about flowers and table settings.

My heart is pounding in my chest, and I don't know what I'm going to say when I see Tally. I just know I can't leave without saying something, anything. Now I know that her mom is gone—I don't know when, but maybe it was recent and that's why she thinks this is sudden. Or maybe it's been a long time, but either way, it still sucks because her mom is gone.

I don't know what I'll do when my mom dies. I don't talk to her as much as I should, but she's only a phone call away.

I knock on Tally's door.

"Come in," she calls from the other side.

I'm not sure what I expected, but opening the door reveals two walls covered with bookshelves, a twin bed in the middle of the room because that's all there's room for, and a desk shoved in the other corner. Beyond the furniture, the room is spotless and very Tally.

"Hey," I say, awkwardly standing in the doorway. She invited me in and is sitting at her desk, so the only place to sit is on her bed, and I don't know if she'd like that. "You really okay?"

Her face is red, as if she's been crying, but her cheeks are tear-free.

"Ish." She laughs. "You'd think that after five years it wouldn't feel like it's such a big deal. They've been dating since the beginning of the year. I shouldn't be surprised. But it makes me miss mom"

I step forward, moving her laptop closer to her so I can sit at the foot of the bed. I don't know how to ask what happened to her mom. "She's your mom. It's always going be a big deal."

Tally wipes a tear from her face, and I resist the urge to pull her into my arms and comfort her. "I guess that's true."

"It's okay to be sad about it."

Tally nods. "I know. It's a weird mix of feelings I have right now. Grief is weird like that—it hits you at the weirdest moments. Like, Beth is great for my dad. She's so different than Mom was, but she makes Dad so, so happy. I know he really loves her. I wish I could have been more excited just now. But them announcing they got engaged makes it more real. It's another reminder that she's not here."

"They kind of sprang it on you," I say. "And I'm sorry she's not here."

"True. Thanks." Tally laughs a little, then her eyes well up again.

"You can be happy for them later and still feel sad."

"Thank you." She gives me a smile, a real one. Even with the tears on her cheeks, she's beautiful.

"You're welcome."

"If you're here whenever they decide to get married," Tally starts, taking a shaky breath, "would you want to be my date? Friend date, I mean?"

"For the wedding?" I ask her, surprise bubbling up inside my chest.

"Yeah." She shrugs like it's no big deal. "I mean, I know Holly will for sure be there, but I could definitely use a friend who won't also be crying and smiling at the same time like she will be."

"It'd be my pleasure." My voice comes out lower than I mean it to, and her eyes darken.

Tally laughs, a low belly laugh. The sound is something I want to capture and take home with me and keep forever. "No one says things like that—'It would be my pleasure.'"

Now it's my turn to laugh. "Last time I checked, I didn't have a British accent."

Tally throws her head back against her pillow. "Oh, gosh. I did do that, didn't I? Remind me never to mimic you."

"I'll try," I say with a laugh. "But chances are, you'll say the words before I can actually remind you."

Tally wipes away another tear, but I think the new tears are from her laughter and not because of her mom. "Fair."

"You good?" I ask again.

"I will be." Her eyes are a brighter blue now, the result of tears, I guess. I still want to hug her. "Thanks for coming to check on me."

"Of course."

"I'll go back up with you so I can actually congratulate them."

She stands, stretching. Her sweater lifts just enough that I see a sliver of her skin and my stomach flips. I remember how perfectly she fit against me when I kissed her. Maybe I could now...

"I don't really do well when big things like that are just sprung on me, ya know?"

"I get that." I stand too. The room seems to shrink now that we're standing just a foot apart from each other, thoughts of kissing her still fresh in my mind. She looks up at me and I wonder, if I kissed her now, would it be like it was all those years ago?

"So just try not to ever surprise me. Okay?" She's staring up at me with puppy dog eyes, and I decide I like this side of Tally. At the shop she's always all business, which isn't a bad thing, but this soft side makes me want to take her home and keep her there so she'll stay that way forever.

I put a hand over my heart. "I promise."

MoReads: Reading anything good this fine Friday evening?
MoReads: I'm almost done with book three. I will totally finish
rereading all four books before next week!
MoReads: Can't wait to meet you!

My empty mug of hot chocolate is on the coffee table, and I'm
nearly done with my chapter when the doorbell to my apartment rings. Mo sits up, looking at me.

"Who do you think that could be, buddy?" I'm not
expecting anyone tonight. I didn't order food, and the only
people who know I live here are Tally and Olivia. But I'm
surprised when I open the door and see Tally standing on my
doorstep.

"Um. Hi." She gives a small wave.

"Everything okay?" I ask her. We worked together all afternoon, so this is a big surprise.

"Yeah. I, uh." She swallows. Her cheeks are pink, but it's not
that cold outside. I can't help but smile at her though, because
she showed up here unannounced and that has to mean something, right? *We're just friends,* I have to remind myself.

"Gran had bingo night at our house, and I just needed to get out. I hope it's okay that I came here. I brought food." She holds up a bag that smells like tacos. "Tacos," she says, as if hearing my thoughts. "Gran had a coupon to get like five free, so I have a lot of tacos."

"Come on up," I say, holding the door open so she can come in. I haven't ever seen her this way since the first day I met her, and I like it. Lately, she's always got some sort of grumpy face or attitude going on, so the fact that she showed up here, of her own free will, with a smile on her face? Yeah, I'm letting her in the door.

Mo barks once as soon as he sees us, then lies back down on his bed cushion by the dining table. I swear he's the world's laziest dog most of the time. But I still love him and I hope someday Tally will too.

Tally drops the bag of tacos on the table, and I grab my mug. "Want something to drink?"

"Water is fine," Tally says.

I grab her a bottled water and then sit across from her at the small table.

Tally unloads the bag she brought with her. She wasn't wrong about there being a lot of tacos. There's way more than two people need.

"Gosh, this is weird." Tally breaks the silence and looks up to find me already watching her. She blushes.

"Why?" The moment she walked in that door, it felt the opposite of weird. I would love to spend every evening with her, relaxing and talking and eating. As well as doing more than that, but I put a stop to those thoughts, even though her lips look extremely kissable tonight.

Tally shakes her head. "I just—I used to come over here when Gran did her bingo nights. Marsha and I would talk about whatever books we were reading, and she'd make us dinner..."

"You miss her." And now I've got another piece to the Tally-puzzle that I'm slowly putting together. She acts tough, and she is tough, but she's also been through hell. I can't imagine what it would be like to lose your mom and then one of your friends a few years later.

Tally nods, biting her lip. *I will not think about kissing her.* "It's not like losing Mom, but it's also exactly the same."

I reach over the table and put my hand on top of hers, and she doesn't pull away. "Losing someone is always hard."

Tally blinks furiously as if she's trying to rid herself of all emotion. When she smiles at me a moment later, it's like she's shoved down all the grief and is putting on a happy face for my sake. I want to tell her that she doesn't need to do that, that I'm not going to run just because she has feelings. But she pulls her hand away from mine and grabs a taco. "Should we eat?"

We need to talk about what just happened, how she doesn't need to hide her feelings from me. But my gut is telling me that right this second is not the time for that conversation. "We can eat."

Tally shuffles at least five tacos toward her and begins opening one. I follow her lead and grab a few and a package of hot sauce.

"So," I say once we're both one taco in, "what have you been reading?"

Tally freezes for a split second before she recovers. "I'm reading Simone's books again. I've got about three chapters left of book three."

"No way!" I jump up and grab my own copy from the couch. After Nora told me a few days ago that she was already on book three, I stayed up way too late the other night to finish the second book so I could catch up. "I've got like two chapters left."

Tally blushes furiously and I have to bite my cheek to hold

in my grin. Apparently, my reading the same book as her makes her blush.

"I'm also reading that book you read last month. The one from book club," I say, watching her reaction closely. She was right, the book has got some serious steam, and I'd be lying if I said it wasn't her I've been thinking about as I've read it. The main character reminds me so much of Tally, trying to be strong and do everything on her own, refusing love, even though it could be a joyous part of her life.

Tally happened to be taking that exact moment to take a sip of water, and now she's choking.

"You okay?" I probably shouldn't bring up steamy books while we're eating.

She waves a hand. "Just—swallowed—water—wrong," she says through a coughing fit. When she recovers, she asks, "How are you liking that one?"

"It's interesting." To say the least. I know romance novels get a bad rep, but so many of them are actually really well written. More people should read them. More men should read them. I don't tell any of this to Tally though, she knows my opinions on them.

"That's one word for it." She grabs another taco, and we eat in silence until there's one taco left. "It's all yours, Jones." She motions for me to take it.

I raise an eyebrow. "Jones, eh?"

"Trying it out," she says with a nod. "People call each other by their last names all the time. Nicknames are fun."

Does that mean she wants a nickname? I could call her Book Girl again, just to see what happens. But I'm not sure I trust myself enough for that.

"True." I grimace. "But my dad was always the guy they called Jones, and I don't want to be associated with him in that way. I have his name, but I don't like to be called by it."

"Oh," Tally says. "Then we'll have to come up with a different nickname."

Ah. Looks like she's going to blow right past the opening I just gave her. A natural flow to the conversation, where I could have told her all about my scumbag of a father who's out living his "best life," pretending he didn't break my mother's heart and leave two small children behind to do whatever the heck it is he does. But she brushes past it. The more time I spend with her, the more I realize Tally is not one to talk about the hard stuff.

"You can always call me handsome." I wink at her, trying to go with her lighthearted mood. I may be the happy-go-luckiest guy in any room, but I also like to get into the deep stuff. I always have. I don't want to shy away from the hard things.

Tally laughs. "Hmm, handsome isn't a nickname I'd give you."

"Rude," I say, and I watch as a blush crawls up her neck.

"I'll think of something." Then we both fall quiet. I'm not quite ready for her to leave because I like spending time with her. As scary as that is, I want to spend time with her. I also don't want her to bolt.

"Want to read for a bit?" I ask, holding up Simone's book. "I could read aloud. My sister is always telling me I should try being an audiobook reader because of my voice."

Tally considers this for a minute. "You do have a pretty nice voice. We could read for a bit. Gran is really chatty, so it'll be a little longer before the house is empty again."

"All right." I'm just grateful she said yes. I never know what's going to happen with Tally. We move over to the couch, where she sits as far away from me as possible. I stretch out and open the book to the chapter she said she was on, then I start to read. We're about to read the first kiss of the entire series, but if Tally knows that, she doesn't say anything as I begin to read.

Tally's breath hitches when I start the scene that I read to myself only an hour before. I try not to let it get to me, but I'm hyperaware of everything she's doing. How she's tucked her legs under herself and is holding her arms as close to her body as she can, as if she's afraid that if she relaxes even a moment, she'll fall for me.

But would that be such a bad thing?

"Noah?" Tally asks, jarring me out of my thoughts.

"Right. Uh. Sorry," I say, startled that I let my thoughts carry me away from actually reading for a moment.

When I finish the scene, I notice that the faint blush from earlier is back on Tally's cheeks and her neck is flushed.

I keep reading and she begins to relax. Her arms fall and she stares at the empty fireplace while I read. She's wiping away tears when I've finished the last page. For a while we just sit in silence. When I realize she's still crying, I move over to her and put an arm around her shoulders, pulling her to my chest.

She doesn't pull away. Instead, she simply cries while I hold her.

I'm not one hundred percent sure what's happening because she keeps so many walls up. The book is emotional, sure, but I don't know if it's this emotional. I catch the scent of her strawberry shampoo when she shifts in my arms. I pull her a little closer to me as her breathing evens out. I don't think she's asleep, but she's not crying anymore.

I'm careful not to move, afraid I might scare her away. Eventually, Tally sits up and shifts away from me. I want to pull her back immediately, but I don't and instead watch as she sinks back into the couch as far away from me as she can be.

"Sorry about that," is all she says.

"It's okay."

"That part always reminds me of my mom. And then being here, in Marsha's old apartment, without her, it all just kind of hit me." She's avoiding my eyes.

"It's okay," I say again.

"Thanks for letting me cry. Please, never bring it up again."

"I promise." And I mean it. I won't bring it up unless she does. Even though I have a million more questions. I'm just hoping that at some point she'll open up to me more than she has. Maybe I should put out a branch.

I let out a slow breath. It's now or never, I guess. "Do you want to know why I'm so positive all the time?"

Tally looks at me with curious eyes, but I can also see the relief in them from the subject change. "You definitely border on annoyingly optimistic all the time. Like, is life really good enough to smile all the time?"

"Is it really such a bad thing to look on the bright side of things?" She's not the first person I've ever asked that question to. I get it, my personality can come off as overly positive at times. But I'm not one to stand and shout about how you always need to look for the bright side of things because sometimes there just isn't a bright side of things. I do make an effort to find the good and take risks and chances. Now anyway.

Tally ponders this for a second. "Maybe not. But definitely right now. There's not really a bright side to our situation."

I swallow. She means The Book Shop, right? That has to be what she means. "We're hanging out tonight. We're friends now. That's a bright side." It's the brightest side in all of this. More than I ever could have hoped for. Well sure, I'd like to be more than friends. But I've spent the last five years wondering and thinking about Tally. Now that she's sitting right in front of me, I can wait a little longer for her to be okay with the idea of us as more than friends.

"Your entire life changed in a week!" Tally cries. I didn't realize she was so upset about this. "You had to move across the country, all because your grandma, who isn't even here now, said so."

I shrug. "It was time for a change."

"That big of a change?" Tally is incredulous and I get why. She's lived here her entire life, and if I were to guess anything about her, it's that she's not planning to go anywhere for a long, long time. "You were just okay with it?"

"Yeah."

"Please tell me, then, why are you so happy and sunshiny all the time? If you weren't anything but genuine, I would truly think it was forced. But you really don't seem like it was that big of a deal to move here." Tally is watching me curiously again.

This is it, time for me to get real with her. Bare a part of me that I haven't even told Annie. Sure, Annie knows what happened, but she doesn't know why it impacted me the way that it did.

"Last summer I went on a camping trip with my buddy Sam," I tell her, and just like when I was reading, I slip into the familiar cadence of storytelling. "I am not a super outdoorsy guy, but we go on some sort of trip together every year. Last year we were camping up in the mountains in Colorado. I couldn't even tell you where we were. We'd hiked almost all day and finally got to the spot that Sam had picked out beforehand."

I pause. If I closed my eyes right now, I'd be right back there. I'd be able to see the small space we'd found in the middle of a grove of trees. How the bugs were so loud that night, which now feels like it was some kind of warning.

"We set up camp, and he got a fire going so we could make dinner. We spent the hours before bed drinking and complaining, which is what we always end up doing when we get together."

Tally laughs. "You complain? I didn't think you had it in you."

"I sure do. I was at this point in my life where everything was making me unhappy, and I was just going through the motions. I was so mad that Sam had decided we were going to go camping for our annual trip. We take turns picking every other year. We'd never gone camping before because he knew how much I don't like it." I pause to look at Tally. "Don't get me wrong, I love being outside. But I also love to go back to a cabin or hotel at the end of the day."

"Same." Tally smiles at me, distracting me for a moment. I could get lost in that smile, the one that fills her whole face and lights up her eyes. It feels like a special treat to get it tonight since I haven't seen it directed at me the whole time I've been here in Provo.

I smile back, then look away. Telling this story feels so incredibly personal, and I want to share it with her. But it feels too intimate to be looking at her while I tell her what happened next.

"I was exhausted by the time we finally went to bed, and we were both asleep within minutes. I woke in the middle of the night, feeling super disoriented. I got up to pee, just to sort of wake myself up because something felt off. When I was walking back to our camp, I heard what I thought was Sam rummaging through our cooler. The one we'd tied up the night before. I was about to head into our campsite when I heard a whistle from above me."

My palms start to sweat, like they always do when I get to this part.

"I looked up and saw Sam sitting in the tree. He gestured for me to climb up there with him. I did. There was a bear in our camp."

Tally gasps.

"That's not even the craziest part." I wipe my hands on my pants. I can do this, I am alive and well and sitting on the couch with Tally. I am so grateful I'm here with her, but there are still some days when I wake up and can't believe that I'm alive. "We sat up there for what felt like hours, waiting for that bear to wander off or fall asleep so we could go to the car, but then it started to rain. The bear by this point had eaten our food, ripped a hole in Sam's tent, and was wandering around our camp chairs. We were stuck and very, very wet."

"You all right?" Tally's voice startles me. I blink and the living room focuses into my view again. Tally has moved closer to me again, her hands still in her lap, concern heavy on her face.

I nod. "I am. It's—it's a lot though."

"You don't have to rush." Tally gives me a closed-lipped smile, and a vision of me pulling her against my chest and lacing our fingers together flashes through my mind. I clasp my hands in front of me to stay focused on my story.

"The rain got heavier and heavier, and then at some point we heard more than saw the flash of lightning."

Tally is like a statue beside me. Mom and Annie both cried when I got to this part, but I don't think Tally will. She's not exactly weepy.

"I didn't realize how close the strike had been until I woke up who knows how long after because I'd been thrown from the tree and knocked out when I hit the ground. By the time we woke up, the bear was gone and the rain had stopped, but we could smell smoke and knew there was a fire."

"Is this real?" Tally interrupts me. "This is kind of a crazy story. I feel like this would have been on the news."

"It was completely insane. Straight out of a movie, but it really happened. It was all over Colorado's news channels for weeks, but I don't think the story went national." I shrug. "We somehow made it back to our car, even though the forest around us was in flames. Sam's ribs were hurting really bad, and by this point, I'd sort of come out of shock and realized that my left arm was definitely broken."

I rub my face. "It was some kind of miracle that we even made it down the canyon and to a hospital, where they told us we definitely shouldn't have been driving. Turns out the lightning was about two hundred feet away from us. If it had been any closer, we would have died."

"Holy crap." Tally squeezes my hand. I never want her to let go.

I nod solemnly. "It could have been so much worse. The doctor who put my arm in a cast said that it was a miracle, if I believed in that type of thing. I guess I started to after that. After that day, I promised myself I'd make the most out of my life. Say yes to things that scare me, look for the good. You never know when it's all going to end."

Tally nods. "It's crazy how things can change so quickly."

I don't reply right away. Instead, I sink further into the couch, bringing Tally with me since our hands our still intertwined. Her head lands on my shoulder and I'm afraid she's going to pull away, like she does every time we get close.

She surprises me by staying.

16

TALLY

Alarm bells are screaming in my head, shouting at me to get up. To move away from Noah, but with every breath I ignore them and settle in closer to him on the couch. His breathing has evened out again, but he's quiet.

While I've lost people, I've never had an experience that brought me face-to-face with death. I can't imagine reliving that, even from the safety of a couch. I should thank him for sharing his experience with me.

I thought about life and death after Mom died and a little again since Marsha died. It's like when you lose someone, you want to try harder to live a little better as a way to honor them. But over time, those old habits come back. That's what it's like to be human though, isn't it? To make changes and then go back to old things and try again and again.

But I've never stared death straight in the face like Noah experienced last year. A lot of things about Noah make sense now. Some things are just bare minimum of being a decent person, like being kind to people. But he seems to go above and beyond, not just around me but around everyone. I don't think I've ever seen him lose his temper before.

He also seems to live life like he's going to say yes to anything, even if it's terrifying or a risk.

I kind of can't believe that he told me all that in the first place. I'm grateful I didn't have to talk more about my mom, but his story surprised me.

He keeps surprising me.

"You never know what tomorrow will bring." Noah's voice is hushed, but it brings me back to the present moment, my head on his shoulder, our hands laced together in his lap. "So why not make the most of today?"

I suck in both my cheeks. "I think that's really nice in theory but a lot harder to put into practice. Most people have to work and do things that they don't always want to do, but what if they have to do those things to survive?"

"What if they don't? What if part of it is them choosing that life? I mean, yeah, sometimes we have to work hard to get to where we want to go and get to the life we want. I don't think life is easy for anyone. But what if we took more time living a life we actually enjoyed, right now, and not worry so much about where we're going to be in five years? We're living right here, right now. Why spend more time focused on the past or the future than actually living?" Noah's words shake me. I want to dive into what they make me feel, but I'm not sure I'm ready to face those emotions.

"What would you do right now if you weren't stressed about the future? What would you regret not doing tomorrow if you didn't do it today?" Noah asks me. He's not taunting me and he doesn't sound like some happiness guru, at least not completely. He actually wants to know what I would do right now if I just went for it. "Nothing stupid though. That's the one rule I gave myself. I'd take risks, I'd go for things I wanted, but I wouldn't do anything that could end up hurting me or someone else."

"I would ask you why you kissed me that day, five years

ago." The words are out of my mouth before I can take them back. It wasn't until he asked that I realized I even wanted to know. More than why he ran away, I want to know why that afternoon even happened in the first place.

Noah rubs his thumb along my hand. I can imagine how tenderly I'd see him looking at me right now if I were brave enough to lift my face and meet his eyes. In the last hour he's held me while I cried and told me a big thing that happened in his life. And all I can think about is how tenderly this man treats me.

"I don't want you to think that I did it because I thought you needed saving," Noah says, and that makes me smile. For a man who doesn't think I need saving, he sure comes to my rescue a lot.

But I don't actually mind.

The thought shocks me.

"I didn't need saving then. I don't need saving now." I'm not even saying those words for Noah. I'm trying to convince myself I mean them.

"Sometimes it's okay if you need to be saved." He squeezes my hand, then continues to rub it with his thumb, waiting for me to respond. When I don't, he continues. "When it comes down to it, I just really wanted to kiss you. I swear I've never been that bold in my entire life. I walked into that café and saw you there and knew immediately I wanted to get to know you. That I wanted to spend time with you and that I really wanted to kiss you. When I saw your face as that guy and girl walked in, it was like my heart ripped in half. I was so angry that any person made you feel that way, and I didn't even know how exactly you were feeling. But the pain was all over your face."

"So what, you kissed me out of pity?"

"What!? No. I kissed you because I wanted to, and making those people jealous seemed like a nice excuse to do that."

"Wow," I say. "Who knew? The guy who reads romance novels is still just a guy like the rest of them and will do anything to kiss a girl."

"That makes it sound so bad." Noah groans. "I swear I wasn't really trying to make any moves. I mean, I totally kissed you and the memory of that kiss, that afternoon, has never left my mind, not that I want it to. But I swear that was the only time I've ever done anything like that."

Not that I want it to.

What does he mean by that? Why doesn't he want to forget? Does he feel the same way I do whenever I see him? Like I'm thrown back in time and wonder what it would be like if we tried something now?

"I know. I was joking. Sort of." My words don't match what I'm feeling at all, but can I tell him how I feel, that it's the same as him? Or at least how I think it's the same?

"I am sorry if I hurt you." I feel a featherlight touch on my head. His lips linger in my hair for a second before he pulls away. "I kissed you. I spent a perfect afternoon with you and then I ran away."

I let out a shaky breath. I hope he doesn't notice how he's affecting me right now. "Yeah, that kind of totally sucked."

"I am sorry for that, Tally."

I look down at our hands. *They fit together perfectly*, I think as I stare at them. *We fit together so perfectly.* The thought makes me want to jump away from him, because curled into his side like this, I almost think that being in his arms is how we were meant to be.

"I like you, Tally." Noah lets out a low laugh. My mouth opens in a tiny *o*. "I know that's probably ridiculous to say right now. It's been only two weeks since I first saw you again, and I told you I just wanted to be friends. But I like you. I want to get to know you better, know what makes you tick and what makes you smile. I want to take you out on real dates. I really want to kiss you again."

I tilt my head off his shoulder so I can look at him. Our noses almost brush because we're sitting so close. If his words hadn't already made my insides turn to goo, the way he's looking at me definitely will. *I like you too!* That's what I want to scream, but I'm still scared to lay it all on the table.

I don't know who moves first, but one second, I'm wondering how I can get my voice to work to tell him how I feel and the next, we're kissing. He breaks away for a beat. "Is this okay?"

"Yes."

His hand slips from mine, moving around my back and pulling me closer to him. I run my hands through his wavy hair, which is just as soft as I imagined it would be. As I remembered it being.

He's got an arm around my back, holding me in place against him, the other in my hair. "Tally," he whispers against my lips, and I kiss him harder.

I've kissed only a handful of guys since our first kiss five years ago, but none of them were ever like this. His lips part, his tongue skimming my lips, and I sigh, leaning into him even more.

I think I've made it to heaven.

Noah's lips are gentle against mine, but there is nothing sweet about this kiss. I can feel the passion flowing from him as he pulls me even closer to him. His lips leave mine as he brushes featherlight kisses along my jaw. I tilt my head and my neck gets the pleasure of feeling his soft lips against it. Then he's kissing my lips again. Hungry and hurried. I am all too eager to match his enthusiasm.

When the kiss slows, it feels like a good time to tell him. "I feel the same."

I'm leaning toward him again, but Noah pulls away and my heart lurches. "But?"

The hesitation I've been trying to keep at bay hits me like a bucket of ice water. How can he know me well enough already to know I've got a "but" coming? I wouldn't have brought it up, but because he did, I have to say something.

I jump off the couch, trying to put some physical distance between us. I can feel the wall around my heart sealing up again.

I need a second to sort out my feelings, to figure out what I should say.

Noah stands, reaching for me. "Tally."

I take a step back, holding my hands up. "But there is kind of another guy. I haven't actually met him in person. We met online through my blog a few years ago and talk almost every day on Twitter. Which I know sounds completely ridiculous, but I'm going to meet him at Simone Sorrows's event down in St. George next week. But I'm also falling for you, so that doesn't feel fair to you or him."

It's the first thing that came to my mind. Better than telling him all that I truly feel. Because I'm not sure what I'm feeling right now.

And it's not exactly a lie, even though what I just told Noah doesn't accurately describe my feelings for Mo. I *do* like Mo. He's my closest friend, and there's a part of me, deep down, that knows that once we meet, things will change between us. Don't they say that you should fall in love with your best friend? I do love Mo, in a way, but before he suggested we meet, I never thought of us as anything more than friends.

Maybe it was just my way of distracting my mind from thinking about Noah, but in the past two weeks I've found myself wondering more if something with Mo could actually work. But what I just said is a stretch, and I feel a stab of guilt as hurt flashes across Noah's face.

I start toward the door.

"Tally, wait." Noah follows me. "We should talk about this."

What is there to talk about? I kissed him and then made it sound like I cheated on another guy with him. I should come clean. Tell Noah I exaggerated because everything about this makes me nervous. Tell Mo that I started dating someone and can't meet him. But I don't. I can't seem to say anything.

I never understood while reading all those romances—and about moments like this—how you can feel so much passion one second and so much regret the next. Now I understand it.

"You should meet that guy before you decide anything." Noah breaks the silence and a tiny part of my heart cracks too. I want him to fight for me, to ask me to pick him. Instead, my heart and my head are ping-ponging back and forth, and I don't know what to say because I don't know what I'm feeling.

I should have told him I needed time. That I need space to figure this all out so I can stop saying things I don't mean. I shouldn't have kissed him.

"Then, after you've met him, we can give us a try, if that's what you want." Noah's voice cracks a little. I want to run to him, to change my mind about what I just said. Instead, I put my wall back up.

"Right. Okay. Sorry." I can't get hurt if there's nothing to hurt. I scan the room for my shoes. Where did I take them off?

My eyes unwillingly land on Noah, who looks so broken standing there, making me regret my harsh apology.

"Let's just pretend it didn't happen," I say stiffly. I turn around, see my shoes sitting right by the door, and make my way toward them. "We can be friends until...after."

"Tally." Noah grabs my hand, tugging me so that I turn ever so slightly. His eyes make me feel like I've been lost in a forest for weeks and finally found a clearing that feels like home. "We don't have to pretend it didn't happen..."

"I think we should," I say, the words rough on my tongue. Why am I acting like the one who's been hurt here?

Noah drops my hand as if he's been scalded.

"I have to go," I say, and then I'm out the door and flying down the stairs. I don't look back because I know that if I see Noah's face again right now, I'll burst into tears.

17

NOAH

TheNoraReview: Ever do something that makes your head and heart so confused? That's what happened to me last night.

MoReads: Want to talk about it?

TheNoraReview: Not yet. Maybe later though. Just trying to figure things out.

MoReads: Let me know when or if you want to talk. You know I'm always here.

"Tally is Nora," I blurt into the phone as soon as Annie picks up, running my hand through my hair. I've done that so many times today, it's a miracle I have any hair on my head. It's Saturday morning and I made myself eat breakfast and walk Mo before I called Annie. I tried Sam first, but he didn't answer. "Well, I don't know that for sure, for sure, but I'm pretty sure they're the same person."

"Why would you think that?" Annie sounds tired, even though it's not even noon in New York.

"Last night she came over and we hung out for a few hours." I want to give Annie the short version, just enough to get her caught up so that she can confirm or disprove my suspicion. "We ended up talking for a while. I told her about the camping trip and asked her what she would regret tomorrow if she didn't do it today."

"Okay." Annie seems distant.

"You all right, Annie?" I ask. My story can wait if there's something going on. My problem really isn't that big of a deal.

"I'm fine, Noah," she says, and I wish I'd FaceTimed her instead so I could actually see her face. "It was a crazy, busy week at work, and I'm ready to sit around and do nothing all weekend."

"You sure?" I push, because my gut tells me that there's more going on than what she's telling me.

"I'm sure," Annie says. "Do you need me to send you a selfie so you know that I also look fine?"

"Would you?"

"Why'd I have to get the protective older brother?" Annie grumbles.

"Hey, you know you love it."

"You're right. I do. Most of the time anyway. I sent a picture, and I really am fine. Now, tell me why you think Tally is Nora."

I don't check my phone to see the picture. I'll look at it when we're done talking. "So, she asked me why I kissed her all those years ago, and we talked about her. Then I confessed that I have feelings for her and then we kissed and it was just as incredible as I remembered, but when she admitted to liking me, she said that there's also this other guy who she's only talked to online. She said they met because of her blog and that they were planning to meet in real life at Simone Sorrows's book event next week. All exactly how things happened with me and Nora, and we're planning to meet next week at Simone Sorrows's event."

"Interesting."

"Really? That's all you've got? Interesting?" I'm trying to stay calm. I don't really know what I'll do if Tally and Nora are the same person. I mean, on one hand, it makes things a lot easier since I tried to distract myself from Tally by asking Nora to meet me, but my heart didn't get the memo because it still fell for Tally anyway.

"I mean, either that's a lot of coincidences or she's Nora," Annie finally says.

"Right?" I ask. There isn't another explanation. It's too weird.

"Has Tally ever mentioned her blog before?"

"No, last night was the first time. From the way she's talked about social media for the shop, I didn't think she was online much."

"Gotcha." Annie pauses. "You could just ask her, clear the air. Then you'd know for sure."

I *could* ask Tally if she's Nora. "I can't."

"Why not? Seems like a simple thing to do, the grown-up thing to do. Communicate." Annie is right, but I can't do it.

"I can't ask her, because after we kissed, everything went south, so I don't think coming clean right now is a good idea. I should have just asked her when she mentioned it."

"You definitely should have asked her," Annie says. "But since you didn't, now is the moment. Isn't that what you and Sam decided anyway? To live in the moment and share your truth with the people around you? You've only got one life, or whatever you guys are always saying?"

I frown. "We're not always saying that."

"You should just tell her. Otherwise, she's going to keep ignoring you as Noah, not because she knows who you are online but because of whatever happened last night."

"I think she's already started doing what she can to avoid

me. She texted me this morning telling me that Olivia, that's the other woman who works at the shop with us, is working today and that I didn't need to come in."

"You need to figure out how to fix this, and the easiest way will be to tell her what you realized, that you've been talking online with her too," Annie says, but I still don't like it. "Look, I've got to go. Mitch just got home from picking up a late breakfast. You'll tell her the truth?"

I bite my tongue as not to share my real feelings that I have about her boyfriend, Mitch. I haven't liked him since day one.

"I will." And I will. Maybe not today though. Now that I know, I want to figure out the right way to tell her. I'm not one for keeping secrets or lying outright, but Tally's embarrassed and I'm embarrassed that I didn't just ask yesterday if she was Nora. Plus I need to figure out a good way to get back on her good side before I ask her.

And maybe I can talk to Nora and see if she can give me any clues.

"Talk to you later," Annie says.

"Bye." I hang up and look down at Mo. "What am I going to do?"

It would be so easy to go down and talk to her right now. We decided last week that we'd take turns working every other Saturday for a half day, and she's down in the shop right now. But the thought makes me anxious. I'm not ready to confront her yet. If Tally really is Nora, what will that mean? That I happened to fall for the same woman twice? I've never had that kind of luck. Maybe someone would call it fate or the universe. I don't know what to call it.

TALLY GETS off work at 3:00, so I message Nora at 2:45. I've been waiting all day, trying to craft the right thing to say.

What do I come up with?

> **MoReads:** Hey. How are you doing this afternoon?

I really feel like Tally is Nora, not only from what she said last night but also because I sent Nora several messages just before Tally showed up the night we kissed and never got a response.

Mo and I go for a walk, walking across the main road and over to the park, where there is more grass than on our street. Someday I'll buy a house with a nice yard so that Mo can go out and play.

I left my phone at home so that I can't pull it out every five seconds to see if Nora has responded. But I do grab it from off the counter the second we're in the door.

> **TheNoraReview:** Hey. Doing all right. Last night I hung out with one of my friends super late and it ended badly. Which is why I didn't respond.

She was out with me. "That doesn't mean it's Tally," I tell myself. I want it to be her, desperately, but I'm also anxious that if it's not her, I've made a terrible mistake. Three little dots appear on my screen—she's typing more. I wait anxiously to see what she's going to say next.

> **TheNoraReview:** I was with a guy friend and he admitted to liking me, and I told him I liked him too. Then when he asked why/if there was any reason I was hesitating, I told him that I might like you. Which then made me super confused because I do like you, I just don't know/think that I like-like you. You know?

TheNoraReview: Sorry if that's all super weird. I just didn't know how to talk to him, and all I could think of to say was that I was meeting you and also liked you. Cause we are meeting and things could potentially change after that...but idk.
TheNoraReview: Just super confused.

My heart pounds in my chest, now sure that Tally *is* Nora. Maybe I can make this work.

MoReads: Dang, it sounds like you were in a super tough spot last night. I don't mind that you used me as an excuse. Maybe that's something we can talk about when we meet (not using me as an excuse, but feelings, maybe?) Cause I've thought about it too.
MoReads: I mean, I made no assumptions that you and I were a thing, so dating or hanging out with other people is totally fair game.

I think now I might be digging myself into a hole.

TheNoraReview: Right. Have you been seeing someone?

MoReads: I haven't. But I'm kind of a homebody, so I don't go out much anyway, so there's not a lot of opportunities for me to meet people.

Oops. Maybe I should have said yes, considering I have been falling for Tally in real life.

TheNoraReview: Okay. Sorry if I made things weird between us, that's the last thing I wanted to do.

MoReads: It really is okay.
You didn't make anything weird.

TheNoraReview: I haven't dated in so long. I always mess things up.
I feel like I'm going to mess everything up, so can we still be friends
after we meet, even if it is completely awkward? My sister tells me
that I self-sabotage my relationships because even though I read a
lot of romance novels, I don't actually believe in love. Maybe she's
right.

Tally doesn't believe in love? I wonder for a split second if *I*
am the reason for that, but I'm hoping it's more than that. Every
time I've interacted with her on a romantic level probably hasn't
helped at all. I left the first time. Last night did not go well in
terms of showing her what love is actually like.

Now I know what I can do. I can be her friend. I can show
her all the love I feel without kissing or getting physical.

Wait.

Am I in love with Tally?

"Yeah, I think I am." Mo runs over to me, barking and tail
wagging. He jumps up so I can rub behind his ears, making him
do his whole-body wag. I wish I could feel that happy right now.
I might be in love with Tally, but I'm worried she might hate
me now.

MoReads: You didn't make it worse. There was nothing to mess up.
You're not going to mess anything up, I promise.
MoReads: You still want to meet next weekend, right?

TheNoraReview: I still want to meet, if you want to. Even though
chances are I'll mess that up too.

I want to call Tally right now and tell her to knock it off, tell
her that she's not going to mess anything up. Not any more than
how the rest of us mess things up. That's a human thing, and

she's not going to mess this—us—up. I won't let her. But I can't call her, so I do the next best thing.

> **MoReads:** Don't say that. You're a freaking amazing human, and you're not going to mess this up.

TheNoraReview: You don't know that.

> **MoReads:** I do, I know you well enough to know that you aren't going to mess this up. It might be scary, sure. You might want to run away, but I'm not going anywhere.

TheNoraReview: Thank you. Truly.

> **MoReads:** You're welcome.

I don't know how long I sit on the couch, thinking about my conversation with Nora and all the interactions I've had with Tally, but when I get up, my body is stiff from sitting in the same position. I stretch my arms high above my head and grab my phone to text Tally.

Hey, Tally. I wanted to say how sorry I am about last night, about how things ended. I can be your friend, if that's what you still want.

It's not what I want, not now that I've realized I'm in love with her, that I've been in love with her this whole time. But if I can't be with her, I'll make myself be okay with only being friends with her.

I look down at Mo, who's been sleeping on the couch. He doesn't move as he blinks up at me. I tell him my plan, even if it's not my best. "I'm going to show up at the event as Mo. I'm going to do exactly what I planned on doing before I knew that Tally was Nora. It'll be fine. I have a terrible poker face, so I'll have to tell her the truth, that I figured it out this week, but it'll be fine. Totally fine."

18

TALLY

We've settled into a normal rhythm at the shop. And by normal, I mean I've been leaving as soon as Olivia gets in at two and avoiding Noah as much as possible. It's Wednesday and I haven't seen him since Friday night, even though Gran invited him over for dinner again on Sunday. I pretended I wasn't feeling well and didn't come out of my room the whole time he was there.

Which made Dad concerned. He came down and talked to me after, asking three times if I was upset about him and Beth getting married. I told him no, even though it does bug me that he still hasn't told Holly. I've known for over a week and he still hasn't told her, not that he hasn't tried. He's called her three times and she hasn't answered.

When I asked her about it, she told me that she's been working on a new art piece, and when that happens, everyone gets shut out except for me, but Dad wants to be the one to tell her. It's killing me that I know and she doesn't and we can't talk about it. I have no idea what she's thinking or feeling about the entire thing because she doesn't know about it yet.

I skipped our Sunday family dinner because Noah was there, and after our kiss and my lie about liking someone else, I couldn't face him. He apologized on Saturday and said we could be friends, that he would be okay with being friends. I'm just not sure that's what I want because I have no clue what I actually want.

This whole situation is the reason why I don't date. Once something more happens than the initial "I like you," things always go south, at least they have for me. Things get serious. I jump in too fast and then the guy always leaves. I've had history repeat itself one too many times.

"You all right?" I look up to find Olivia standing in front of me, a lollipop in her hand. I must have zoned out. I didn't even hear her come in.

"Yeah, fine."

"Noah showed me what he was working on for our website last night. I think it'll help our sales out a lot." Olivia sits on the stool beside me behind the checkout counter. "And I know you don't really want to talk about him, but he talked about you."

I sit up straighter at this information. "What did he say?"

"He mostly was asking how you're doing because he hasn't seen you since you left his apartment on Friday night. Which you haven't told me about yet."

I groan. Of course Noah would mention it.

"It wasn't like he brought it up on purpose, but you didn't work last Friday, so I asked when he'd seen you that day." Olivia licks her lollipop. "But I am very curious about what happened. Is that why you've been rushing out of here so fast every time I get here this week? He hasn't even come down till almost five the past two days. He's been working on the website."

I cover my face as I squeak out the words, "We kissed on Friday."

"YES!" Olivia shouts. "I love a good kissing story."

"Then you're going to hate this one." I look down at my feet because I can't bear to look at her while I tell her what happened. "We kissed and then I freaked out a little and told him that there was this other guy I've been talking to online who I'm going to meet this Friday at the Simone Sorrows thing and that I kind of like this guy too...and then I sort of ran away."

"And what about Mo?"

"Yeah...what about Mo?" I sigh. "But until I said something to Noah about having feelings for Mo, I'd never thought about it before. But now I can't stop thinking about it and how I think that falling for Noah would be a bad idea because Mo is perfect. Literally perfect."

"No one's perfect, Tally. At the beginning of a friendship or relationship, it might seem like that, but no one is perfect."

"Perfect for me, I mean," I say softly. "He gets me. He knows exactly what to say when I've had a bad day that will make me smile or help me not feel so down. He's got great taste in books and movies, and talking to him has always been so easy. But I've never seen his face. Can you fall for someone you've never seen?"

I look out the wide front window that looks out on Provo's Center Street, just to give myself something to do. There are a few golden leaves clinging to the tree across the street, but the rest of the trees are bare or nearly there. We've slipped from fall right into winter, even though I know it's technically still autumn for another two months. It feels like I've blinked and missed the fall weather completely.

"Maybe you can," Olivia says. "I know this probably isn't what you want to hear, but I think you should take a good look at what your heart is telling you and trust it. I promise when you do that, everything will go the way it's supposed to."

There's movement outside that catches my eye as someone walks past the windows. Not just someone, but Noah. He's walking his dog. For a few precious seconds I'm able to simply look at him. I'm not worried about having him catch me staring, like I'm always thinking about when we're working together. His cheeks are pink from the cold and he's looking at his phone. He pauses in front of the shop as if he hadn't realized where he was.

Noah is the kind of guy who stops and smells all the flowers. I've seen him on walks before and he never has his phone out. I wonder what's happening today that's so important.

Noah slides his phone into his pocket. He looks up and sees me through the window—sees me *staring* at him through the window. I give him an awkward wave and receive his charming grin in return.

"Listen to your heart," Olivia whispers, like she's some kind of love guru, as Noah comes through the door with his dog.

"Hey, ladies." He says it so casually. As if the past week hadn't happened. As if I hadn't told him that I might like another guy right after I kissed him like I needed him as much as I needed air. As if Olivia and I weren't just talking about him.

"Hey," I say back, because apparently, I can't come up with the words. I'm also slightly mortified that he caught me staring, even though he probably doesn't know how long I was watching him.

"I like your sweater," Noah says as his dog lies down on one of the many rugs we have in the shop.

I glance down. I'm wearing a brown-and-orange sweater that just feels like fall. "Thanks." It's actually my favorite sweater. I am trying to see if telepathy is a thing by screaming at Olivia in my mind to say something, but she seems perfectly content to watch us while she enjoys her lollipop.

Noah stares at me for a moment. So long that I have to turn away because I'm not sure what's happening inside his head. I want to know; I want everything to be fine between us. But we pushed the gas from zero to sixty, then I brought it back to zero and I don't know how to change it.

"Let me take Mo up and I'll be back down to work," he tells us, then he's down the back hall and out the door.

I'm pretending to update our inventory spreadsheet in the office and Olivia is helping a customer when he comes back down, wearing another one of those waffle-knit sweaters that just seems to hug his body. Gran's right, he does look a little like Chris Evans, especially when he wears sweaters.

"How's the morning been?" he asks, grabbing one of the folding chairs to sit in the already cramped space.

"Really slow." I don't tell him that I've been bored out of my mind most of the day.

"Are most Wednesdays like this?" he asks, picking up a stack of bookmarks and straightening them. Which I did two hours ago.

"Depends on the time of year. We get busier leading up to the holidays, and in the summer most days are pretty much the same. But for a few weeks in the spring and fall we have some pretty dead days."

"And the shop makes enough to cover all the costs?"

I shrug, because honestly, until he showed up and started asking questions, I never actually thought about it. Marsha was always in charge of the numbers and the money. She said she had a guy who did our taxes every year and looked over our accounts. She never gave me any reason to think that we were struggling. I don't make a ton of money, but I'm able to save a lot of it since I live with Gran.

"I'll look at the numbers later," Noah says. "But from the

things I've seen so far, my guess is that Grandma Marsha used some of her own money out of pocket to pay for things like taxes and bills since she owned the place."

I slump slightly. "Do you really think she would have done that?"

Noah nods. "She would have. She loved this place and probably would have done anything to keep it up and running."

"I can't believe she never said anything."

"She kept a lot to herself."

"Yeah, like how you were her grandson," I say sarcastically. I slap a hand over my mouth. "That sounded way worse than I meant it."

"Did I ever come up in conversations?" Noah asks.

"Yeah, you did. She loved you and Annie so much. But you know how she wasn't one for pictures, and if she did try to show me one, I often had to be somewhere else right that second." I feel my face grow warm at these words. It's not something I ever planned on telling anyone.

"Why?"

"I mean, I met a guy named Noah, who was in town visiting his grandma." I look at him for the first time since he came into the small office. "I wasn't ever ready to take the chance that you might have been just out of reach the whole time."

"I'm sorry I left that day, so quickly." Noah runs a hand through his hair.

I lean back in my seat, the question on the tip of my tongue, but I'm still not sure if I want the answer.

"You want to know why." Noah is watching me. "I guess now is as good a time as any. Grandma Marsha called me."

"That's who was on your phone?" I'm grateful it wasn't a girlfriend, but it doesn't make any sense.

"It was my last day in town, I'd been hanging around the

shop for two days and I was driving her crazy. She told me to get out for a while, so I did. When I saw her name on my phone, I kind of panicked. I'm pretty sure she meant to get out for a half hour or so, not for four hours."

Four glorious hours of his hand in mine, walking down the street. Pushing me against the brick walls in front of so many stores simply to kiss me.

"I realized I hadn't checked in at all with her, and while Grandma Marsha was never much of a worrier, I am. I completely went into 'she's going to kill me' mode and took off running. About twenty seconds later I realized I was a complete idiot, so I turned around, but you were already gone." Noah's gaze makes me warm all over. "I've regretted running like that every single day after because I thought I'd lost you forever."

"Why would you be worried about that?" The words come out as a whisper because I *am* terrified to know the answer.

Noah laughs like what he's about to say next is completely insane. "I fell in love with you. That probably sounds crazy; you can't fall in love with someone in a single afternoon, but I did."

I did too.

I'm about to tell him this when Olivia appears in the doorway. "There's a woman here claiming that after she donated a box of books, we promised not to shelve them for a few weeks in case she changed her mind. I don't recognize her. Did you tell anyone that?"

I go over the past few weeks in my mind. "Nope, did you?"

Noah shakes his head.

"I think she said she dropped the books off at the end of August," Olivia tells us. "He wasn't even here yet."

"I'll see if I can help her." I stand and follow Olivia out. A woman I know I've never seen before is waiting for us at the counter.

Ten minutes later she leaves, yelling about how she'll never do business with us again because we lost her books, even though the titles she mentioned are pretty rare, and I would have remembered seeing them in our system. She definitely didn't come here.

"Do you want to drive to St. George together?"

I jump out of my skin at the sound of Noah's voice.

"Sorry, didn't mean to startle you," he says, and I turn to face him.

For a split second I think I've imagined it. It's completely one hundred percent something that my brain would come up with. We're both going to the Simone event, so it'd make sense for my brain to imagine Noah asking me that. In fact, I'm pretty sure I dreamed about it the other night before our kiss.

"Tally?"

I blink. I look up from my shoes to meet Noah's gaze. "Huh?" I know my face is pink again.

"I asked if you'd want to drive to St. George together since we're going to the same event."

Yup. Didn't actually dream that just now. That was completely real, and now I'm mortified that it seems like I zoned out and said "huh" like an idiot.

"Why would we drive together?" My brain can't seem to catch up, and I regret the question as soon as it's out of my mouth.

Noah's lips turn down. I look at his eyes because looking at his lips always makes me imagine kissing him. "You're joking, right?"

"Uh, no?" I say, but it comes out more like a question. Why do we keep doing this? Swinging from heartfelt conversations that never get proper closure to these awkward ones where I feel like I can't ever say the right thing.

"We're both going down there. Olivia already said she could cover the store on Saturday. I thought we could leave after we close on Friday," he says, and for a split second I'm filled with panic.

"I, uh..." I swallow. I can do this. I'm Tally Nelson, I am a mature adult who can communicate what I'm feeling. "But I'm meeting that guy at the event."

Noah's face doesn't change. "That's fine, it's just a car share. I meant what I said in the text, we can be friends."

THEN WHAT WAS THE POINT OF OUR CONVERSATION TEN MINUTES AGO!? I want to scream. I don't though. I keep my cool.

I swallow again. It's just a car share. And friendship. Even though I kind of want more than friendship and I know he does too.

"Uh, right. Sure, then," I say, because how can I say no after that? Even though it's going to be the most awkward four hours of my entire life.

"Great. We'll leave Friday at like eight?" Noah asks cheerfully. How is he not feeling as weird about this as I am?

"Sounds good," I say, grateful that my voice sounds normal. As if I'm a normal human being who's not completely freaking out about the fact that not only am I going to meet my online friend of two years this weekend, but I also have to be in the same car for four hours (eight, if you count the drive home) with my real-life crush. The one that I'm trying really hard not to crush on.

I'm trying really hard not to crush on him, but if he keeps smiling at me like he's doing right now, I'm toast. If I were completely honest with myself...nope. Not even going to go there tonight. I can't handle any more feelings today.

"Awesome," Noah says. "You're staying at the hotel across from where the event it is, right?"

"Yeah, how did you know that?" I ask, because that's borderline creepy.

"Everywhere else was booked. I guess there's some big convention or something also happening this weekend, and everything was full except that hotel. I booked right after I got my event ticket." Okay. Less creepy.

"Yeah, same." I had been wondering why everything seemed to be booked. St. George isn't exactly a super hopping place at the beginning of October. At least I wouldn't have thought it was. I'd just been too lazy to look up why everything was booked. I got a room, that was enough.

"Well then, do you want to take your car or mine?" Noah asks.

"Uh, would you mind driving?" I ask. Up until this point I've been thinking only about how incredibly awkward this will be. Even though it's only awkward if I make it awkward; that's something I feel like Mom would say. I'd completely forgotten about the fact that I hate driving on the freeway.

"Sure," Noah says. "Oh, and do you think that Gran or your dad could come let Mo out a couple of times each day?"

"Gran would probably love to just watch him at her house, if that's all right." Gran talks about getting a dog about three times a week. It truly is surprising she doesn't have one yet.

"That would be so great! I'll bring him over Friday night when I pick you up?"

"I'll check with Gran, but that should be fine," I tell him. "I'm going to head out now."

Noah nods. I grab my purse, waving to Olivia as I head out of the shop and to my car. Then, after this weird day, I'm finally headed home.

I accidently honk my horn when my phone vibrates from somewhere in my purse that's sitting on the passenger seat.

This earns me a middle finger from the person in front of me. "Sorry," I say, even though I know they can't hear me. Since I'm at a red light, I pull out my phone.

There's a string of texts from Holly.

DAD'S GETTING MARRIED!!??!
I'm trying to process. BUT HE'S GETTING MARRIED?!
ANSWER YOUR PHONE, WOMAN!!!!!!

I also have seven missed calls from her. Oops, guess I should turn my ringer on more often. Holly is probably combusting. I am combusting. I call her and she answers on the first ring.

"Dad called you?" I say when she picks up.

"On my lunch! I had to have the teacher across the hall cover my last class since he has a prep period."

"How are you feeling?" I ask.

"A million things." Holly sounds like she's about to cry. She was twenty-two when Mom died, and while I sort of got really realistic about love and how it ends, she dove deeper into her fantasy of finding the perfect guy who still has yet to appear. But I'm not going to bring that up right now.

"Same." I feel myself deflate a little. At least we're both feeling a million things. "Like, Beth is so good for Dad. I think they'll be happy together."

"But she's not Mom." Holly says the words perfectly.

"Yeah."

We're both quiet for a minute.

"I just can't believe he's going to get married," Holly finally says.

"I know."

"And I don't want to go to another wedding without a date," Holly says, surprising me. She may be a bit of a hopeless romantic, one with a list a mile long with qualities she wants in a man. But she's never complained about being single before.

"I've got one!" I burst out. This is probably the wrong thing to say in this moment. I should have told her that since Dad hasn't picked a day to get married yet, she still has time to find a date.

"Wait. Who?" Holly asks, completely alert to what I'm about to say. "Mo? Noah?"

"Noah, actually. Just as friends though. He was there the night Dad announced it, and I kind of didn't react well. I think I made Beth cry."

"Oooh," Holly says. "He seems to be your knight in shining armor a lot, Sis."

"Are you just going ignore the fact that I might have made Beth cry?"

"No. But this is bigger. Did you ask him, or did he offer?"

"I'm pretty sure I asked him."

Holly squeals. "That's so great!"

"How is it great?" I ask. "I went over to his apartment last week when Gran had bingo and we made out, and then I left after telling him I might like someone else. But now it doesn't matter because we're going to be in a car for four hours on Friday."

"Wait. What?" Holly asks. "I really need to get better at not shutting out the world when I'm in creative mode. I feel like I've missed everything."

"Yeah...we kissed. Then I told him about Mo. Now it's awkward, but he still asked if we could ride together to St. George this weekend. Even though I told him I'm meeting another guy there. But I also kind of really like Noah, even though I don't want to. What am I going to do?"

Thankfully, I've made it home. I turn the car off and sit in the driveway.

"Noah's going to the event?" Holly asks. I swear she cares about the weirdest details. That is not at all what I would have asked first.

"Yeah. He bought a ticket too. Turns out he also likes her

books, and now we're driving together. Well, he's driving so I don't have to."

"Well, yay for not having to drive!" Holly cheers.

"Holly," I say with a groan. "I'm riding with a guy I've had a weird crush on for the past five years to meet a guy I've never actually met, but ever since I told Noah that I also like Mo," I'm rambling now. "I think I've started to like Mo after I realized how good we would be together, even though we've never seen each other in person."

Holly's quiet for a minute, and while I wait for her to respond, Gran opens the front door. I hold up a finger.

"Well, maybe you can figure out which one you actually want to date," Holly says.

"Not super helpful." Even though she's probably right. This weekend could be good. I get to spend some alone time with Noah and see how things go. And I can meet Mo for the first time. "Or maybe you're right."

"I'm always right." Holly laughs.

"UGH." I put my head against the steering wheel, causing it to honk again. "What am I going to do?"

"Not kiss Noah again until after you've met Mo?" Holly offers.

"Great plan." I was already planning on that. Should be easy, seeing as he'll be driving most of the time we're together. "But it's still all so confusing. The 'what if I actually have feelings for Mo,' and all these feelings with Noah, and Noah is *right* here, and I just don't know what to do."

"Trust yourself," Holly says, just like Olivia told me, which surprises me. Unless it has anything to do with her art, she's never been a "go with the flow" kind of person. Holly always has a plan and five million rules to go with it. "You'll figure it out. See what happens this weekend. See what happens with Mo and if there are sparks or not. See what happens with Noah."

"But isn't that being disloyal to both of them in some way?"

"Noah knows you're going to meet another guy, right?" Holly asks.

"Yeah."

"So just try to be friends with him, see how it goes. And maybe tell Mo you're getting a ride with a guy friend but that he's just a friend."

"Does saying that sound overkill though? Like I'm trying to convince everyone that he's just a friend?" If someone was trying to convince me they were coming with "just a friend," I'd probably question it.

"No. It's just being honest. He is a friend and that's all he is right now." For some reason it feels like she's stuck a knife in my gut, even if what she said is true. It still hurts.

"Okay," I say, more for myself than her benefit. "I'll just be honest with both of them about what's happening. At least the part about me riding with Noah and also going to meet Mo. I'm not sharing my full feelings with anyone yet."

"Probably smart," Holly says. "And you really shouldn't kiss Noah again unless your heart tells you to do that."

"Yeah. Planning on that not happening." Except now all I can think about is how good it feels to have Noah's arms around me and how comfortable I feel with him.

"Okay," Holly lets out a deep breath. "Dad's getting married," she says. "It'll take me a bit to get used to that."

"Same."

"Text me updates this weekend?" she asks.

"Of course." How else am I going to do this if I don't have Holly walking me through this? She's the one who still watches rom-coms. I haven't seen one since Mom died. I may read a lot of romance, but right now I'm not sure how to apply anything I've ever read in real life.

"Good. Now go get your guy."

"Ha," I say. "Talk to you later."

"Talk to you later." She hangs up and I'm left wondering just which guy I'm going to get. My phone vibrates.

MoReads: Can't wait to see you on Saturday.

                              TheNoraReview: Me too.

19

NOAH

I use my nervous energy about Tally finding out who I am to go on a run before I head to work on Friday. I never run, but today it feels refreshing.

I'm surprisingly calm about the idea of being in a car with her for several hours. I still haven't figured out how I should set up a meeting between the two of us. We confirmed yesterday that we'll both be there and that we'll figure out where exactly to meet tomorrow.

Tally leaves the bookstore almost as soon as I start my shift—to go and finish packing is what she tells me, but personally, I think she doesn't want to spend any more time with me than she has to. The longest I've talked to her all week was when I suggested we drive to St. George together and confessed that I fell in love with her five years ago, which she seemed kind of horrified by, not that I can totally blame her. She is planning to go meet a guy that she really likes or at least thinks she likes.

I just hope she's not disappointed when she learns that I am Mo.

I head over to Gran's house just after eight to drop off my dog and pick up Tally. I've called him Mo in front of Tally before, but I did it the other day, just to see if she'd pick up on the name and make the connection. But the only connection she's made is that he's named after the main character in Simone's books, which is also the reason behind my Twitter name.

"Oh, look at you!!" Gran squats down to pet Mo. She's talking to my dog, not me. I'm in sweats and a hoodie. "Well, come on in, dear. I think Tally is peeing for the twelfth time."

"Gran!" Tally grumbles from the bottom of the stairs, a carry-on-sized suitcase next to her. "I did not pee that many times."

"Sure seemed like it." Gran winks at me and then picks up Mo. He looks at me with horrified eyes, and yes, a dog can make that expression. "You two have fun! We're going to go snuggle and watch a Halloween movie."

I reach over and scratch Mo behind the ears, just where he likes it. "You be a good boy," I tell him. He licks my face, seeming calmer now that I've spoken to him. "I'll be back, you be good for Gran."

I turn to Tally, whose expression is unreadable. "You ready?"

She nods. "Guess so."

The first ten minutes of the drive are painfully quiet. It's only eight, but I'm worried she's going to fall asleep on me.

"Want to turn on some music?" I say, and at the same time she says, "I've been listening to the fourth audiobook, want to listen?"

I smile and glance at her as she tucks her chin to her chest as if she's embarrassed. "Definitely the audiobook." I'd love to have music so we could have a chance to talk, but I don't want to push her too much right now.

We're friends. Friends that listen to audiobooks together. Friends who made out a week ago. I am totally good with friends because after this weekend, maybe we can finally be more.

Tally connects her phone to the Bluetooth, and soon we're swept away into a world with faeries and giants and a little bit of romance. I'm itching to talk to her, to hear her laugh and make her smile, but I'm also trying to remind myself to be patient. I can be patient. I think.

We're about to Beaver, Utah when Tally says, "Could we have a little pit stop?" It's almost ten, and I need a good stretch and some caffeine. We still have two hours to go.

"Sure," I say, taking the next exit. I fill up the tank with gas while Tally goes inside the combined McDonald's and gas station.

I lock the car and head in to grab a Pepsi. Ten minutes later I meet Tally by the door. She's holding a McDonald's bag.

"I got us some fries."

"Perfect." I smile at her, suddenly remembering how a woman I once went on a single date with told me that my smile was sure to make any woman weak at the knees. I wonder if it has that effect on Tally.

Tally hands me a medium fry when we get into the car, which I set between us in the cup holder in the middle console.

"Music?" she asks, scrunching her face up as she watches me take a sip of my Pepsi.

"What?" I ask back, giving her a look that says, "Who cares what I'm drinking?"

"I'm more of a Coke person, but to each their own, I guess." She looks down at her phone. "So, music?"

"Sure. Want to be the DJ? I've got a lot of songs." I pass her my phone. I've turned off all my notifications so that even if she does happen to message Mo while she was holding my phone, she'll be none the wiser. I want her to find out on my terms, and reading a message that she sent to Mo wouldn't be exactly ideal.

"This could be fun," Tally says, grinning at my phone. She's still tense, but I can tell she's starting to relax as she scrolls through my music.

Soon familiar chords fill the air. "Backstreet Boys, good choice."

Tally laughs. "You think so?"

"Yeah. I may not be the average listener, but their songs are good."

"All right," Tally says, then she grabs her phone. "Let's see. Oh, yes!"

"What's happening over there?" I ask as I pull back onto the dark highway. She's relaxed and is in a better mood than before.

"One hundred and sixty-nine questions for couples...or two people on a road trip." I can hear the grin in her voice as her legs bounce up and down. "This could be fun, right?"

Does this mean I'm forgiven? That we're actually going to move on from the awkward moments we had after we kissed last week? "That sounds like a good way to get to know each other better since we're friends and all now."

"Yup. Friends." But there's something in the way the word catches that makes me wonder if she doesn't want to be just friends. It sparks a tiny thread of hope in my chest. Maybe I can turn things around this weekend before she even meets Mo. "Let's start with a would-you-rather question," she says, reading from her phone. "Would you rather be twenty minutes early or ten minutes late?"

"Wow, I for sure thought you were going to pick a harder one than that." I smile, teasing her. Tally punches me in the arm. "Hey. Fine." I take a fry before answering. "I'd rather be early than late."

"I am almost always late." Tally takes a sip of her drink. "I don't mean to be, but if I'm late, it usually means I'm in the middle of a good book. Or it's just in my genetics, because my older sister is always late to everything too. I'd like to be on time though. But twenty minutes early...that's so early."

"You could always get places early and read there, then you wouldn't be late and you still get to read."

"True. Or I could just keep being late," Tally says. I have a feeling that she'll always be running late. "Next question. We'll make it harder, Mr. 'That's Too Easy.' Worst first date story. Go."

This time I laugh. Then I think for a moment. I've been on quite a few bad dates, which story should I tell? "Once I showed up on a blind date, but the woman thought that it was a bring-your-own-date, so she had another guy already with her."

"That's not too bad." Tally is laughing now, a sound I am grateful for.

"I mean, it was super awkward when the three of us got a table together and the other dude wasn't really into her," I tell her. "He even offered to leave when he realized what had happened."

"He didn't!"

"He did, I felt super bad." I smile a bit at the memory because the whole thing was a little ridiculous. "But I don't think she actually noticed that he didn't want to be there. She had serious heart-eyes for him the entire time. It was so awkward."

"That's awkward, but I don't know if it's worst-date materi-al." Tally pulls her legs up onto her seat. She is always so put together, it's different to see her with a messy braid and in sweats. I like seeing this side of her. "Do you not remember my date fiasco just the other week? When my date ordered for me because he saw me eyeing the burgers?"

"Oof, yeah, you definitely win that one." I laugh. Tally is totally a burgers-and-fries lady, and I love that about her. "Next question?"

"Who is the person you trust the most, and why?" Tally asks this question carefully, maybe because this question is moving into more meaningful territory.

I eat a few more fries before answering. "This one is tough. Not because I don't have someone like that, but because I have two. My younger sister, Annie, is the first. I know a lot of siblings don't always get along, but we've always been pretty close. I swear she knows me better than I know myself sometimes."

"I feel that way about Holly too," Tally says. "And the other person?"

I think about Sam, how he might not always answer his phone, but as soon as he knows what's going on, he comes running in to save the day. "My buddy Sam. I'd trust him with my life. You remember our camping trip?"

"I don't think I'll ever forget about the time you almost died," Tally murmurs, and I wonder if she's grateful that I'm still here, like I am. "And I guess I sort of answered that already. Holly, my sister. I don't have that many people that I'm close to that I'm also not related to."

"How come?" Maybe it has something to do with the fact that she seems to push every single person away. Olivia and I are already what I would consider to be pretty good friends, but when I see Olivia and Tally together, I see how Tally puts up the same walls she puts up around me. At first it made me feel better, knowing that I wasn't the only one who she keeps out. Then it made my heart break, because, yeah, people can hurt you, but there's also a lot of joy that enters your life when you let someone in.

"I don't know." Tally sighs. "Or maybe I do. I have always been the quiet, bookish girl. I'd rather stay home and read a book than go out with friends. I had some close-ish friends in high school, but I don't think I've talked to any of them in at least three years. After my mom died, everything sort of shifted. I was suddenly the nerdy bookworm girl who also had a dead mom. I don't think people at school knew what to say to me. And in college I lived at home and kind of stuck to myself. Marsha was the closest thing I've had to a real friend in a long time. The ladies from book club I guess I'd call friends. I see them a few times a month, but I don't think I'd trust them with my life."

"That sounds kind of lonely." In nearly every city I've been in, I always have guys I can call and go out with if I want to on a Friday night. I haven't found anyone here beyond Tally and Olivia, mainly because my focus has been the bookstore, but it's kind of killing me.

Everyone needs some good friends.

Tally laughs, but I don't think that she thinks this is funny. It's another way of her putting up a wall. "It is pretty lonely. The funny thing is, I really like having friends. Even though most nights I'd prefer to stay home and read, if I don't have some form of human interaction every day, I go a little nuts. I loved it when Olivia started working at the shop, even though I don't know if we'd be considered friends."

Yeah, I want to say, because you don't ever ask anything about her. Do you know that she's lonely too? And would love to hang out with you after work? But Tally doesn't know because she hasn't asked, and Olivia can feel the wall between them just like I can.

"When Gran goes out of town, I don't know what to do with myself in the evenings. I just don't feel like I fit anywhere, which is why making friends is hard. I don't know. Now I'm just rambling." Tally trails off.

"Rambling is fine." What I want to add is that maybe she fits right here, right with me, with Olivia and her family and the book club ladies. That maybe she doesn't need to fit anywhere else. She seemed so self-assured and fine with her life when I first got to Utah, but now that I've been getting to know her, it makes me want to try harder to show her that loving people, whether a friendship kind of love or something more, doesn't have to be scary.

"I'm embarrassed I shared all that. I trust Holly the most," she says, and I know the game is over, or at least she's ready to be done.

"Would you rather have a million dollars right now or get that money over time?" I ask just to keep her talking.

"That's a dumb question." Even in the dark, I picture her crinkling her nose.

"What's your answer?" I prod.

"Over time, I guess. I don't know what I'd do with that kind of money."

"I'd buy a boat," I say confidently. A few years ago I got it in my head that someday I'd be the kind of guy who had a boat and took it to lakes on weekends with my family.

"A boat?" Tally asks. "What is it with guys and boats?"

"They're cool," I say, suddenly defensive. "It's not like I want it as a way to show off any money I have; I just think they're cool."

"If you like getting seasick, sure. Sounds super cool," Tally says, and suddenly my dream of going boating on the weekends vanishes. I'll find another dream, one that fits with Tally.

"Okay, no boat. What would you buy?" I ask, suddenly hyper aware that I want to know what her answer is.

Tally's quiet for a minute. "I'd buy a plane ticket. To Scotland. Mom always wanted to go, but she never got to before she died."

Now my boat answer really does sound dumb. I already knew this too because she told me as Nora.

"Scotland is amazing in the winter." I grin. "And the summer."

"YOU'VE BEEN!?" Tally shrieks so loud, I'm positive she's burst one of my eardrums.

"Yeah, twice." I rub my ear. "My buddy Sam? He's a traveling YouTuber. I went with him a few years back."

"That is so cool." I see Tally cross her arms over her chest. "I am really trying not to hate you right now, but I kind of totally do."

"You should definitely get the ticket."

"I can't exactly go to Scotland this year," she says quietly.

"Well, why not?"

"Dad's getting married—sometime this year I'm assuming. And Marsha left me a bookstore that I have to keep running for eleven more months."

"We're going to St. George right now."

"Yeah, but that's for the weekend."

"You deserve a vacation. You said it's been a few years." If I could, I'd nudge her leg with mine to motivate her to take the leap. "You can always go once you get the money Marsha left you."

"I know," Tally says. "I think that's the first thing I'll do once I have the money. If we can make it, working together that long."

"We will." And now I'm smiling, even if she doesn't believe me, because I can picture us walking hand in hand down the streets of Scotland, and I'm not going to let that vision go.

But I keep these thoughts to myself.

———

IT'S JUST after midnight when we pull into the hotel. After we talked about Scotland, Tally declared she was tired and took a short nap for the last hour of the trip. As we get out of the car, she looks exhausted, so I grab my duffel and pull her suitcase behind me. She doesn't make a peep about it.

We enter the well-lit lobby. Tally blinks up at the bright florescent lights as we make our way over to the desk.

"Noah Jones," I say, pulling out my ID.

"Room three-thirty-seven," the teenager behind the desk says, popping her gum as she slides me a key.

"Tally Nelson." Tally slides her ID to the girl. The girl types in her name and frowns.

"Sorry, ma'am, it doesn't look like you have a reservation," the girl says, handing back her ID.

I can feel Tally's panic.

"What do you mean?" Tally's voice comes out high-pitched, like she might cry. "I booked it three weeks ago. Let me pull up the email."

I watch her search the name of the hotel. A confirmation email comes up, along with another one. "Wait. I got an email yesterday saying it was canceled. Why would you just cancel my room?"

The teenager shrugs. "Who knows. Maybe someone over-booked the hotel."

"He still has a room!" Tally's voice has gotten considerably louder.

"Look, lady." The girl blows a bubble and pops it before she starts chewing again. I grimace. "You don't have a room. We could offer you a free stay another time?"

"No...that won't work. Everywhere else is booked. Every-where was already booked when I got this room. Where am I going to stay?"

"With me." I look at Tally, trying to convey silently that I have no hidden agenda here. She just needs a bed to sleep in and I've got an extra one. The teenager rolls her eyes and then looks at her phone again as if the issue is resolved and there's no

THE LUCK OF FINDING YOU 185

need for her anymore. Technically, there's not, but she's still being rude.

"With you?" Tally asks, her eyes as wide as saucers.

"Yeah. The room has two beds, should be fine. It's just two nights." Totally not a big deal. Even though part of me is thrilled I get to spend a little extra time with her.

"I don't think it's a good idea..." she trails off, yawning.

"Because of the guy you're meeting?" I ask, and she nods. "Don't tell him. Or do and just show him the email."

"I can try to find somewhere else." Tally pulls up Google on her phone.

"Tally." She looks up at me with her tired blue eyes. "It's late. You're exhausted. Let's just go sleep."

Tally bites her lip. Is it really that big of a deal? Why is this such a hard choice for her? We're friends. I'm not suggesting we sleep in the same bed, just the same room.

"Okay, fine." She points a finger at me. "But I get the bed by the window, and we don't close the curtains because otherwise, it's too dark."

"Deal." I hold out my hand to shake hers. To my surprise, she slips hers into mind. It's warm and small and gone all too soon.

20

TALLY

I'm silent as we take the elevator up to our room.

Our room.

Oh, gosh, what am I even doing? I'm too tired to even think straight though, so when Noah offered to let me sleep in his extra bed, I said yes.

I want to call Holly, but I can't do that because for the next twelve hours, at least, I'll be in the same room as Noah. I can't call Holly to have her help me when my problem is going to be only a few feet away. I'll send her a text once we get up to the room.

I catch my reflection in the mirror across from me. I look exhausted and slightly frazzled. My hair has started to come loose from the messy braid I put it in hours ago. At this point though, I no longer care.

"This elevator is so slow," I say as the number changes from one to two after almost a minute. "We should have taken the stairs."

Noah smiles and I ignore what the smile does to me because I am here to meet Mo and Simone Sorrows. I will not be distracted by Noah right now, even if he is super distracting.

"We can remember that tomorrow." Noah is still smirking, and it makes me want to punch him in the shoulder. Or rest my head on it.

"No. Not going there." I mutter to myself.

"What was that?" Noah asks, raising his eyebrows.

"I said that out loud, didn't I?" I am awake enough to know that the words did, in fact, come out of my mouth. "This happens when I'm tired. I say things out loud that I should have only thought."

"And what exactly where you thinking about?" Noah teases as the elevator finally comes to a stop. "Just now. Where aren't you going?"

I look at him for a split second while we wait for the elevator doors to open. "Nope."

"Nope what?" Noah asks as we step into the hallway. It looks like the hallway from the movie *The Shining* that I once watched with Dad. Dad, for reasons that I still cannot comprehend, is a horror movie fanatic. It's the one and only horror movie I've ever seen. I'm still scarred from watching it and that was when I was in high school.

"Are you sure we're not going to die here?" I ask, frozen in place. I do not do horror movies. Or creepy hotels that look like the set of a horror movie.

Noah laughs, at least until he realizes that my question is serious. "I don't think we're going to die here, Tally."

"Promise?" I ask, even though it makes me feel pathetic to ask.

"I promise to protect you from any threats." Noah is dead serious.

I am actually grateful, but I do punch him this time.

"What the heck was that for?" Noah rubs his arm, even though I know I didn't hit him that hard.

"Have you never seen *The Shining*?!" I gesture toward the carpet and the wallpaper. Recognition dawns in his eyes.

"Like I said, I think we're safe. But if creepy twins appear, I promise I'll protect you." Noah suddenly stops. We're at our room.

I've read enough books and seen enough movies to know that waiting behind that door is just one bed, because that's always what happens. This is real life though, and when Noah pushes open the door, I see two twin beds in the cramped space. I'm grateful and disappointed at the same time.

"Ah, cozy," Noah says, tugging off his jacket as he looks around the room. The two beds are pushed against one wall. There's a door to my right that I assume is the bathroom. A tiny fridge is humming in the corner, but that's the only other thing in the room.

"At least there are two beds," I say, pulling open the door to reveal the tiniest bathroom I've ever seen. Most of the room is taken up by the huge vanity. Then the toilet and glass shower are squished across from it. Noah and I look ghostly in the lighting. We're definitely going to die here.

"Ah, didn't want to snuggle with me?" Noah grins and I blink. Why does he have to be flirty with me when I'm tired? I want to flirt back, but I won't.

"You wish." I walk past the first bed and sit down on the second. It feels slightly softer than a rock. I don't think I'll be getting any sleep tonight. Though the comfort of the bed probably wouldn't have changed that at all.

"I'm going to shower, that okay?" Noah's still got an amused expression on his face.

"That's fine." I yawn. I can change into my pj's while he's in there, maybe forget the fact I'm sharing a room with him, and possibly fall asleep before he comes out. The likelihood of that happening is pretty low, but I'm still going to try. Noah nods once, then disappears into the small bathroom.

I have to SHARE A ROOM with Noah.

I turn my phone over after I send Holly the text. The girl loves her sleep and has been going to bed before ten every single night since she was in high school, so I know she won't respond. But at least someone besides me and Noah knows that I'm alone in a room with him. And at least he doesn't know how strong the feelings I have for him are.

The water starts in the bathroom, and to distract myself from thinking about Noah in the shower, I quickly change into my pjs and grab my laptop to open Twitter. Mo and I have been talking like normal again, after our weird week of near silence when I told him about how I hung out with Noah and then sort of ghosted him. I was mostly ignoring him because I've been trying to figure things out, which I haven't. But I miss talking to him. We talked a little again last night and it almost felt normal, but maybe he doesn't think anything is wrong. Maybe he's completely fine and I'm the one projecting my own anxiety onto him and the conversation.

MoReads: Got to St. George :)

I check the time stamp. I wonder where he came in from because he just got here a few minutes ago too. I can't believe that we're in the same city.

TheNoraReview: Same.

MoReads: Wow! You're still awake!

TheNoraReview: Yeah, just got in, so I haven't exactly had time to
sleep.

TheNoraReview: And talking to you is pretty fun ;)

I rub my sweaty palms together, immediately wishing I could take the winky face back, but it's too late, he's seen it.

MoReads: I hope you think so once you meet me tomorrow :)

TheNoraReview: I will. I know I will. You get me like no other person has, even if we've only talked online so far. You're my best friend.

Now I'm wide awake. My fears take over and come out of their own accord.

TheNoraReview: Do you think that it's weird we've waited so long to meet in person? I hope you're not disappointed. I hope I don't mess it up.

MoReads: I won't be. And you won't mess it up. If anything, I will be the one that messes it all up.

MoReads: I also don't think it's weird. I think we've both really liked this place where we are. We're friends. We're close. We talk about so many things, and we're about to change everything by meeting in person. I think it's okay that we both waited so long before even asking the question. I was so nervous to do that.

TheNoraReview: I'm so glad you did.

TheNoraReview: And for the record, I don't think you'll mess this up either.

The text bubbles appear, then disappear. The water in the bathroom turns off. When Noah comes out a few minutes later, brushing his teeth, there's still nothing from Mo. He must have fallen asleep. I close my laptop and turn off the light.

It's not until I'm curled up on the rock of a bed that I realize Noah's hair gets curly when it's wet and it makes my stomach flip. But I'm too tired to think about what that means for me. For us.

His breathing slows faster than mine, and pretty soon I know he's asleep. I'm wired from the weird situation and the fact that he's less than three feet away from me in this dark room. But eventually, exhaustion takes me, and soon I fall asleep.

21

TALLY

Our room is empty when I wake up the next morning. I hurry to the tiny bathroom to get ready for the day. The event isn't until six tonight, so we really could have just driven this morning instead of last night. But I still wouldn't have had a room for tonight, so I guess it doesn't really matter.

It would have meant less time with Noah. A thought that makes me both happy and sad. I could have spent time without him, but I also want to spend time with him.

I'm curling my hair when I hear the room door open and click shut. "That better be you, Noah!"

"I grabbed some breakfast," Noah calls back. "I wasn't sure when you'd be up, but I was starving."

I let out a relieved and grateful breath. "I'll be out in a second." I run my fingers through my curls, trying to convince myself that the only reason I'm putting more effort into my look today is because I'm meeting Mo later, as well as my favorite author. It has nothing to do with the fact that the next eight hours are just Noah and me.

I put everything but my curling iron back into my toiletries bag, which I leave on the spacious vanity so it can cool off, and then head out into the room that now smells like grease and hash browns. My mouth waters.

"I wasn't sure what you'd get for breakfast, so I got a few burritos, cinnamon rolls, a couple hash browns, and pancakes. Pick whatever you'd like." Noah has all the food spread out on his bed, which I notice he's made. It looks so tidy next to my unmade bed. I move over to my bed, pulling the covers up so that I won't get crumbs in the sheets. Then I face the food.

I grab a burrito, two hash browns, and a cinnamon roll and take my food to my own bed. "This is the weirdest hotel ever."

"No, 'thanks for the food, Noah'? Just going to keep mentioning the hotel?" Noah asks, but he's smiling. Teasing me again.

"Fanks for the food," I say through a mouthful of hash brown. I swallow. "I swear the pictures online looked a lot nicer."

"To be completely honest, I thought I was getting a room with two queen beds, a desk, and a deck." We both glance to the window that can't be more than two feet wide and a foot tall. There is no deck outside that window. We're on the backside of the hotel. The front looked like the pictures I remember looking at.

"Not exactly what they promised," I say, then I laugh. I must still be tired because once I start laughing, I can't seem to stop.

Noah smiles, but he clearly can't figure out what's going on in my head.

"I'm sorry," I say, trying to catch my breath. "Nothing is even funny. Everything about this isn't funny and yet..."

I continue to laugh after my very bad explanation. Why can't I be normal around this man? Why am I laughing like a toddler hyped up on sugar?

"Are you ready for tonight?" Noah asks, and I sober immediately.

"I think so," I say, reality rushing into me. I don't do this. I'm not the girl who goes out of her way to meet internet strangers. I'm not the girl who kisses one guy one week and then goes out to meet another the next week. What am I doing? Would Mom be freaking out if she were still here?

"I just hope that you get everything you want," Noah says quietly. I swallow and a piece of the hash brown scratches my throat. Somehow I manage not to cough. I grab my water to swallow the rush of emotion I feel that is more painful than the food.

His eyes haven't left me since I sat down, and I shift, feeling hot all over.

"I hope so too," I tell him, even though I'm not exactly sure what it is I want.

"Just remember that he's not going to be perfect." This comment surprises me and reminds me of Olivia's words. "You might have hyped him up in your head, and he might not be what you expect. Just know that's okay."

I try to hold back my confusion. I don't understand, but from what Noah's saying, it's like he wants me to like Mo and that he's worried I won't.

"I've most definitely hyped him up in my head. I used to do that a lot; I'd jump way ahead and plan a whole future with someone that I'd never even talked to. I like to think I've gotten it more under control."

Noah nods as if he understands exactly what I'm talking about.

"But I will keep an open mind, and I promise to tell you everything I'm feeling so that I don't hurt you. Or him." It's a huge promise to make, but I feel like I can't go through any of this unless I put it all out on the table.

"Either way, someone will get hurt." The heartache in Noah's words makes me lose my appetite completely.

I push away the half-eaten cinnamon roll and untouched burrito.

"I'm sorry, I'm not trying to make you feel guilty or anything. I know you told this guy you'd meet him before you and I ever had a conversation about our feelings." Noah's apology jars me, but it doesn't completely take away my guilt. "I just hope you get everything you want."

To his repeated words, I simply nod. I want to go back to a couple of minutes ago, before the air in the room felt heavy. "I hope so too."

"What do you want to do today?" Noah moves away from our more intense conversation, and disappointment hits me like a ton of bricks, even though the feelings don't make any sense. I want to make sense of it, but I don't think Noah is going to want to talk about my feelings until after I've met Mo.

"No idea," I say, reminding myself that for today, we can be friends. I can do friends. It's more than we've been since he got here. Too bad I don't really know how to be someone's friend. It's been too long since I started a new friendship. "We could always explore the creepy hotel."

Noah laughs. All the tension he was holding a moment ago is completely gone. "Then we'll for sure end up in *The Shining*."

"I told you it was creepy." My eyes widen. "Did I not tell you it was creepy?"

"You were right." Noah says. "We could go catch a movie, go to the outlet mall, hike."

"Do I look like someone who hikes?" I ask, holding up my foot that has a three-inch heel on it. Yes, I'm someone who always is wearing shoes, and most of the time they are heels.

"Not really, no." Noah smiles and puts his trash in the now-empty food bag. "Just throwing out suggestions based on the limited things I know about this place."

"We could go see a movie." Then I think of the two of us siting close in the dark theater. "Or shopping. You could help me pick out an outfit for tonight."

"You didn't bring something to wear?" Noah looks surprised.

"I did. But I could always find something new." I did bring a dress that will work, but you can't go wrong with something new, most of the time.

"Or you could wear what you brought and we could find something else to do. Did you bring your swimsuit?" Noah asks me.

"It's October! That's hardly a good time for a dip in the pool. Why would I have brought a swimsuit?" I shiver, thinking about how I wore a sweater yesterday and it was still cool out.

"It's St. George. I think it's nearly eighty outside already." Noah holds out his phone to show me the rising temperature on the weather app.

"I could buy a swimsuit." If I can even find one. I feel like it's almost impossible to find a swimsuit you like and that's in your size during the regular swimsuit season. It will be slim pickings, if there are even any available.

"The pool actually looked nice," Noah says, and suddenly I want to spend the day in the pool with him. I don't think about why this is the activity I'm most comfortable with out of all the things he's suggested, but now I'm a woman on a mission.

"Where do you think I'll be able to find a suit this late in the year?" Do they even sell swimsuits after August?

"Again. St. George. People have pools in their backyard, and they swim in them almost all year round. It shouldn't be that hard," Noah assures me. I'm pretty sure he has no idea whether or not people here actually swim all year round.

In the end, I'm the one who ends up being right, and the only suit I can find in my size is the brightest shade of neon orange. I feel like a walking Fanta ad, but I buy it anyway. Maybe it's good that I don't look attractive in orange, maybe Noah will take one look and make life simple by telling me we'll just be friends forever.

Sweat is dripping down my back as I pay the forty dollars for it. I can tell Noah is trying not to laugh as I tuck it gingerly in the bag.

"Not a word," I say as we make our way back to the hotel. "About the suit or about the color."

He bites his lip to keep from laughing. "Orange is my favorite color."

"It is not!" I smack his arm. "It's the color of a pumpkin. I'm going to look like a pumpkin."

The laugh he's been holding back comes out. "You will not. Plus, we'll mostly be in the pool anyway—it will be harder to see when you're underwater. But not impossible. It's like the color of a traffic cone."

He can't contain his laughter now, but I can't either.

"I can't believe it was the only swimsuit we could find." Each word comes out between a laugh, because now we're both laughing so hard that we can't breathe.

When I put it on, I realize that not only is it orange, but it also has ruffles that I hadn't paid much attention to in the store. The ruffles are everywhere. What is the point of them? They do not make the swimsuit more feminine or attractive. I mean, if anything, they make it worse.

Noah doesn't say anything as we take the stairs down to the swimming pool. He doesn't say anything when a little kid at the pool says, "Mom, that lady looks like orange juice!" Though I do see a hint of a smile again, and now I'm trying not to laugh.

"I personally think I look more like a Creamsicle," I say as I step into the pool. The water is cooler than I'd like, but it feels kind of nice against the blaring sun.

Noah lets out a deep belly laugh, and I watch his shoulders move. I try not to look at his sculpted chest. Who knew the man had all that under all his Chris Evans sweaters? "A Creamsicle is an appropriate description. Why are there so many ruffles?"

"That's exactly what I was thinking!" I splash him with water. "So, do you take all of your lady friends swimming?"

Noah splashes back, then goes under the water; coming up, he says, "Geez, that's cold." He shakes the water from his hair. "You're assuming I have lady friends."

"Do you not?"

"I mean, yeah, I guess there's a couple who I'd say are strictly friends. I have a lot of acquaintances. I don't settle down in one place for too long, so it's hard to have real friends everywhere I go. Staying in Utah for a year is going to be the longest I've been in one place for the past five years."

We've made our way to the deep end of the pool. The kid who said I looked like orange juice is swimming around, and his mom is sitting on the pool steps. Other than that, the pool is empty. "Do you really not want to settle down anywhere?"

"I guess eventually." Noah makes a wave with his hand as he moves it across the water. "I just haven't found the right place yet."

"Does there have to be a right place?" I ask. I've been in Utah my whole life. I love it and don't really want to move, but I'm also not opposed to the idea. Holly moving to California showed me that you can find roots anywhere, even if it means putting them down yourself.

"Sometimes it feels like there needs to be a right place," Noah says.

"I thought you were Mr. 'Go With the Flow.'" I shove some water in his direction.

"I am," he says. "But this feels like one of those things that I don't need to do on an impulse."

"That sounds kind of lonely," I say, thinking back to our conversation last night about how lonely I am. Maybe lonely people are just everywhere.

"Says the lonely girl." Noah's eyes are gleaming, so I'm only slightly prepared for what happens next. His arm snakes around my waist, pulling me close to him. "And who said I was lonely now?"

Before I can answer, he dunks both of us. I come up sputtering, pushing him away so that he doesn't pull me under again. I shiver, now that my hair is wet. "I'm going to have to shower again."

"What did you expect? We're swimming." Noah's laughing as he treads water. I can't help it, I start to laugh too.

We manage to stay in the pool for almost an hour before we both get out, our fingers pruney and purple. "How can I be so cold?" I ask through chattering teeth. My hands are shaking so badly that Noah has to help me wrap the towel around my shoulders. I'm instantly warmer with it around my body, but I can't stop shaking. "It has to be eighty degrees out here."

"If the water isn't warm, it doesn't matter how hot it is outside," Noah says, wrapping his towel around his waist so all I can see are his beautiful abs. I'd like to run my hands across them, but given the circumstances, I don't think that's a good idea.

When I look back up at Noah's face, he's got a half-smile, like he knows exactly what I was just thinking.

"How can the water not be warm?" I try to change the unspoken subject about how I want to touch his skin. "The pool is in the sun."

Noah shrugs. "I don't know how it works. But since you're cold, you can shower first when we get back up to the room. Or we could hop in together to save some time." Then the man has the nerve to wink at me. Wink!

"We will not be doing that," I manage to say and wonder how I'm going to get *that* thought out of my head. Plus, now I'm like five thousand degrees, thanks to that comment, so at least I've warmed up.

Noah shrugs like it's not a big deal and that I didn't just turn him down for something pretty big, so I try to act like it's not a big deal either.

DRIPPING WET, we make our way back to our tiny room, taking the stairs instead of the creepy elevator. I shower quickly, singing the lyrics of "The Best Day" by Taylor Swift to think about my mom instead of Noah. I hang my neon swimsuit carefully over the shower door to dry and twist my hair up in a towel.

Noah is reading on his bed when I come out of the steamy bathroom.

I do my makeup with my small mirror while he's in the shower. When he finishes, I brush out my hair, deciding I'll straighten it after it air-dries. I'm painfully aware that we now have three hours to fill and we're just sitting a few feet away from each other on our own beds.

I need to message Mo, but the thought makes my stomach roll. What if today, of all days, I say something that makes him not want to meet me? Why would I want to ruin something before it has even started?

"You okay?" Noah asks, interrupting my thoughts.

"What? Oh yeah. Totally good." I'm mortified that not only was he watching me but that he also could read how I was feeling.

"What's going on?" he asks me. "We don't have to talk about it, but you're looking a little green."

"I'm nervous about meeting Mo." No point in keeping it a secret I guess; Noah knows that's going to happen tonight.

"Mo. That's the guy you're meeting?" Noah asks, and I realize I've never told him Mo's name. Not that it matters. But it's weird to hear him say it. "Want to practice what you'll say?" He sits up, facing me. I turn to face him and in the cramped space, our knees brush. I tuck my legs under me. No touching Noah. I have to remind myself of that rule. I wish Holly would text me back, but the only thing she said this morning was *Go get your man!* Which was the opposite of helpful.

"I guess."

"Okay. So how are you meeting him?" Noah asks, and my stomach drops.

"We, uh, haven't planned that yet," I say, realizing how stupid that sounds. "We need to make a plan though, right? Because otherwise, how will we find each other? We don't know what each other looks like."

"A plan would be good." Noah pauses, rubbing his chin. "Are you sure this is a good idea? He could be a creep or something."

"There will be like six hundred other people around. I think I'll be okay," I say, even though now I'm questioning everything. Maybe this really is a terrible idea. I reach for my phone. "I'm going to message him. I'll tell him what I'm planning to wear and that we can meet at the main entrance at 5:30 so we can go in together."

I am not as confident as I sound.

Noah nods. "Okay."

"You think this is a terrible idea." It's not a question, even though I want to know his answer.

"I like you, Tally," Noah says, and there's a burning in my

belly. "I think you're beautiful and strong and absolutely incredible. You don't laugh often, but when you do, man, it lights me up inside, so I keep trying to find new ways to get you to laugh or even just smile. I like you a lot. You know that—I haven't tried to keep my feelings for you a secret. So while I don't love the idea of you going off to meet another guy, if it's what you want to do, I'll support you in that."

Does he really support me, or is he only telling me that to ease my anxiety?

"You don't have to respond to that." Noah chuckles. "I just wanted to tell you that yeah, I like you. I like spending time with you. And it's probably not the greatest idea to have me help you get ready to meet this other guy, since I'm already a tad bit jealous."

Where is all this honesty coming from? Why now? I can't help but wonder, but I don't ask. Instead, I just sit there, staring at him as if he just confessed that he was in love with the Queen of England and not that he likes me.

My heart picks up a notch at the thought, even though I have had this information for a week now. Even though he told me just the other day that he *loved* me all those years ago. There's still something here between us, but I already agreed to meet Mo and I always follow through.

"You were the one who suggested helping me." I frown at him. "Why would you do that if you're jealous?"

Noah runs a hand through his hair, a habit that I didn't realize he had until this trip, but now I remember him doing it over and over at the bookstore. He seems frustrated with himself. "I just. I don't know. But give me a chance if things don't work out with this guy?"

My heart twists. He can't ask that of me, can he? It feels like if I answer, that means I'm putting him second, like he's just my backup plan, which doesn't feel fair to him. But if I don't answer, that will hurt him too. So I say, "Okay."

"Okay." There's something real and raw and a lot like hurt in Noah's eyes. He blinks and it's gone. "We could practice your kissing skills."

The room shrinks. We're back to the teasing and flirting.

"I think you just want to kiss me," I say, even though my mind is swirling from the emotional whiplash I've had all week.

"I definitely won't disagree with that." Noah smiles at me and I'm a goner. I mean, when a man like Noah comes into your life, you keep him, right? If he keeps staring at me like this, I'm going to lose all my resolve.

"I haven't kissed anyone in a while." Apparently, I've already lost all my resolve. "I mean, besides you last week. It had been a long time before that."

Noah shifts, and then he's sitting on my bed, a foot away from me.

"Practice would be good, then?" he says slowly. He moves his hand, almost as if he's afraid to touch me, but his fingers graze my face as he pushes my hair behind my ear. He just told me that he wanted me to give Mo a chance and then him a chance if Mo didn't work out, and now he's making a move on me?

No wonder my heart is a complete mess.

"Yeah." It comes out all breathy, and I don't know what just happened, but I've completely lost my grip on reality. Maybe I really do just want Noah to kiss me again. I tilt my head, angling it toward him.

After tonight, there may not be any more of this. I know deep down that what I have with Mo is real, and yeah, if he ever finds out that I kissed another guy hours before meeting him, it would probably crush him. But I may also never get a chance to kiss Noah again. Because if I do get together with Mo, I've got to stop daydreaming about Noah forever.

A face pops into my mind as my eyes flutter closed. Mo's face. I open my eyes wide, realizing I've always given Mo Noah's face, just with darker hair. But the face I've always imagined was Noah, especially since he started working at the shop.

Noah's leaning toward me—he's watching my every move, but I'm a statue. He gets half an inch away. I can feel the heat from his lips.

"I want to kiss you, Tally," Noah says. "But I'm not going to unless you say it's okay."

We're frozen.

"I want you too," I whisper. I'm surprised by the tears springing to my eyes.

Noah eases back. "But?"

"But it wouldn't be fair to you." I look down at my hands. "Or to Mo." Or me. But I don't say that, because that thought seems selfish.

Noah reaches for my hand and squeezes it. "I hope he's good to you" is all he says, then he leans forward, his fingers sliding into my hairline at the base of my neck, and tenderly presses his lips against my forehead. Tears stream down my face as he lingers there, longer than a brotherly kiss. After everything he just said, there's too much emotion in this.

He eases away far too soon, looking into my eyes. He brushes away my tears with his thumb. He gives me a half-hearted smile and my heart cracks into a million pieces.

I know I've made the right choice by not letting him kiss me. But why does it also feel like I've just made the biggest mistake of my life?

Noah goes back to his own bed and grabs his phone. "I'm going to take a walk, clear my head. I'll be back soon." He leaves without another word.

I message Mo to tell him that I'm wearing a dark-pink dress with matching heels and ask to meet him at 5:45 at the main entrance. Guilt prickles through me the entire time I send the message. What am I even doing? Stringing two guys along? That's not who I am. I have to figure this out. Hopefully, by the end of the night, I'll have my answer.

22

NOAH

The tension in the air when I get back to the room is palpable. I have to come clean. I've almost told Tally three times today that I'm Mo, but I keep chickening out. And the longer I wait, the worse it's going to be.

"Tally, I need to tell you something."

She's watching something on her laptop, so she takes out her earbud and looks at me. I'm standing way too close to her bed because there isn't really a place for me to stand.

"It's okay. You don't have to say anything," Tally says, and I stare at her. Nothing is okay, and it won't be okay until I tell her that I am Mo. "I'm sorry that I'm putting you through all of this," she continues, not giving me a chance to speak. "If I were in your shoes, I would be so upset too. It's not fair at all, and I'm sorry."

Tally isn't wrong, but because I was so focused on what I was going to say and not expecting her apology, I don't end up saying anything.

"I'm going to go get something from the vending machine. I'll be back soon." Tally gives my arm a squeeze as she passes me.

I should grab her and pull her into my arms and tell her everything, but for some reason I cannot understand, I'm frozen in place until she's gone.

"UGH!" I throw myself onto the bed. "I'm actually Mo. See? It's not hard to say those words!"

So why can't I tell her in person?

I pull out my phone like the giant chicken I am.

> **MoReads:** Sounds like a good plan. See you then.

I don't want to feel this way, with jealousy coursing through my body and shame for not telling her right underneath the jealousy.

She's still going to meet him. Even after our day together. Even after I keep admitting my feelings. I shouldn't be jealous. We've been talking online for two years; she has every right to want to meet her online friend. I'm regretting not having told her earlier though. I should have just come clean as soon as I figured it out, and then we could have enjoyed this weekend a whole lot more.

<<Group message with Annie and Sam>>

> *I can't do it. I can't show up as Mo.*

Annie

YOU HAVEN'T TOLD HER THE TRUTH YET!? YOU CANNOT LEAVE HER HANGING.

Sam

She's right, you have to tell her.

I think she's going be really mad that it's me, especially now that she's told me the guy she's meeting is named Mo. Like, why didn't I tell her then???

Annie

Yeah, why didn't you??

Sam

You should get her flowers or something.

Annie

Flowers do not fix everything. Why do guys think flowers fix everything?

Sam

I thought you liked flowers???

This conversation is not helpful. I have to tell her the truth, even if now it's going to be extremely awkward because I've had so many chances to come clean and I haven't taken any of them.

I run my hands through my hair. It's probably sticking straight up at this point, but that is the least of my problems.

Annie

Not the point. You have to tell her, Noah.
You like her, right?

Yeah, I really like her. Like a lot.

Annie

Then tell the woman. It's always better to be honest than to lie and hide things.

Annie's text makes sense, but I wouldn't say that I've been intentionally hiding things for too long, right? Does that make it less bad?

Annie
Just tell the woman how you feel.

Sam
Tell her, man.

I'm really afraid she's going to hate me.

Annie
I would. Good luck.

The door unlocks and Tally comes back into our room, arms full of chips and chocolate bars. I put my phone down as soon as I see her. I can try again.

"I was thinking, can we talk about everything after tonight?" Tally asks as she hands me a chocolate-covered granola bar, my favorite. This is a truce, I think, or maybe a peace offering, even though she doesn't need to be offering this.

I'm not mad at her at all; if anything, I'm mad at myself.

"We can talk after." When I say it, I can picture us lying on our own beds, staring up at the ceiling and chatting late into the night like you would a roommate or sibling.

It won't be like that. Because either she'll be so thrilled that it's me or she'll be so mad that I'll never see her again.

"Okay." Tally smiles at me and opens a Kit Kat.

"Okay." Okay? That's what I said? Not my big confession? I am really screwing this up. "It will be good to talk."

"Okay, then, it's a date." Her cheeks turn pink. "I mean, you know what I mean. So, what do you think is going to happen in this next book?" Tally changes the subject, and my window is gone.

MY PLAN IS A STUPID ONE, but I'm committed now. Simone's event is being held in one of the big conference rooms at the hotel across the street from where we are staying. Tally looks great—she's wearing a dress I've never seen before, and I feel very underdressed in my joggers, which look slightly high-end but actually feel like sweats, and a T-shirt. I would change, but this is what I brought, so I'm going with it.

Tally ended up curling her hair and putting lipstick on, only to take it off because she said it didn't make her feel like herself. Which is true; it was the only time I've ever seen her wear lipstick.

I run over my plan as we walk across the street.

We're going to get through the main ticket entrance, which is also where we get our books. Then Tally is going to wait outside the event's main room, at the doors. I am going to go in, letting her know I'll save her a seat just in case. But really, I'll go get our seats. I brought a jacket to cover them. Then I'll sneak out a different door and approach her, laughing and saying something like, "Oh my gosh, wait, no way! I'm Mo." As if she hasn't told me his name, as if I haven't talked about him like he's some mystery man that I don't know anything about.

She'll probably punch me. No, I think she'll definitely punch me. But it'll be fine. I hope it'll be fine because at this point, I just have to go through with it this way. If I tell her now, I know she'll hate me for a million years.

My stomach is a ball of nerves and I really feel like I'm going to be sick. I am not this guy. The one who keeps secrets.

It's my own fault I'm in this mess, and I can't tell if I'm more nervous that Tally is going to be mad that it's me and that I knew and didn't tell her or that she's just going to be mad that Mo is me.

She almost kissed me though...

I'm clinging to that thought, hoping it soothes some of the nerves.

It doesn't.

WE GET our books after they scan our tickets.

"I can't believe this is real!" Tally clutches the book to her chest, then holds it out again to look at the cover. The book officially released on Tuesday, and beyond talking to Nora—well, Tally—on Twitter, I've avoided the internet.

If it were any other day and not the moment she finds out that I'm Mo, I'd probably feel the same way. I've been excited about this book since I read and loved the rest of the series. Plus, this one is going to be signed. I'll get to meet Simone Sorrows, if only for a moment.

But I won't be able to even comprehend any of that until I come clean with Tally.

"Okay, this is where I told Mo I'd meet him." Tally looks at me, almost apologetically.

"Cool." I give her an easy smile, even though I think I might be sick. I really hope I don't look green. The event starts in twenty minutes. Mo is supposed to meet Tally in five. "I'm going to go grab some seats over there." I point into the main room off to the right side. It seems less empty. "I'll save you a seat, just in case."

"Thanks." Tally smiles at me, it squeezes my heart. "That won't be necessary though."

"I'll see you back at the room, then?" I ask sadly. I have to be disappointed right now or she'll figure it out a little too soon, and at this point, I'm all in for sticking with my plan.

"Yup." Tally wipes one of her hands on her dress, and that's when I know she's nervous too.

"You look great," I tell her. I want to hug her, give her some sort of comfort, but I can't touch her. "He'll love you."

Tally bounces up and down, scanning the crowd before looking back at me. "Part of me wanted it to be you." She laughs. "You know, like the whole *You've Got Mail* thing. Silly, I know." She looks down.

Now. Now is when I tell her the truth, that it is me. It is that moment!

"But I'll see you later." Tally grabs my hand and gives it a little squeeze, then lets go, turning away from me.

Missed my moment. Again. Why is it so hard for me to say what's on my mind? I've always been able to do that when I'm around Tally. Speaking up and sharing my truth has been easy until this.

Now I have no choice but to go grab us seats. We're early enough that I get some pretty close to the front, which is actually really cool. Then I head back out through a different door. Only instead of finding myself in the main hallway, I'm in a different hallway that's full of people waiting to get into the event. I turn around to go back through the door I just came through, but it's locked.

"Sorry, sir, you have to wait in line," a security guard who's walking by tells me.

"No, I just came from in there." I show him my stamped hand. "I was, uh, looking for the bathroom."

"You'll have to wait in this line to get back in. I'm sorry," he says apologetically. "The bathroom is at the other end of the hall." He points toward the end of the line. "Then you have to wait to get back in."

Panic rises in my chest. "I've got a friend waiting for me at the main door—I told her I'd just be a few minutes."

"You'll have to wait in line. Just text her."

That's when I realize that my phone isn't in my pocket. I don't even know if I brought it with me and it's in my jacket that's now strewn across the chairs saving our seats, or if it's back at the hotel. I don't have the time to go check at this point. Now I really am going to be sick. I make a beeline for the bathroom, saying a prayer of gratitude that they are singles and that there's an open one.

I barely lock the door before I'm dry heaving.

This. Cannot. Be. Happening.

"At least I have my book." I hold up the brand-new hard-cover and see my pale face in the mirror. If anything, this makes me feel worse.

I don't think I'm going to actually puke. But I really want to.

I splash some cold water on my face and take a deep breath.

How on earth am I going to get to Tally in time if I have to wait in that line again?

ONCE I STOP PANICKING, I rinse my face with cold water. "You can do this," I tell myself in the mirror. I take a deep breath. It's now or never.

I go over to the door and turn the knob. I hear the click of the automatic lock unlock and I pull. Nothing happens. I twist and pull again. The only difference the second time is there's no click. I rattle the door, but it doesn't open.

I'm locked in.

"No. No, no, no, no," I moan as I bang on the door. Maybe

someone that was standing in line will hear me. Or that useless security guard. "Hello! HELP! I'm stuck."

I don't have my phone, and I'm stuck in the bathroom. I guess now is a good time to remember that I'm not claustrophobic. It doesn't help my predicament, but at least I'm not stressed about that.

"TALLY!" I yell against the door and hit it with my hand again, even though I know she won't be able to hear me. Dread fills my stomach; I'm not going to make it to her in time. She's going to think that Mo stood her up. "Crap. HELP!" I yell again and bang on the door.

Stopping to listen, I realize that the chatter I heard when I first came in the bathroom has completely stopped. The line has moved enough that most people are in the main event hall.

"Okay. It's fine," I tell myself. I try to figure out what time it is, because of all days to forget to wear my watch, today is apparently that day. "I came in here at what, 5:40? It can't even be six yet, right?"

I bang on the door again until my palm is raw and then sit down against the door. No one is coming. I am officially stuck. I catch a glimpse of the book that I brought in here with me. I wonder if I stare at it long enough, it will turn into my cell phone.

When that doesn't work, I stand up again, trying to be as quiet as possible to see if someone outside will help me.

There's no sound coming from the hallway. I have no way of knowing for sure, but at this point I'm guessing that the event has officially started.

I sink back to the floor, leaning against the door so that if anyone walks by, I'll be able to hear them.

After what feels like fifteen minutes, I stand up and grab my book, resigned to the fact that I am officially stuck in this bathroom. I'm full of guilt because I can't stand Tally up, even if it is on accident. She's the kind of woman you fight for and try to be the best person you can be, if only to actually deserve her. She makes me want to be a better man, to settle down and have a huge family and live in a big house with a wraparound porch where we drink hot chocolate together in the mornings.

And I might have ruined it all by not telling her the truth—and by taking a detour to the bathroom and getting locked in.

23

TALLY

I watch countless people walk from the line into the conference room. Men, women, even a few teenagers. No one stops to talk to me. A few offer me an awkward smile after I make eye contact. I've been standing there for fifteen minutes when a security guard walks by. "You waiting for someone, miss?"

I nod.

"You'll want to go in soon to get your seat. We close these doors five minutes before the event starts, and I can't guarantee you'll get a seat once they do shut," the guard says, but what he says doesn't make sense. This is a ticketed event; shouldn't they have seats for everyone who bought a ticket?

I nod politely and he moves on.

I'm thankful for the heavy book in my hands that's keeping me from fidgeting too much. I pull out my phone at 5:47. Do I message Mo? I wonder if he's said anything. I open Twitter. Nothing.

I don't want to sound desperate. But this was his idea. He's the one who suggested we meet and that we meet here. The unsettled feeling I've had all day falls on me in full force. What if he doesn't show?

TheNoraReview: I'm at the main entrance, are you here?

At 5:54 I put my phone back in my pocket, with no response. "I will wait three more minutes, and then I'll go in," I say out loud, which earns me a side-glance from a mom and her teenager walking in the doors. Watching them, my heart pangs in my chest, followed by an ache that fills my entire body. I bite my bottom lip in an effort to hold back the tears that I know will come.

I miss Mom. I ache for her to be here with me. I wish more than anything that I could be sharing this moment with her. She would have loved coming to something like this. When we were growing up, she would take us to any author events that our local library hosted. There weren't very many, but it was always a thrill to be there with her.

My eyes unwillingly fill with tears. I'm tempted to bolt, to text Noah and tell him being here was too much and then call Holly so we can talk about Mom and cry. It's been a long time since we've done that, too long. What I need right now is a good, long cry. My soul needs to do that, to call Holly and go over my memories of Mom, making her feel more alive, even though I can't see her again.

"Are you okay?"

I blink away my tears and see an insanely gorgeous man standing in front of me. Could this be Mo?

I shake my head, then let out a little laugh. So much for first impressions. "Got in my head for a second there, but I'm okay."

The man smiles at me.

"Are you Mo?" I blurt out the question like I'm a dog who just saw a squirrel.

The man's charming smile slips a little.

"No. I'm Chase." His voice is deep and rich and my heart

sinks. "Are you waiting for someone?" The stunning smile is back.

"Yeah, I am." As good-looking as this guy is, I don't need any more men in my life.

"Well, I hope they come." Chase waves before heading into the main room.

A minute later, they shut the doors. Just like the security guard promised.

I tap my foot as I look around the lobby area one more time. Besides the security guard and an older woman, it's completely empty. I bite my lip. No matter how I feel, I am not going to cry. Not about my mom being gone, I can do that later. And most certainly not about Mo standing me up. I'll go in and find Noah, and we can meet Simone and then make out all night. That might technically be using him to eat away the consuming embarrassment that's building in my chest, but maybe he won't mind. Maybe he'll be ready and willing to comfort me, and when we get back to Provo, we can give us a shot. Because despite everything, I really would like to give us a shot.

I slip into the room, still trying to hold my composure. I scan the back of heads and realize there are a lot more people here than I thought there would be. I pull out my phone as the moderator gets up to introduce Simone and text Noah.

Where are you sitting? Could you wave or something?

He leaves me on delivered. He must not be looking for his phone. But he's got to be looking for me, right? Waiting to see who I come in with?

"Ma'am, you need to find a seat," a woman standing near the door tells me.

"My friend saved one for me, I'm just looking for him," I tell her. People are clapping and I watch as Simone takes the stage.

"You need to sit down," the lady tells me again. "If you need help, I can direct you to a seat."

"I'm fine," I say, because she's only making this worse. Humiliation is taking over and I'm blinking back tears again. "You can do this, Tally," I whisper to myself, wishing it could give me the confidence I pretend to have most of the time. It doesn't work and I feel the same.

The door opens behind me. I turn, hoping to see Mo walking in with some explanation, but it's a group of teenage girls. The woman moves to help them find seats. Which gives me another moment to scan the room. I try to find Noah's wavy dark-blond hair, but I can't see it. There are too many people.

I find a single chair in the last row; I'll find Noah afterward. It's better this way—I don't have to sit next to him pretending everything is fine. I don't have to tell him right this second that I got stood up, which is good because I think if I had to tell him that right now, I would actually cry and he'd probably insist we leave, which would be so sad if we missed this. Not that I've heard a single word that Simone has said in the last five minutes.

I have an hour or so to let some of the embarrassment settle, if it ever will, and to figure out what I'm going to say to Noah.

My heart physically aches. Simone says something and everyone laughs, but the world around me is muted, like it isn't as bright as it was a few minutes ago.

He changed his mind. He saw me, and he changed his mind and left.

The thought slams into me, and it's the one that makes the first tear fall. I try to wipe it away discreetly, but it doesn't matter; my eyes are like a river now. I couldn't stop the tears if I tried.

Simone's talking about why she did a surprise release as I pop up out of my seat. Thankfully, I'm in the last row, so only a handful of people notice as I make my way out and through the door. I skip the elevator and hurry down the stairs that I saw while I was waiting for Mo. Tears stream down my face the entire time. I can't get out of there fast enough.

24

NOAH

If I weren't so irritated about being locked in a bathroom without my phone, I probably would have fallen asleep from boredom. I tried meditating, but that is not something that's for me. I also tried counting, but once I hit nine hundred I stopped because it was too discouraging. Reading Simone's new book is an option I considered. But because I tend to zone out when I read, not picking it up seems like the best option here.

I nearly fall over when I hear someone walking in the hallway outside.

"HELLO! HELP! I'M STUCK IN HERE," I yell as loudly as I can and bang on the door again. I wince as I pull my hand away, which is still tender from all the banging I did earlier.

"Hello?" I hear a woman call tentatively back.

A person! I could cry in relief. "Hi! Yes! I'm stuck in the bathroom; the lock won't unlock. Could you find someone to help?"

"Yeah...just a second." The sound of footsteps fades, and I'm alone again.

"Sir?" a man asks through the door, and I think it's the security guard from earlier.

"Yeah! I'm stuck." I try to keep my voice calm, but the truth is, I'm mad. Mad that the door locked. Mad that I didn't have my phone with me. Annoyed that the guy on the other hasn't tried to open door from the outside yet.

"Have you had any alcohol to drink?" he yells through the door.

"What? No! I just want to get out of the bathroom. I twisted the knob and heard a click, but it seems to be locked still," I yell back.

"All right." I hear muffled radio sounds. "I'm having someone bring the master key. This happens every couple of weeks."

It happens every couple of weeks? So why don't they get it fixed?

I sit on the counter while I wait, and a few seconds later there's a knock on the door. "I've got the key. You're clothed?"

"Yes!" Does this guy really think I'm drunk? I'm stuck in the bathroom, not for funsies or because I'm so intoxicated that I can't get out. Plus, he said this happens every couple of weeks. Why would he assume I'm drunk?

"The key doesn't work," the man calls. "The door seems to have locked itself. I have to call the fire department."

I throw my head back in frustration. "Can someone get me out!? Please?" No one answers my question.

What I think is twenty minutes later, there's another knock on the door. "I'm Ned from the fire department. We'd like you to stand away from the door. We're going to take out the bolts to remove the door." I hop off the counter and move to the corner farthest away from the door.

After another eternity, the door slowly moves open, off its hinges. I grab my book and rush forward as an EMT rushes toward me. I hold up a hand to stop him. "I'm totally fine, I've just been stuck in here for—what time is it?"

Ned looks at his watch. "Almost seven."

"I've been stuck in here for over an hour," I tell the group of people staring at me. "Now, if you don't mind, I need to go find a friend."

The people move at a sloth's pace to let me through.

I have to find Tally.

I sneak into the main event room, where Simone is at the front, talking and laughing and answering audience questions. I scan the backs of heads for Tally. Where would she have sat after she realized I—Mo—wasn't coming? She would have looked for me, but if she couldn't see me, she'd probably just have found a spot. I'm still scanning the crowd when there's a flurry of movement.

"You going to get in line?" a woman asks me, nodding to the desk that I failed to notice before. I'm standing right by the autograph station.

"What?" I ask, distracted.

The woman hands me a sticky note. "Write your name on this if you want it personalized." She moves on to the person behind me and tells her the same thing. Simone gets to the table and grins up at me. I hand her my book.

"Anything specific?" she asks, holding a Sharpie.

"For Tally." Her name comes out because she's all I can think about right now. I hold up the sticky note. "Sorry, she just gave me this."

Simone smiles at me. "Not a problem, dear." She signs the book and hands it back to me. I scan the crowd of people, waiting for Tally to see me or call out to me. If she was in here, she'd be able to see me or I would be able to see her at this point since the line wraps around the room.

Disappointment hits me like a ton of bricks. She must have gone back to the hotel when she got stood up.

It's only when I'm running out of the hotel and across the

street to where we're staying that I realize I had her sign my book to Tally.

I burst into the room, ready to explain myself, only to find it completely empty.

My phone is on my bed, right where I left it.

I have three missed calls from Tally, from right before the event started, and about seven texts from her.

Tally

Where are you sitting? Could you wave or something?

Tally

Where are you??

Tally

Noah!! He stood me up. Where are you sitting?!

Tally

Answer your phone!!!

Tally

I'm back at the hotel. I just couldn't be there anymore. Text me when you read this.

Tally

I just saw your phone in our room.

Tally

I'm really sorry, but I just...I called an Uber. Gran said she'd pay for it. On my way home. I'll see you Monday at the store. Thanks for earlier today, I had a really good time with you.

There are two messages for Mo.

TheNoraReview: I'm at the main entrance, are you here?

TheNoraReview: I think it would be best if we don't talk anymore.

When I click on her profile, it no longer shows her following me.

I drop my phone, sinking into the bed and burying my head in my hands. "No. No, no, no," I groan.

She left. I didn't get a chance to explain and then she couldn't find me when she needed someone. I grab my stuff as quickly as I can. Maybe if I drive fast, I can get to her house tonight and explain everything.

I'VE BEEN in the car for an hour when my phone rings. "Tally?" I answer without even looking at the caller ID.

"Noah? It's Annie." My heart drops.

"What's wrong, Annie?" I ask, noting the distress in her voice.

"Could you come help me?" Annie's voice is quiet. "I need to move out tomorrow."

"Out of your apartment?" I ask dumbly.

"Yeah." She sniffs. "Mitch, he...well, I don't really want to talk about it. But I'll need some help so I can be out of here by Sunday."

"I'll be on the next plane," I promise her. I take the next exit so I can look up flights and grab some food. The quickest flight leaves from Salt Lake in six hours. I book it and drive straight to the airport.

I'M SO anxious the entire flight that I don't sleep a wink, even though I'm exhausted. I've lost Nora, and I don't know what to do so I don't lose Tally too.

As I take a cab to Sam's apartment, where Annie texted me

she was staying at, I try to clear my head. I need to be able to focus on helping Annie, at least for the next twenty-four hours, then I can figure out how I'm going to fix everything that I messed up with Tally.

I'm grateful that Sam left Annie a key to his apartment, even though he's in Europe for the next five months.

I let myself into the apartment and find Annie asleep on the couch.

"Hey, Annie," I say, gently nudging her. She opens her eyes sleepily. It's dark, but I can still see a bruise on her left cheek. I'm going find Mitch and murder him if he's the one who gave it to her.

I might murder him anyway.

"Noah," Annie says, wincing as she gets up off the couch and falls into my arms. "Thank you for coming. I'd really like to go get my stuff as soon as we can. Mitch is at the office today, so we have until about seven if you want to sleep first."

I just hold my sister. I'm so full of anger. The emotion feels foreign to me. I was such an angry kid after Dad left until Mom got me into therapy. Anger isn't something I feel very often these days. But now? Someone hurt one of the people I love most in the world, and I don't know what to do with this rage.

"He..." Annie starts.

"You don't have to say anything," I tell her. "He was garbage. We didn't see it—it's not your fault."

I don't think she believes me, so I hug her tighter.

"He slept with one of the new line cooks," she says, and somehow I know that's not the worst of it.

"Trash," I say through clenched teeth. Mitch always rubbed me the wrong way, but now I really hate the guy. I force myself to push my anger down because Annie is already hurting. She doesn't need to see how mad I am about this.

Annie weeps in my arms, and I hold her until she's nearly

asleep. I help her lie back down on the couch and cover her with a comforter I recognize from Sam's high school days. Once Annie is asleep, exhaustion hits. The sun is already high in the sky, but I need at least an hour of sleep if I'm going to help Annie move her stuff out of the apartment later. I go into Sam's room, where he hasn't slept in months, and I'm out as soon as my head hits the pillow.

25

TALLY

Gran is up and waiting for me when I get home. It's past midnight and I'm completely exhausted from the past twenty-four hours.

"It's going to be okay, sweetheart," she whispers again and again as she runs her fingers through my hair, and I cry like I haven't since Mom died. I managed to hold it together in the Uber. If I thought the tears at Simone's event were a lot, this is a waterfall.

Everything that happened seems so out of character for the person I thought Mo was, for who he was online. But I guess you really can't know someone as well as you think you do when the only words you exchange are on a screen.

"Everything's a mess." I look up at Gran when the tears finally stop, her fingers going through my hair. I'm lying across the couch, my head in her lap. I don't think I could move even if I wanted to.

Gran's fingers pause. "What happened?"

"I waited and waited and waited," I tell her, the humiliation of it all filling me up again. "I messaged him and he never responded. I went into the event right as it was starting to try and find Noah, but I couldn't see him because there were too many people, and it was all too much so I went back to the hotel. Which is where I saw Noah's phone on his bed, so that's why he hadn't told me where he was, but still. It was all too much. I just couldn't deal, so instead of waiting for him to come back, I just called you and packed up, and now here I am."

Gran runs her fingers through my hair again in a way that reminds me so much of Mom that I start to cry again. She pulls me into her, giving me a big awkward hug since she's sitting above me. "I know that tonight was really hard," she starts. "We don't have to worry about Mo or Noah until the morning—well, later this morning."

Gran helps me up and leads me down the stairs. She braids my hair, just like she used to do when I was younger and I slept over here. She kisses my cheek softly and tells me to get some rest.

Before I fall asleep, I look at my phone one last time, willing there to be a message from Mo, even though I told him I don't think we should talk again, but there's nothing. If I had any tears left, they would fall now. I might have told him not to talk to me and unfollowed him, but that's not actually what I want. I got my hopes up tonight, and in the end, I lost my closest friend.

I SLEEP UNTIL NOON. My phone fell off my bed at some point in the night, but my growling stomach forces me to go straight upstairs before looking for it.

"Morning," Gran says with a smile as she slides a pancake onto the plate sitting at the counter that I assume is for me.

"Morning." I yawn.

"Technically, afternoon, but you had a late night, so we can pretend it's morning." Gran passes me the syrup.

"Maybe I shouldn't have left," I say as I take a bite of the sugary goodness. Gran's pancakes are to die for. If I had to pick one thing to eat for the rest of my life, it would be these.

"You shouldn't have. You could have had a long, romantic night with Noah." Gran sighs. She's always been a romantic too.

"That's not what would have happened." I didn't even tell her about our almost-kiss yesterday, but I swear she has a sixth sense for these kinds of things, just like Mom did.

Gran eyes me carefully. "You really trying to tell me that you and that boy were alone in a hotel room and nothing happened? I've seen enough movies to know that's not a thing."

I curse silently when I feel my cheeks grow warm. "Nothing happened." It's true, nothing *actually* happened. Even though things *almost* happened. Then they didn't, and I have Noah's hurt face permanently stuck in my brain.

But I'm not going to tell her any of that. It'll just give her the satisfaction of being right. Which isn't what she needs right now.

"He kissed you!" Gran grins.

"He did not kiss me," I say, stuffing my mouth with another bite. And I am not going to bring up the kiss from last week. "He was a perfect gentleman. Just like he always is."

"But you wanted him to kiss you?" Gran asks, waving the spatula around.

"Gran!" I groan. "It wouldn't have been fair to either of us. I was there to meet another guy."

"And your favorite author." She smiles.

"But also another guy," I grumble. Suddenly nauseous, I push away my plate. "I'm not hungry anymore."

"Oh, sweetheart." Gran reaches across the counter and touches my hand softly. "I'm sorry he didn't show. Maybe he texted and told you why?"

I nod slowly. "Maybe." My stomach is in knots as I move

away from the counter. "I'll go check, I guess. And I'll see when Noah is going to come pick up his dog." Noah's dog, Mo, lies on the rug by Gran's feet. He was sound asleep when I got home and didn't even jump up to greet me until this morning.

"He's picking him up tomorrow. That was our deal. I am not giving this dog back till then," Gran tells me, eating her own pancake.

"Oh-kay," I say, dragging out the word. "Maybe you should just get your own dog."

"Too much work," Gran says, swatting her hand in the air. "Maybe you should just date Noah and I can see this one all the time."

"Gran."

"Fine, fine. I'll be quiet. Go see what your men have to say."

My heart skips a beat when I see the notification from Noah.

I'm in New York. Family emergency. Could your grandma watch Mo for a couple more days? I owe you one. <3

I stare at my phone for several minutes, trying to interpret the text. It must be his sister he's visiting, since his mom lives in Colorado. I try to ignore the butterflies I get when I see the heart at the end of his text, but I can't stop looking at it. I don't know how to process how it sparks a tiny bit of hope within my chest. Maybe I didn't mess everything up with Noah by trying to meet Mo and then leaving when I got stood up.

Gran will love to watch Mo for a couple of days. Hope everything is okay.

I delete a heart before I push send though. I'm not sure I'm ready to go there just yet.

There's also a message from Mo.

MoReads: I know you don't want to hear from me, but I can't end things like this. I am so, so sorry. I would love to explain what happened last night, but I understand if you don't want to hear it.

The message is from two hours ago. I sigh. I'm still embarrassed and angry. It would have to be something huge for me to be able to forgive him.

I put my phone on my bed facedown, only to pick it right back up again. I start to type out a response, but then I realize that I don't have anything left to say to Mo. He didn't show, and that said more than any words ever will.

26

NOAH

Annie doesn't cry as we pack up her things and get them out of her and Mitch's apartment. Which is weird, because out of the two of us, she's always been the weepier one.

We make quick work of grabbing her things. It takes a little over an hour to fill her two large suitcases with her clothes, cookbooks, and the handful of novels she brought with her to New York a few years ago.

"Everything else is his problem now," she says as we slowly carry the suitcases down the stairs and load them into the back of Sam's truck, which we borrowed after finding a set of keys in his bedroom. "He bought most of the furniture anyway, and anything I bought I can easily replace."

I want to tell her that she shouldn't have to do that, that she should be able to take whatever is hers. But when I mentioned it when we first got to the apartment, she shut me down quickly, so this time I keep my opinions to myself.

We unload everything into Sam's apartment, in the spare room where his parents stay when they come to visit.

"I kind of want to burn all of my clothes, but I don't really have enough money for an entirely new wardrobe." Annie sighs as we look at her clothes hanging in the closet.

"I could loan you some cash."

"Nope," Annie says, just like she always does when I offer. "I do not want your pity money."

"Is it really pity money if I'm offering it as a gift?" That question earns me a smack in the arm, which makes me miss Tally. I sent her a text before I fell asleep this morning to let her know I'm in New York. I also sent her a message as Mo, but she never replied to that one.

"I don't need your money," Annie repeats.

"Okay, fine. I'm just trying to help."

"I know, but you've done more than enough, flying out here right after I called. Thank you. You really are amazing." Annie pulls me into a hug. Her praise fills me with guilt because I'm really not amazing.

"When are you going to go to Colorado?" I ask her. I'll figure out a way to get her some extra money. I know she makes a decent amount as a chef, but she lives in New York City. Not exactly the cheapest place in the world.

Annie is silent for a moment. "I don't know if I want to quit my job yet. Even if it means seeing him a few times a month. Because I love working at the restaurant."

"You shouldn't have to deal with that," I argue.

"He shouldn't have the kind of power over me that forces me to quit my job and move across the country." Annie's fierceness reminds me of Tally in this moment, and there's an ache in my heart.

I want to call her, but I don't know what I'd say.

"I think I'll stay here until I figure out my next step. Sam already said I could stay here for a few months while I get things figured out. He won't be back till March or April anyway, so there really isn't a problem."

"Okay," I resign. Annie is too stubborn and I'm too tired to try and convince her to do something else. "And you're sure you don't want to file a report on Mitch?"

I gesture to her black eye. She's been wincing all day whenever she turns too suddenly, and I would bet money that her ribs are bruised as well.

"I already filed a report," Annie tells me, scowling. "The lovely cops at the station told me that they would write it up and keep a record of it, but that they couldn't do anything else right now."

"They said what?" I growl.

"Noah." Annie steps away from me and gives me a look that's so much like our mother when she's about to say something serious that I have to remind myself I'm actually looking at Annie. "They did what they could. Which isn't enough, obviously, but I'm exhausted and I just want it all to be done, so I'm dropping it. I'm not going back there."

"But—"

"No. Noah." She plops onto the queen bed, surrounded by her books that we haven't put away yet. Then she sits up. "Wait. How did telling Tally who you are go?"

I groan. I was hoping to avoid this conversation for longer.

"It didn't." I sit on the bed next to her and tell her what happened. From our road trip to my personal series of unfortunate events about getting stuck in the bathroom and then finding Tally gone when I got back.

Annie jumps up, searching for my phone amid all her stuff. "You need to call her. Call her right now."

"But I'm here with you."

She rolls her eyes. "I'm fine. I'm safe. Mitch didn't ever come here, so he has no idea where I'm staying. He's already got a new girl to do whatever the freak he's gonna do, probably be sweet to her for a while." I give her a look. "And I promise I'll warn her, but he's not going to hurt me again. I won't let that happen. But Tally needs to know where you are. Especially since you told her you'd come see her." Annie is looking at me like I'm the one in trouble, as if she didn't have someone hit her. My gut sinks as I wonder if this has happened before.

"I did text her and tell her that I'm here," I finally say, but the weight of my transgressions makes me feel like I've been tied to a boulder and am sinking in the ocean.

"But she doesn't know that you're Mo?"

I shake my head. How am I going to explain everything to Tally in a way that doesn't make her hate me when I can't even find the words to explain it to Annie?

"I can't exactly tell her that in a text. I need to figure out how to tell her." I rake my fingers through my hair. "I didn't expect all of this to get so complicated. I got so freaked out when I found out that Tally was Nora that I kind of avoided mentioning it. But then I had plenty of chances to tell her once the initial shock wore off, but I didn't tell her. I just hoped to meet her, just like she and Mo planned—until I got locked in the bathroom."

If I needed any moment to go right in my life, it was that one. I can't help but feel that I've missed my one and only shot at an actual chance with Tally.

"Why were you going to the bathroom anyway?" Annie asks, tossing me a chocolate bar that she had in one of her bags. "It doesn't seem like that was the best timing."

I shake my head. Annie's always been the bolder one out of the two of us. She takes risks again and again, even after she's been burned. I've followed her lead since the camping incident, but I still struggle to actually do thing things that are most important to me. I hope that what happened with Mitch doesn't stop that for her. "I had to nervous pee."

It's not exactly a lie. But when I couldn't easily get back

around to Tally, I got anxious, and naturally, that was the perfect time to hide in the bathroom.

Annie laughs. A laugh that fills her up completely. "You would" is all she says. Maybe someday I'll find this situation funny, but right now all it does is make me want to vomit.

"I feel so bad." I bury my face in my hands. "Obviously, she was super hurt and embarrassed about being stood up. She said as much in her texts after she left."

"Well, duh," Annie says. "Anyone would feel that way. Plus, she's also been talking to you online for several years, and for you not to show up, that's gotta hurt. What did you—Mo, I mean—tell her?"

"Nothing." Annie's eyes go wide. "Well, not quite nothing. She said we shouldn't talk anymore and unfollowed me. I sent a message; it was a pretty sad excuse of an apology though. I asked if I could explain." Annie pulls out her phone.

"Now she's really not gonna respond," Annie tells me. I groan. "You're gonna go home and sweep her off her feet. There's a flight back to Utah in three hours. We can get you on that one. You can sleep on the plane."

"How exactly am I going to sweep her off her feet?" I ask. I'm pretty sure Tally doesn't really want to see me. I think she's embarrassed from our almost-kiss in the hotel and the fact that I, well, Mo, didn't show up. And she really isn't going to want to see me when I tell her that I've been Mo the entire time.

"You can figure that out on your flight. I just bought you a ticket." Annie smiles at me. "So now we need to head to the airport."

I feel so guilty leaving her. "You have money to buy me a plane ticket but not new clothes? Are you sure you don't want me to stay a few more days?"

"Mom's gonna come stay for a little bit," Annie says, biting her lip. "I'm going to be okay. And I want you to get your happy ending, so the plane ticket is worth it."

"You deserve a happy ending too," I tell her.

Annie ponders this for a moment. "Maybe it will come, in its time." The thought hurts my heart, but I don't have time to dwell on it, not right now.

"Did you say my flight leaves in three hours?" I jump up.

"Yup." Annie grins. "You'll eat at the airport?" I nod and we scramble to get my bags, which have been sitting untouched since I got here. Annie drives Sam's truck again, since she doesn't have a car and taking a taxi could take too much time, and we make our way to JFK airport.

"It was good to see you, Sis." I give her a hug across the middle console when we pull up to the airport doors.

"Maybe next time I see you, my life won't be falling apart," Annie says with a smile. I know Tally talks about how I'm Mr. "Sunshine" all the time, but she's never met Annie. Annie, who always has been able to see the bright spots, even in the darkest moments.

"I don't know how you keep it all together, even when it's falling apart," I tell her.

"I don't know if I would say that," she says, her face darkening. "But I'll get through it."

I give her another hug. "I'll see you soon?"

"Soon." Annie waves as I get out of the car, and then she's gone.

I type out a text to Tally, telling her that I'm on my way back and asking her if we could go out to talk. Two hours later, as I turn off my phone, there's still no reply.

For the first hour of the flight, I try to sleep. I hoped it would come quickly, seeing as I've only slept for two hours in two days, but I'm too wired. In the end, I pull out Simone's new book and try to distract my brain with someone else's problems.

27

TALLY

"You can't ignore that boy forever," Gran says as I help her set the table for dinner. It's Monday and I called in sick today like the chicken I am. I'm not ready to face Noah yet, even though I know that at some point I will actually have to. He got back sometime today but hasn't come to pick up his dog yet, which I'm secretly happy about. Mo has turned out to be a really great snuggler when I've been reading or watching movies, which is how I spent the afternoon yesterday.

I kind of want to let him hang out in the shop when Noah's working. I might take that to my grave. I don't want Noah knowing I've gone soft for his dog.

"I can." I stick my tongue out at her. I've become a child. I feel like I need to go on a run, which is very weird for me but feels like something I should do so I can plan what I'm going to say to Noah when I see him tomorrow. And make a plan of how I'm going to survive the next ten and a half months of working with him.

"Tally." Gran looks at me, and there's a feeling in my gut that says I'm not going to like whatever she's about to tell me but that I also need to listen. "When I fell in love with Gramps, I knew he was it. I'd never wanted a man, yet there he was."

I nod, because this is a story I know. Not that I really want to hear it again, but I don't think I have much of a choice.

"I was happy, life was good. Then Charles, your grandpa, moved in next door. I was a senior in college. My mother was horrified that I was still attending school, that I hadn't gotten married and started popping out babies. My roommate told me that there was a cute boy next door that I had to meet."

Gran has that doe-eyed look that she always gets when she talks about Gramps. "I managed to avoid meeting him for almost two whole months. I paid attention so I could come and go when he wasn't around. Then one day, my car wouldn't start." Gran sighs, like she's still inconvenienced by this moment that happened sixty years ago.

I smile. This is my favorite part of the story; it always has been.

"Then this guy I'd been trying hard to avoid came up to me and said, 'Need help?' I told him no, even though if I couldn't get my car started, I would miss my final exam. He said, 'Want a lift somewhere, then? Then you can fix the car when you get back.' I hate admitting that this was what made me look up, that made my heart race just a little faster. Here was a man who had offered to help, and when I told him no, he offered exactly what I needed. He didn't say that he'd fix my car or anything. Just offered a ride."

"And you were smitten." I smile.

"I was not," Gran snaps, but then she's back in time again. "I was, however, running very late, so I accepted his offer of a ride. He didn't say a word to me, nor I to him, as he drove me to the testing center. I told him thank you as I got out, and he waved and then was gone. I took my test, wondering how I'd get home when I was finished. When I walked out, there he was. Leaning against his car right outside the exit."

I smile. I can picture Gramps doing this. He was probably smiling, a smile that I inherited but don't use as often as him. But even though I see him in my mind with wrinkles instead of a twenty-year-old guy, he's still Gramps.

"I walked right up to him and said, 'What are you doing here?' And he just kept smiling and said, 'I knew you'd need a ride, Ginny. Want to get an ice cream?' I was a little peeved that he already knew my name and I didn't know his." Gran sighs. "Then I always tell everyone that after that, the rest was history, but that isn't quite true."

I sit up a little straighter. What part of this story has she left out?

"Gramps was never proud of what happened next, which is why when you grandkids started asking about us and our story, we took this part out."

Now I'm intrigued. "What happened?"

"We dated until I graduated. Charles still had a year left, and we had a whirlwind of a summer romance together." Gran sighs. "Then one day in August, I woke up with a note taped to my door. He'd left."

"He left? Left where?" I've never seen anyone love someone else as much as Gramps loved Gran. He was devoted to her more than anything else in his life. She always came first, before work, before kids, before anything.

"He went back home. Left without a number to reach him." Gran gives me a sad smile. "I'd always said I didn't need a man, then the only one I ever loved ripped my heart in two."

"But the two of you got married." I'm struggling to figure out how the rest of the story worked out.

"We did." Gran takes my hand gently. "Sweetheart, this Noah man, he hurt you in the past, didn't he?"

I nod.

"And Mo, he hurt you too?" Gran asks.

I hadn't thought about it in ten minutes, dang it. My heart aches. "Yes."

"Do you love either of them?" Gran watches me closely. "You don't need to tell me that answer, but all I'm going to say is that the people who love us the most can often be the same ones who cause our deepest heartache. But when there's love and mutual respect and both people are willing to try, you can have a good life together, if you give them a chance."

"Is that what happened with you and Gramps?"

Gran smiles, and I know that she's not going to give me the details of what happened next. "Something like that."

I'm about to ask her to tell me more when the doorbell rings. Mo starts barking wildly, and I have a feeling that the person on the other side of the door is exactly the person that I'm trying to avoid. I walk down the stairs and Gran sits back down. "I'm going to my room," I yell to her as I walk right by the front door. I am not ready to see Noah yet. I want to, but I'm not ready. I need to figure out what I'm feeling first.

Gran sighs. She's probably mad that she already sat down and that her story did nothing to my heart. I won't give her the satisfaction of knowing that it *did*, in fact, do something to my heart; I can't even admit that out loud to myself. Let alone her. Or Noah.

I slip into my room just as Gran opens the door. "Noah!" There's a moment filled with Mo barking wildly, and I take a tiny peek around the corner and up the stairs and see Gran giving Noah a hug. I take a step back into the dark hallway as they part.

"Thanks for watching Mo for an extra day," Noah says, and I smile at the sound of his voice. "Hey, buddy," he says to the dog.

"It was my pleasure. How's your sister?"

"She'll be all right." They're standing on the landing, the front door still open, which I'm grateful for because that means that I won't have to hide out in my room for more than a few minutes. "How's Tally?"

I move a step closer to my room. They wouldn't have been able to see me from where I was standing anyway, but I don't want Gran to know that I'm eavesdropping.

"She'll be okay," Gran says happily. "She's a bit torn up that that boy didn't show up. She also wouldn't tell me what happened between the two of you, so I made a few guesses."

My face burns. I couldn't tell Gran about our almost-kiss.

"You need to call her," Gran says.

I imagine Noah's running his hands through his wavy blond hair just about now. "I was going to." I will my heart not to drop, but it still does. What does he mean that he was *going* to call me? Is he not anymore? "Could you tell her to meet me at the shop at eight tomorrow morning?"

"Of course, dear," Gran says. "Would you like to stay for dinner? I made plenty."

Please say no. Please say no.

"I'm sorry, but I already ate. Thank you though." It hurts a little. Even though I was hoping he'd say no, I didn't think he actually would. "Tell Tally I'll see her tomorrow. Tell her it won't be like the last time."

"I will," Gran says, then the door clicks shut. "You can come out now."

I step sheepishly away from my doorframe.

"What did he mean it won't be like the last time?" Gran asks as I head back up the stairs, my stomach growling.

"I honestly have no idea," I tell her, my mind spinning, trying to piece together what he was talking about and what I'm going to do when I see him.

"UGH," I moan as my alarm goes off an hour earlier than normal. I am not a morning person. I've never been a morning person. Which is why I get up at a quarter to eight every day to make it to the bookstore by nine. Today, though, I am, for some unknown reason, getting up an hour earlier to be there at eight, just like Noah asked.

I haven't responded to any of his messages. I probably should, but I also have no idea what I'll say. I'm pretty sure Gran told him that I'd be there this morning.

Standing under the scalding water does little to wake me up. My stomach is in knots by the time I make it upstairs for breakfast. I grab a granola bar, promising myself that I'll eat it after whatever happens with Noah, and then I'm out the door. People who say that mornings are the best time of day have never met me. Obviously. Noah should know that mornings are not my jam and that whatever this is he's got planned definitely could have waited until later in the day.

Like in the evening.

The shop looks quiet when I pull into a parking spot out front. Technically, I should park in the back because this spot is prime real estate for any customers, but parking in the back is a pain and I'm not in the mood.

The front door is locked. "Of course it is," I grumble as my hand moves through my overcrowded bag to find the keys I just dropped into the abyss. I find them and the bell above the door makes its familiar sound as I enter, and I flip on the lights.

"Hello?" I call out, because I don't see Noah right away. I move to the counter out of habit and set my bag by the register. A flutter of movement catches my eye and I turn to see Noah standing there, holding a bouquet of daisies and is that the fifth Simone Sorrows book? I haven't even cracked my copy open yet.

"What's going on?" I ask, taking a cautious step in his direction.

"I know that last weekend didn't go the way you planned." Noah's eyes pierce mine. He gives a tentative smile and takes a step in my direction. "It didn't go the way I hoped either."

"You knew I was going to meet another guy," I say softly, thinking of our almost-kiss in the hotel room.

"I know," Noah says. He's right in front of me now. I can smell his cologne. Pine something. "But that's not what I'm talking about. I'm sorry you got stood up and that you felt like you couldn't wait for me, that you had to get out of there. I'm sorry I wasn't a better friend to you so that you could have trusted me."

That is not what I was expecting. He hands me the daisies. My favorite.

"I did get this signed," Noah says, holding the book out to me. "I didn't even know you'd left the hotel already, but I knew you weren't at the signing, so I told her your name."

I let out a small gasp as I flip open to the signed page, where it's signed to me. "Thank you, Noah."

I give him a quick hug, not trusting my own emotions.

"I do have one more surprise for you." He tilts his head to the back of the shop. "Trust me?"

28

NOAH

Tally follows me up the metal stairs that lead to my apartment. I can tell she's dying to know why I'm bringing her up here, but I stay silent as I unlock the door.

"Surprise!!" the book club ladies, Olivia included, all yell as Tally steps inside. I'm nervous about how she'll respond, especially knowing that she hates surprises. But I thought she could use some friends after the weekend she had.

To my delight, she starts to laugh.

"You did this?" she asks me as she steps forward to hug Donna and Collene.

"He did all this." Olivia smiles at Tally, and the two share a look that I wish I could interpret.

"Did you guys kiss yet?" Pam shouts from across the room. She's sitting on the couch and Mo is curled up in her lap.

"Oh! Give him a kiss now!" Shirley grins at both of us. Tally laughs uncomfortably.

"How about we eat?" I suggest instead.

"I guess food is fine," Gracie grumbles. "If we don't get a show, we should be able to eat all that food we've been smelling for the past half hour."

"Noah made you wait?" Tally asks the ladies.

"It was fine," Olivia assures her. "He told us you could use some friends and invited us over for breakfast."

"Did he tell you anything else?" Tally glances at me with wide, worried eyes.

"No." Now Shirley's grumbling. We really need to get some food into these women. "He didn't tell us a single thing."

"Food is in the kitchen," I call out, and the women move together in that direction. Tally stays back, and when the women are in the kitchen, she faces me.

"Thank you, for everything." She ducks her head shyly.

I reach out, lifting her chin. "You're welcome."

Tally offers me a small smile, then steps back and heads toward the kitchen to get herself a plate of food.

WHILE THE BOOK club ladies and Tally are eating in the family room, I sneak away for a minute to send a message. The last message I ever plan on sending as Mo. This morning was just phase one—tonight, I'm telling her everything.

> **MoReads:** Hey, so this might be a little weird, I'm going to be in Provo this evening. Would you meet me at Nielson's Grove Park at seven tonight? I know I didn't show last time, but I promise I will this time. I'd really like to meet you in person and explain what happened on Saturday. If not, I understand, but I hope you say yes. I'll be standing by the reflecting pool holding a bouquet of flowers.

I stick my phone back in my pocket and come out of the kitchen with a tray of orange juice. "Who needs a drink?" I ask and every woman raises her hand.

Tally has perked up a bit. I knew that having her come in

early would be risky since she hates mornings. And I remember our stay at the hotel when she slept until almost ten and still needed an hour to get going. But now she's laughing and talking, and I hope that means that all is going well.

Maybe my plan might actually work.

"Are you sure you're not together?" I hear Collene ask as I take my own seat across from Tally. Her cheeks flush, and if I had to guess, she's trying to avoid looking at me. I hide my smile behind a glass of orange juice.

"I'm sure," Tally says.

"Pity," Collene says. "If he wasn't so smitten with you, I'd throw my hat in the ring."

Tally's cheeks go even redder, if that's at all possible.

"Give it time, dear." Collene pats Tally's knee. "You'll come around."

I certainly hope that she does.

At nine thirty Tally stands, declaring it's time for her to head down and get the shop ready for opening.

"I'll open today," I tell her. "You stay up here awhile."

"Are you sure?" Tally asks, seeming almost nervous. I know changing her schedule up on her last minute isn't her favorite thing.

"I'm sure," I promise her.

She nods once, then sits back between Pam and Collene. "I'll be down in a bit."

"No rush," I say as I head back down the stairs and into the bookstore, unlocking the door and flipping the sign to open.

WHEN THE SHOP has been open for an hour, I'm hanging out in the back office, finalizing some things with the website I hope to launch in the next few weeks, when my phone chimes.

THE LUCK OF FINDING YOU 249

TheNoraReview: I'll be there.

"Yes!" I throw a punch up in the air. She said yes!

Now I just hope she's not disappointed or angry when she sees me standing there. A few seconds later I shove my phone back into my pocket when I hear the back door to the shop open. Tally is saying goodbye to all the book club ladies and Olivia. I smile at her when she appears in the doorway.

"Thank you." Tally's watching her feet more than she's looking at me. "I owe you one. I didn't know how much I needed that until I showed up."

"You're welcome."

"All good down here?" she asks. I love how much she cares about how the shop is doing.

"All good down here," I tell her. "We've had a grand total of three customers this morning, so I've been working on the website."

"We're going to have to do more to keep this place open, aren't we?" she asks, sitting on the old wooden chair in the corner. I want to show her the website now, but I know waiting until next week when Olivia can be here will be better.

"A few minor things could make a big difference," I tell her. "But the online shop will help a lot, I think. Maybe we'll even be able to get you to Scotland."

Tally laughs and it makes my heart beat faster. "That would definitely be nice."

"And we may have to change a few more things, but I think the shop will be okay." I want her to know that I'm going to be here to take care of it and her.

"Okay. But I get to keep the unconventional book club." Tally laughs.

"Of course. I'll be there every time."

Tally throws her hands up in the air. "Men are not allowed!"

"Donna thinks I should be a permanent member. She said the other ladies are taking a vote."

Tally groans. "Of course they are." She bites her lip before looking at me. "Thank you again for this morning. It was exactly what I needed."

"I'm glad." I look at her, taking in everything from her curled blonde hair to her black heels. "You really do deserve the best, Tally."

Tally's quiet a minute. "I'm going to meet Mo tonight."

"Oh." I expected her to bring it up. It doesn't surprise or hurt like it did over the weekend. "That's good?"

"I think so. I hope so." She picks at a stray string at the bottom of her sweater. "I really want some closure. A face to the name. Maybe an apology face-to-face. I don't know. It's probably a bad idea."

"Want me to come with you? Scope him out before you meet him?" I ask her. If she takes me up on the offer, that could make things a bit more complicated, but I'll make it work.

"What! Of course not! I've already got a nosy older sister who acts like a momma bear all the time. I don't need an older brother."

"So you think of me as a brother now?" I really hope she says no.

"What? No. That's not what I meant." Tally shakes her head, her cheeks turning red. "Thank you for the offer, but I'll be just fine."

"Okay," I tell her. "The offer still stands though, if you change your mind."

"If he doesn't show again, I'd rather be humiliated all on my own, thank you very much." Tally frowns.

"I hope he shows," I tell her.

"Why?" she asks, surprising me. "I mean, if he doesn't, I'll know for sure he's a jerk and wasn't the guy I thought he was. And then you and I will have a talk about what we are, and I'll feel guilty that you think you're just my second choice..."

I look at her expectantly when she trails off.

"You were going give me a chance?"

"Ugh. I cannot seem to talk around you today. I'm not going to answer that question. We just decided to be friends. I can do friends. I've got to stop putting my foot in my mouth." Tally's face is a deep red that I hope she'll always have, even when we're old and gray and have been together for sixty years.

"I sure like it," I tell her. "What other things shouldn't you be saying that you might accidentally blurt out while we're sitting here? We could have a conversation to determine our relationship right now."

That comment earns me a glare.

"I'm going to go shelve some of the books we got last week," Tally says, standing.

"I'll see you out there later." Because even though I do want to hang out with her, Olivia will be back here soon, and I've got a few more bills to pay.

Tally nods and heads out into the store. I hear her singing along to the radio a few times. The unease I felt this morning when I woke up is mostly gone. Now I'm just full of nerves. I really want tonight to go well. It needs to go well.

She likes me, I can tell, but I don't know what to expect when she shows up and finds me, Noah *and* Mo, waiting for her.

Noah left several hours ago, but I keep glancing down the back hallway, willing him to reappear. It's a quarter to seven, and Olivia is closing tonight so I can go meet Mo. I want Noah to come back down so I can ask him to come with me because suddenly I'm nervous about going alone.

I could always text him, I think to myself as I grab my jacket. Instead, I find myself taking the stairs two at a time and knocking on the door at the top of the stairs. It's silent. No TV sounds or dog barking.

"He must be walking the dog." The words taste like ash in my mouth. I'm wishing that I was brave. Instead, I just keep remembering how it felt to stand waiting in the entrance on Saturday night. Waiting and waiting for a guy who never came. "You can do this," I tell myself as I make my way back down the stairs and through the shop, where I wave to Olivia.

"Good luck!" she calls out to me as I step outside. "It's going to be great!" She's already given me three pep talks today. I'll have to send her flowers as a thank you, because I am freaking out right now and have been all day.

I take another deep breath, which is supposed to calm me, but it does little to do that.

It's officially cooler—the sun is setting, and now that it's October, there already seems to be a hint of what is to come.

I'm not ready for fall to be over. It always goes to fast. It sneaks up on you. At least that's how I feel. One day all the trees are green, and the next day there's nothing but yellow and red leaves covering the ground.

We wear sweaters without coats for a few weeks and then bam, the cruel winter air cuts through the morning instead of the crisp fall air that I love so much.

I make the ten-minute drive to the park that Mo suggested, grateful that traffic is light and I make it in time. I park in the parking lot opposite the reflecting pool where he said he'd be, just because I don't want to be able to see from my car if he's standing there or not.

My hands are shaking as I pull the keys out of the ignition.

"I can do this," I tell myself again as I get out of the car. "I can do this."

With every step I take through the ever-darkening park, all I can think about is Noah.

I see him in the café, the first time I met him. The first time I kissed him. I feel his lips on mine and warmth rushes through me. I let out a weird sob-and-smile combination as I think about when we kissed a few weeks ago and how much has changed since then. I think about the way he says my name in such a reverent way all the time and how he's always trying to make me either laugh or blush.

A leaf crunches under my foot and my mind is thrown back to the day at the lawyer's office when I learned my new fate and ran from the building. That was really the first day that leaves had been on the ground. I was so angry that day. Mad that even though I get to keep The Book Shop, I still don't have the money or the time to take a break and go to Scotland like I wanted to next summer.

I remember the night of the book club, when the ladies—my friends, though much older than me—all flirted with Noah and he took it with such ease.

He's so kindhearted and makes me want to curl up under a blanket and listen to him read to me for hours.

I stop short just before turning the corner where I know Mo will be standing. I let out another half-laugh, half-sob and force myself to calm down. I wipe the tears from my cheeks, mentally preparing myself to meet Mo. It doesn't matter what he looks like because I know now that I'm in love with Noah.

It doesn't matter what Mo looks like or that we like the same types of books or think that hot chocolate is a better drink than coffee. All the things we've talked about over the past two years? They don't matter, not really. He's just been an internet friend, and yeah, I'm finally about to meet him, but then I've got to tell him that I fell in love with someone else. Someone real. Someone who I've been falling in love with since I saw him again. Someone who runs his hands through his hair a million times a day, and how I'm always in awe that it never fails to still look perfect.

A man who's charmed his way into my life and my heart, even though I don't think that was his intention at all. It just happened.

And yeah, maybe it's a little fast because technically, I've only truly known Noah for three weeks, but it feels like a lifetime.

Dad knew Mom one whole week before he asked her to marry him. He always said that he just knew that it was her who he was going to spend his life with, so why wait?

"Dang it." I wipe way at the tears that won't seem to stop. I take a deep breath and go around the corner.

My eyes must be really blurry because I think I see Mo barking and running toward me. I squat down. "What are you doing here, little buddy?" I ask him. A realization hits me so hard that I nearly fall over. "Mo?" I whisper suspiciously, and he licks my hands in response.

I stand slowly and walk over to the twinkling lights surrounding a gazebo that's near the water. Noah is standing in the center, holding a bouquet of daisies, just like the ones he gave me earlier today.

I stop a foot away from him.

"Why are you crying, Book Girl?" Noah asks, his voice so gentle that I nearly start sobbing again. He hasn't called me that once, not since that first day five years ago.

"It's you," I say through another sob, even though now I'm smiling.

"It's me." Noah moves closer, the gap between us almost gone. He doesn't reach out for me yet.

"But. Wait. Did you know in St. George?" I push away from him, but he catches my arm.

"I guessed the day that we kissed, when you told me about your internet friend," Noah confesses. "I knew for sure that week after."

I'm stunned. "And you didn't think it was a good idea to let me in on that information?" I'm so relieved that it's him. I wanted it to be him. I hit him in the chest because I have to let out some of my anger, but I also want to wrap my arms around his neck and kiss him.

"I kind of freaked out when I figured it out," Noah tells me, his eyes never leaving mine. He squeezes my hand and takes a small step forward so we're so close that I can feel his chest move as he breathes. "I already knew I was falling for you. It felt like the right thing to meet Nora and figure it all out. But then you were going on and on about this guy that you were meeting, and I felt so much pressure."

"Why didn't you show up?" I hate that my voice cracks, but I have to know.

Noah's eyes fill with tears. "I got locked in the bathroom without a phone for an hour. I went in to splash cold water on my face and just mentally prepare to face you as Mo, but then I got locked in. I only got out in time to get the book signed. I ran back to the hotel to explain everything, but you were already gone." Noah presses his forehead against mine. "I'm so sorry. I never meant to stand you up."

I let out a small laugh. It's not funny—really not funny. But relief fills my body because now I know that he didn't stand me up on purpose.

I wrap my arms around his neck, trusting my heart for the first time. "I'm glad it's you."

"Really?" Noah's voice cracks this time.

"You want to know why I've been crying like a fool for the past ten minutes?" I ask him, and cautiously he nods. "I was trying to figure out how I was going to tell Mo—who is your dog, by the way, how did I never put that together? Anyway, I was trying to figure out how to tell Mo that I was in love with someone else. That I love you."

Noah's arms tighten around me. "I wanted to be the first one to say that."

"To say what?" I ask coyly.

"I love you, Tally Nelson," Noah says the words, and it's like I'm breathing air for the first time in my life. "That for years and years I've been running scared. Terrified that I'd never find a woman who I'd be able to love so completely as I did that first day I spent with you. But I found you, again and again. I just keep finding you. I love you, Tally."

I'm crying again, this time because of his confession. "I love you too, Noah Jones."

And then he kisses me.

His lips are soft and tender, his hands in my hair, pulling me up against him. It's better than any kiss we've shared before, and I know this time it's real. There's no guy to make jealous in a café, no unspoken feelings in a small apartment over a book shop.

It's just me and Noah, the way it was always meant to be.

EPILOGUE—ONE YEAR LATER—NOAH

"Hey, big brother!" Annie gives me a hug, and I grab her bag as we walk toward the airport doors. Mom is doing Thanksgiving with her new boyfriend's family, so Annie decided she'd come visit me and Tally for the holiday. We'll be eating with Tally's family.

Somehow Tally failed to mention that nearly all of her extended family members live within an hour of Gran's house. Which means everyone will be there today. Though I've met most of them already at various Sunday dinners, I'm still not used to being around everyone on holidays.

"Hey yourself." I wrap my arm around Annie's shoulders. Tally brings me so much peace and joy, but Annie has been my constant since the day she was born. I feel slightly less nervous now that she's here with me.

She looks good, better than when I last saw her. There's something different about her, but I can't put a finger on it.

"Stop looking at me like that." Annie looks up at me.

"Like what?" I ask innocently.

"Like I'm about to break into a million pieces." Annie sighs. "I'm okay, Noah."

I only half believe her. It's been a year since everything with Mitch happened, but I still worry about her. She's not quite the same as she was before. "Really?"

"Ish." I give her a squeeze, then let her go so we can get in the car. She still hasn't told me everything that happened to her, but I'm trying to be patient because I know she'll talk when she's ready.

"I'll be okay soon," she says optimistically, as if she can be fine just by thinking so.

"I hope so." I'm still remembering that I have to bite my tongue. There are a million things I'd like to say, mostly to Mitch, but Annie's asked me to let it go, so I'm trying to. Even though Sam and I have had plenty of conversations about the things we'd like to do to Mitch to make sure he stays out of Annie's life for good.

I know I'll feel better in a couple of months when Sam's back in New York for good since Annie refuses to leave.

"I can't wait to see Tally!" Annie says, changing the subject as we pull out of the parking garage.

"She would have come, but her grandma said she needed help with the food." Tally was so disappointed that she didn't get to come with me to the airport to pick up Annie.

"That's fine," Annie says, pulling out her phone. "I'm just excited to meet her in real life as my future sister-in-law, not just a random stranger at Grandma's will reading!"

Tally and Annie have been texting like crazy since Tally and I got together. They FaceTime at least once a week. I have a big suspicion that Annie is happy to have another friend close to her age who isn't part of Mitch's friend circle.

"Oh! I almost forgot." Annie reaches into her bag and pulls out a little black velvet box. "Grandma Marsha's ring."

"Are you sure about this?" I ask her. Grandma Marsha may

have left us both The Book Shop, but she gave Annie her wedding ring.

"I'm sure," Annie tells me, putting the box on the middle console. "I don't think I'll be ready for marriage for a long, long time. In fact, I might never get married. Tally and Marsha were really close. I think it'll mean more to her than it will to me. And I've told you all of this about a thousand times since I offered the ring to you."

My fingers catch in my hair, a habit Tally pointed out I do often, whether I'm nervous or happy or excited or stressed. I'm trying to stop though, because now I'm self-conscious about it. "Okay. If you're absolutely sure."

"I'm absolutely sure," Annie says. "Now drive. I want to hug my future sister-in-law."

"You can't call her that," I warn.

"Not for a few more hours," Annie says in a sing-song voice. "After that, I officially have a sister."

Yup. That's right. I'm going to propose to a woman I've been dating for the past year. Some people might say that's fast (those people probably haven't read a romance novel.) Some might say it's crazy. The ladies in the book club will say I took too long.

I say it's perfect.

I SLIP the ring box into my pocket and get out of the car. Annie heads into The Book Shop just like we planned, and I make my way over to the little café. They aren't actually open today, with it being Thanksgiving and all. But when I told the owner my story and my plan, he agreed to let me in for a little while this afternoon.

I call Tally. "Hey, uh. Annie wanted to drop her stuff off at the apartment and fix her hair or something before we came over. But now my car won't start."

"What!" Tally whisper-screams into the phone. "Gran is going to kill you if you aren't here in an hour to eat."

"I know. Can you come get us? I'm really sorry." My car did break down two weeks ago, and the mechanic told me it would be fine. But when I told Tally about it, I might have told her that he said something like this could happen again. I needed to get everything set up for today.

"Okay. Yes. I can come. Gran will not be happy. Are you guys just at the shop?" I hear her keys jingle as she grabs them.

"Yup, just at the shop," I tell her. "See you soon."

"See you."

"I love you," I tell her, because I am now incapable of ending any conversation with her without saying these words.

"I love you too, Noah," Tally says, her voice softer now. "I'll see you in a few."

I set my phone on the table in front of me. Now all I have to do is wait.

After what feels like eternity but is really only fifteen minutes, I see Tally through the window. My heart thuds furiously in my chest, only not out of nerves. Out of all the things I have imagined since that day I walked in here and saw her sitting in this booth, I never let myself hope that this moment would happen.

I watch as she pulls open the door, glancing around the empty café, her eyes falling on me and our little booth. I grin and wave to her.

"What's going on?" She hurries toward me, her eyes wide. "What are you doing here? Annie said I'd find you here. Gran will kill us if we don't get back."

Gran actually knows exactly what's happening right now. I

knew I wouldn't be able to steal Tally away for more than a minute unless I told Gran exactly what was going on.

"Sit for a second." I gesture to the seat across from me.

"What's going on?" Tally asks again as she slides into the booth.

"I just wanted a minute alone with my lady," I say.

Tally snorts. "My lady? That makes me sound so fancy."

"You are pretty fancy," I say, laughing. I'm grateful she's relaxed a tiny bit since she walked through the door.

Suddenly the table between us is too much. I jump up and slide in next to her.

"I feel like I'm experiencing déjà vu. Only this time is much better than the last." Tally leans in for a kiss, but I pull back slightly. I know myself well enough to know that if I kiss her now, I won't be able to stop.

"Tally," I whisper.

"Noah," she whispers back. She's oblivious and I love her for it.

I slip a hand into my pocket. I want to kneel for this, so I get out of the booth. Tally tilts her head at me, reminding me a little of Mo.

"Noah?" she asks as I slide down to one knee. Her eyes grow wide.

"Tally Nora Nelson," I begin, and that's when the tears appear in her eyes. Who would have guessed that she was a crier? "I think I fell in love with you all those years ago in this tiny café when I first walked in. I kissed you and then walked away. I wish I hadn't. I'm so glad that you are back in my life. In so many ways, Marsha brought us together that day back then and again last year. I love you, Tally. I keep falling in love with you every day. Will you marry me?" I open the box.

Tally lets out a gasp. "Is that—?"

"Marsha's ring? Yes."

"Wow," Tally breathes.

"Is that a yes?" I ask. I don't want to rush her, but it's killing me that she didn't say yes right way. Why didn't she say yes right away?

"Yes!" Tally says, touching my face. "I love you. I want to marry you!"

I smile and pull her into my arms again to kiss her. I slip the ring on her finger; it looks perfect there, and I kiss her again. It looks like I will get that picket fence after all and someone to grow old with.

Tally is wiping at her tears when she pulls away, but she's got the biggest grin on her face. "I have to call Holly!"

I tug on her hand, toward the door, where Annie is waiting on the sidewalk. "You can call her on the way back."

"Dinner! Gran!" Tally moves faster.

"It's okay. Gran knows." I smile at her and she smiles back, glancing down at the ring on her finger. "But we still might want to make it back soon."

Tally nods.

We head out onto the street, the one that now feels so much like home. The trees are bare, and the clouds in the sky mean there might be snow later today. Tally already has plans for how we'll decorate the shop for Christmas, which we'll do next week.

I can't wait to see all the trees and shops lit up with lights, but right now, as I watch Tally and Annie hug each other, I know that even the magic of Christmas won't beat this moment.

Annie offers to drive, and Tally lays her head on my shoulder once we're in the back seat.

When she sits up abruptly, I look at her, our noses brushing.

"What?" I ask.

"I'm just so lucky to have found you. Several times." Her ocean-blue eyes are so serious. We are going to have to work on that—she really does need to learn to laugh a little.

The Bluetooth stereo in the car connects with Tally's phone, and Annie yelps at the loud audiobook that fills the air.

I just laugh as she turns it down and press a light kiss on Tally's forehead. Tally might think she's the lucky one, but if she's the lucky one, then I'm the luckiest.

ACKNOWLEDGMENTS

Ahh! How is this real? I'm writing the acknowledgements for my first book! I have so many people to thank, but I'll keep this short.

First, I am so thankful to God who has been a steady hand in this entire process. I would not be here without Him. I have to thank my sister and best friend McKenna. Without her, this book wouldn't exist and I might not be publishing books at all, so thank you for being my biggest fan and cheerleader.

Next, I have to thank all of my fantastic early readers. Kristen, Ashley, Erica, Alexis, McKenna, Cassie, Grace, and Bethany. I am beyond grateful for every single one of you. Thanks for falling in love with Tally and Noah and helping me make this story even better.

I also have to thank my incredible editor Jana, you helped bring this book to the next level. Also, a big thank you to Meghan for proofreading my book.

And to my parents, thank you for cheering me on and listening to me talk about the publishing world for hours. Dad, thanks for telling me back when I was twelve that I'd be an author some day, you were right.

For Griffin and Von, thank you for loving me and supporting me as I chase this dream of mine. I love you both so much and could not do any of this without you.

And lastly, dear reader, thank you! Thank you for taking a chance on me and reading my book. I am forever grateful for you!

ABOUT THE AUTHOR

Taylor Epperson has dreamed of writing books since she was a kid. She firmly believes that every story needs kissing and romance. Her stories will make you swoon, laugh, and maybe cry. But hopefully they'll always leave you feeling a little happier.

When she's not writing, you can find her curled up with a good book and a bag of potato chips or playing with her daughter. She enjoys binge-watching cooking shows and crime dramas. She lives in Northern Colorado with her husband, daughter, and very anxious black lab.

 twitter.com/tayeppwrites

 instagram.com/authortaylorepperson

ALSO BY TAYLOR EPPERSON

The Luck of Finding You (nelson sisters book 1)

Holly's Book (nelson sisters book 2) *coming soon*

Made in the USA
Middletown, DE
27 October 2023